THE ASCENT

THE ASCENT

CHRISTOPHER WALKER

Hardback ISBN: 979-8-9934998-0-2

Paperback ISBN: 979-8-9934998-1-9

Ebook ISBN: 979-8-9934998-2-6

PART I

THE DOOR

CHAPTER 1

Screeching tires, metal crunching, glass shattering—thankfully, those three sounds are the only lingering memories John Atwater has of that fateful car accident some three decades earlier. The trajectory of his life changed entirely after that day, and with the loss of his parents, how could it not?

John's uncle, Randy—his last living blood relative—took him in at the age of seven and raised him as his own. They lived together on his sprawling ranch in Alabama until John was eighteen years old. At the ranch, he learned how to be disciplined, how to work hard, and a few other skills he never would've learned if he'd grown up in the suburbs of New England where he was born. How to ride a horse, for instance, he learned at the age of ten, and he learned how to hunt at age twelve—shooting his first deer at thirteen.

As John reminisces about his uncle, he's reminded of how lucky he was. Losing his parents at such a young age—and in such a horrific way—could have sent him down a completely different path, the wrong path. But instead, the difficult journey molded him into the man he is today. A strong, confident, and only slightly troubled man—although that last one had nothing to do with his uncle, and everything to do with his life after college.

Top of his class at MIT, he was a brilliant young engineer. So brilliant, in fact, that the army picked him up right after he graduated. With the promise that he would see the world if he joined, and the instant approval from his uncle, he didn't think twice. However, at six foot six and two hundred forty pounds, they saw more than just a gifted engineer in John; they saw a soldier.

Soon after he was accepted, he started training to become part of an elite group of individuals who called themselves "The Undesirables." The training was rigorous and technical. Sixteen hours a day for twelve weeks takes a physical toll on any person, but worse than that was the mental toll it had. Some people would break in the first week; for others, it took several. This training was meant to harden any individual who went through it, and it did.

Once John solidified himself as a team member of this elite group, he got the obligatory tattoo that the rest of the team had—THE UNDESIRABLES—which he chose to put above his left pec. The missions that followed brought him to every remote part of the world you can think of, to carry out all sorts of tasks: search and rescue missions, assassinations, and even full-on assaults on enemy territories. This team was disciplined, precise, and most of all, reliable. Until they weren't …

After being honorably discharged a year ago, he had no idea what to do with his life, as was the case with most people who left the Service. He had spent fourteen years doing whatever was asked of him—training, fighting, killing—and when he got out, he had the scars to prove it. John had physical scars all over his body, including the jagged cut along his torso from a serrated bowie knife in Senegal, and the bullet hole in his lower abdomen—courtesy of a search and rescue mission gone wrong in Vietnam. Those scars he could handle; it was the mental scars that caused him so much anguish.

Anxiety attacks were infrequent at first, but eventually, they became a daily occurrence that would render John a shell of himself. That, mixed with the PTSD that would rear its ugly head at a moment's notice, was all too much to handle on his own. He started seeing a therapist on a doctor's suggestion; to say he was hesitant was the understatement of the century. After all, in the military you push down your feelings, so as not to affect the mission. However, after only a few sessions, he started to enjoy his hour-long talks, even looking forward to them some days. He gained useful tools he could call upon at any time to help deal with his anxiety, his PTSD, and his bouts of depression.

"It will never go away. You are going to live with this forever. But I assure you, it will get easier to deal with as time goes on," his therapist would tell him.

These tools helped John rebuild his confidence and helped him secure his current job as a facilities engineer for a shipping company in Alabama. His daily routine is a fond reminder of the military: He wakes up at 5 a.m., arrives at work by 6 a.m., starts his one-hour lunch at 11 a.m., and then leaves by 3 p.m. This routine and his crew cut hairstyle are the only things he cares to hold on to from that time in his life.

Today marks one year to the day of his discharge, and he's using his lunch break to peruse a local market, hoping to find some ingredients he can use for dinner. He basks in the ninety-two degree Alabama heat, his tanned skin glistening in the sunlight as a bead of sweat slowly makes its way down his chiseled jaw. He'll never complain about the heat, though. After experiencing every climate imaginable with The Undesirables, he knows there's always something worse out there. A hot day in Alabama beats the hell out of the subzero temperatures he endured during an extended trip to Russia six years prior.

As he walks, he takes in the scents of the market: raspberry pastries drizzled in vanilla icing, homemade cedar picture frames, and the distinct scent of a hazelnut cold brew. John stops at a table with various fruits and vegetables arranged in small wicker baskets. As he picks up a plump tomato, he notices an older woman staring at him out of the corner of his eye. He avoids eye contact, knowing full well what's coming. While the local market is a great place to get fresh produce, it's also a great place for people to push their bogus and overpriced healing herbs and oils. At least that's how John sees them.

He slowly puts the tomato down, hopeful she won't make a move. Just as John begins to turn away, the woman's shrill voice pierces his ears: "Sir! Have you ever thought of trying patchouli oil? It has a calming effect on most people and has been proven to reduce anxiety."

John smirks, and without turning around, he replies, "No thanks, ma'am, a shot of whiskey and a cold beer are all I need to calm my nerves."

The woman is left speechless, her mouth agape, as John strolls confidently away from the table. He's in no way a big drinker—although he does like the occasional glass of single malt scotch—he just likes to be a bit dramatic when people take that sort of stuff so seriously. It's not as if he's a cynical man either; he's just always preferred Western medicine over Eastern, science over mythology, and facts over fairy tales.

It's 12:05 p.m. when he finally makes it back from his lunch break. He sneaks in through the back door, knowing he'll be spotted, and also knowing exactly who he'll be blaming for his tardiness.

John's fresh out of college coworker and fellow engineer, Jayden, is sitting in a folding chair waiting for the door to open, with one leg crossed over the other. He has the unmistakable grin of someone who is about to say something smug. "Well, look who decided to show up . . ."

John shakes his head. "Before you say anything—"

"'If you're early, you're on time, and if you're on time, you're late!' The John Atwater motto for being punctual!" Jayden interrupts sarcastically as he follows John back to his office.

"You say anything to the boss and I'll chop that little man bun right off the top of your head," John jabs back.

"Whoa . . . uncalled for, *Johnny*. But let's hear your wonderful explanation, and I'll see how I feel about it."

John's eyes squint together. He's never liked nicknames, but what can you say to an immature twenty-something who likes to stir the pot? "Listen up, I was cruising through the market, grabbing everything I needed for my homemade pasta sauce, when out of nowhere this woman comes up behind me and tries to sell me patchouli oil. Can you believe that? *Patchouli oil.* Like I'd ever be dumb enough to waste my money on that."

"Whoa, whoa, whoa . . . 'Waste?' Patchouli oil is a gift from Mother Earth."

John scoffs, "Next you're going to tell me you believe in elves."

"Elves?" replies Jayden, confused.

John mimes pulling back the drawstring on a bow. "You know, elves, with the bows and the arrows?"

"Okay . . . that is a huge jump in logic, comparing a mythical creature to an essential oil."

John smirks. "Alright, alright, why don't you settle down and go get another *Reiki* massage while you're at it?"

"Dude, you know I don't like to get frazzled, but you are really starting to irritate me. Reiki is very relaxing and *so* emotionally healing. You have *no* idea."

"Oh, please . . . if I want emotional healing, I'll try yoga, or maybe even meditation, but I draw the line at Reiki. That is some voodoo nonsense."

Both of them are standing outside John's office now. Jayden's face has become red with anger, but before he can reply, their boss yells down the hall, "John, I need five minutes with you. *Now.*"

Jayden chuckles to himself as he walks away. "That's karma, bro."

John sits across from his boss, a sturdy mahogany desk separating the two of them. His boss, Bruce, isn't an imposing man in stature, but he more than makes up for it with gravitas. When he speaks, you listen. "John, we need to discuss something."

John quickly interjects, "Before you say anything, I know I was late returning from lunch. It won't happen again, and I will make up the five minutes at the end of the day. That's a promise."

Bruce raises his eyebrows. "You think I care that my most reliable employee was five minutes late? I'm the one who's always telling you to take long lunches. If I were disciplining people for tardiness, Jayden would have a rap sheet longer than a shipping container."

John can't help but smile. A dig at Jayden and a shipping container comparison—classic Bruce. "So, why did you call me in here?"

Bruce looks down at a dark blue binder in front of him. "There is a meeting taking place at one of our branches in Edinburgh, Scotland. It's an annual event where we discuss ways to streamline the company, and we look into alternative ways of running the business. I'm going to be honest, John, not much ever gets done at these meetings. The best part is the four days of *networking* they give you to gallivant around Scotland and do whatever your mind compels you to do. As fun as that is, this would be my seventh trip to Edinburgh, and I'm getting tired of the long flights. So, I was wondering if you would go in my place?"

John is taken aback. He's traveled many places in his life, but Scotland remains uncrossed on his bucket list. "Are you serious? Boss, I'm just a facilities engineer. I don't know how qualified I would be to discuss business needs."

"Trust me, you'll be fine. It's just an excuse for a couple of bigwigs at the top to expense a bunch of scotch and pretend they're helping the company. Just go to the meeting, take some notes, try to look as inquisitive as possible, and then enjoy the paid vacation. I'd recommend the Isle of Skye if you're interested in an adventure. It's a magical place."

Routines are great. But sometimes if you get stuck in a routine for too long, you can forget that there's more to life than a nine-to-five. And John—realizing how much he's missed the travel and excitement that he once took for granted—waits only a moment longer before responding.

"I'll do it."

CHAPTER 2

A few days later, and after a brutal travel itinerary—Bruce wasn't lying about that—John arrives at the warehouse where the meeting will take place. He walks into a spacious room with cement floors, aluminum siding, and tall metal shelving pushed to the side. What clearly used to be a storage space has been temporarily converted into the meeting room. Wooden circular tables are set up around the room rather haphazardly—about fifteen of them—with four chairs to a table. At the front of the room, there's a stage, a microphone, and a projector screen pulled down. John scans the room and locks eyes on a long buffet table filled with everything he's heard is included in a Scottish breakfast: coffee, eggs, sausage links, hash, bacon, scones, toast, fried tomatoes, and even the famous haggis. *Finally,* John thinks.

As he grabs a cup of coffee and piles food sky-high on a paper plate, the rest of the group start funneling in. They're all in their late fifties, with silvery hair, and dressed to the nines. Some of them are even wearing bow ties. John looks down at his skintight white T-shirt, buffalo plaid flannel, and ragged blue jeans . . . *Probably a little underdressed.*

John takes a seat at the back of the room as the presentation begins. Hours go by as the man drones on about quarterly reports, cost-saving initiatives, and the "team mentality" that their company strives for. John is barely listening as he scarfs down his food and writes in his notebook—not notes, however, no; he's making a list of ingredients he'll need to make dinner when he returns home the following week.

"Alright, let's take a fifteen-minute break. We will pick back up where we left off after that," announces the presenter.

"Nope," John mumbles under his breath as he gets up and makes a stealthy exit, stepping outside into the pouring rain. *Now this is the Scotland I've heard so much about.* He hustles over to a small glass hut where he can escape the rain, located at a bus stop just down the street. While sitting on an uncomfortable wooden bench, he scans over the many flyers taped to the inside of the hut, offering an array of opportunities, including bagpipe lessons, language classes, and even stand-up comedy. As he scans, his eyes lock on one flyer in particular, advertising a guided hike:

THE ISLE OF SKYE
MAJESTIC SCOTTISH HIGHLANDS
TOWERING STONE CASTLES
BREATHTAKING VIEWS
COME WITH ME AND YOU'LL SEE IT ALL

John stares at the flyer for a moment. A small but noticeable smile forms on his face as he remembers what his boss said to him: *"The best part is the four days of networking they give you to gallivant around Scotland and do whatever your mind compels you to do."*

Scottish Highlands, stone castles, breathtaking views. All I need is a three-finger pour of a single malt, and that's the perfect Scottish getaway, John thinks.

***

After several hours of driving the following day, John arrives at the meeting spot stated on the flyer. Excited to get to the hike, he stopped only once to purchase a lighter and a cigar from a nearby gas station—the perfect addition to any hike. The rain has subsided, but the weather remains overcast and humid, with clouds as far as the eye can see. He looks out to see a man standing on a large, flat rock, addressing a group of about twelve people. The man is on the shorter side—about five foot four—and is sporting a long red beard and a traditional Scottish tartan kilt. As John gets out of his rental car and approaches the group, he can hear the man speak, his voice booming with a thick Scottish accent.

"This trip I have planned is not for the faint of heart. Sure, the views are spectacular, and the mountains majestic. But make no mistake, this is a treacherous climb with animals that will want to rip your head off at every turn! Rains so hard, you'll think you're at sea! Winds whipping by you so fast and loud, you'll think you're at the Daytona 500! Ha! Ha, ha, ha!"

The small crowd—all clearly American tourists—erupts in laughter.

"Well, let's saddle up, folks; the tour begins now!" booms the guide.

The hike begins on a thin, rocky, and very slippery path. Even though the guide was clearly embellishing for laughs, this is not an easy hike by any means, and John is thankful he remembered his hiking boots. They pass a well-kept pasture of Scottish Highland cows, stopping to take pictures. As they move farther along, they stop at a dilapidated castle for more pictures. All the way up the path, there are breathtaking views of the countryside. The guide is going through his spiel he must've given a thousand times, trying to seem energetic, but often coming up short—but that all changes when they pass under a massive stone arch where the path flattens out.

To their right is the side of a mountain—a jagged stone wall standing well over fifty feet tall. Rocks jut out, moss and vines are stuck to the side of the cliff, and steady streams of water pour down over everything. But directly in front of them stands what looks like a door—not a big door, just an average-sized door—inlaid into the cliffside. It stands out in its contrast to the rest of the rock—smooth, uniform, with not an ounce of vegetation growing on it.

The excitement in the guide's voice is evident as he speaks. "Hundreds of years ago, a group of men and women, not unlike yourselves, left their village in search of something . . . a door, but not just any door, however; this door was said to lead to a magical new world—a world shrouded in mystery and intrigue among their people—a world known only as 'Mhorelia.'

"The journey was treacherous, and they would face many obstacles along the way. For some in the group, the hunger and thirst were simply too much, and they turned back. For others, it was the menacing storms, the bone-chilling temperatures, and the ever-towering, seemingly unscalable mountainsides that stood in their way. But one man would not turn back, determined at all costs to discover this magical world. His name was 'Balloch MacNicol.'

"One morning, as he was making his way up a mountainside, the wind began to blow. It started as a slow whisper, but before long, it was howling all around him. This was the start of a ferocious, tempestuous storm; Balloch could feel it. The wind, accompanied by a never-ending barrage of piercing rain droplets, deafening thunder, and blinding lightning, was becoming too much to handle for Balloch.

"As he made his way under a stone arch, lightning struck the cliff above him. Rocks started raining down from above, and he lunged toward the wall of the cliff. Suddenly, the rain, the wind, the temperature, the noise, the rocks careening down all around him, and the thought that this really could be the end for him . . . it was all too much. A tear began to fall down his face as he sank to the ground. But when he leaned back against the cliff, he felt something unexpected . . . nothing. The cliff gave way, and he fell backwards, rolling inside.

"As he stood up, he looked around in amazement. There was no wind, thunder, lightning, or rain, just vast fields, showered in sunlight. In the distance, he saw lofty mountain ranges, some snowcapped and some lush with greenery. Balloch couldn't believe it; the tears began streaming down his face, but this time, they were tears of joy. He had done it; he had finally done it. He had found *Mhorelia*."

A round of applause erupts from the group as the guide finishes his story. An overzealous man in the front perks up: "So, this is the door? This one right in front of us?"

John can't stop his eyes from rolling as the guide responds, "Oh yes, lad. This door right here is where Balloch entered, and this is also where he sealed it with a magical spell. Nobody has entered since, and nobody will enter ever again. Well, no one except . . . the Chosen One." The guide then tears down an overgrown bunch of vines just above the door, revealing an inscription in the rock:

FOREVER SEALED, NONE SHALL ENTER
EXCEPT FOR ONE, THE LONE DISSENTER
THEY'LL LIVE TO FIGHT, AND NEVER RUN
AND THUS BE NAMED, THE CHOSEN ONE
THEY'LL STAND THEIR GROUND, AND NEVER WAVER
TO ALL AROUND, A TRUE LIFESAVER
WHAT HAPPENS NEXT, CANNOT BE UNDONE
THE ASCENT BEGINS, FOR THE CHOSEN ONE

Everyone in the group—except for John—stares at the inscription in awe. *Magical spells . . . The Chosen One . . . They're eating this nonsense up,* John thinks.

"Well, who wants to go first? Step right up and lean back against it, just like Balloch did all those years ago," the guide says with a smile.

One by one, members of the group walk up to the stone door, cross their arms, and slowly lean back until they hit the rock. Most of them laugh it off, knowing deep down they weren't going to fall into some mystical land. Some faces do, however, show mild disappointment. The guide had shown such passion in his storytelling that they believed, if only for a moment, that they might just be the Chosen One.

As the guide waves John to give it a try, he shakes his head. "No thanks, I'll pass. Not really my cup of tea."

"Unfortunately, I can't take no for an answer, my friend," the guide replies, clearly annoyed but attempting to sound lighthearted.

"Really, I'm not interested," John says.

"Oh, but you must," the guide insists, trying but failing to remain lighthearted.

There is a palpable tension growing as John looks around the group, and then back to the guide.

Fine, if it'll shut you up, he thinks, amusing himself.

"Fine, if it'll shut you up," he says aloud.

The guide brushes the comment off as John slowly walks to the door. He turns around and crosses his arms, even slower, trying to milk this whole ordeal in an effort to annoy the guide.

It clearly works, as the guide blurts out, "Oh, get on with it, lad. We haven't got all day."

"I'm sorry to disappoint you all, but I am no Chosen One," he says as he leans backward toward the door, "and there is no such thing as—"

John's sentence is abruptly cut short as nothing breaks his fall, and he disappears into the mountainside.

CHAPTER 3

Trust falls are nice when someone's there to catch you. But if nothing breaks your fall, all that's left to be had is a throbbing head and a ringing in your ears—both of which John finds on the other side of the mountain wall.

Disoriented from slamming into the ground so abruptly, it takes a second for him to assess what just happened. After which he jolts up, looking frantically around for the door he just collapsed through. But, to his surprise, there is no door to be found. In fact, nothing looks right to John; it's as if he's been transported to another world. But he actually has, hasn't he?

His heart starts pounding, and he feels a tightness in his chest as the anxiety sets in. *What is this place? Where am I? How am I going to get back?* The thoughts start taking over his brain. Luckily, another thought pops into John's head: *"Quick inhale, long exhale, quick inhale, long exhale."* It's the voice of his therapist and one of the many tools she taught him in order to quell his anxiety. That tool, along with the simple phrase, "Everything is temporary," has gotten John through a lot of panic attacks over the last year.

As John feels his body loosening up, he takes in the world around him. The sun is shining brightly down upon him, and a soft breeze blows over his body. Behind where the door should be standing, spans a well-kept grassy meadow that goes on for about a hundred feet before making a steep drop to what looks like an ocean below. As he turns, he sees that this meadow meets up with what appears to be a field of grain, stretching out in front of him and standing about waist height.

In the distance are mountain ranges for miles and miles, each peak higher than the previous. Just to the left of where he fell stands a single tree—rather large, topped with a canopy of green, and with what looks like bright yellow melons hanging from it. This tree is most peculiar to John. Not so much the tree itself, but its placement, as there is nothing remotely like it nearby.

Curious, he walks toward the tree, stopping to look closer at one of the melons hanging down from a branch. Just after picking one of the bigger melons, he stiffens up, sensing something that he used to feel while on missions in the military . . . like he is being watched. At that moment, a blur comes from the top of the tree, and there's a *thud* behind him. He spins around and throws the melon as hard as he can toward the creature that now stands before him.

The creature—having dodged the melon by effortlessly leaning to one side—lets out a sigh before saying, "Is that any way to treat your host?"

It's a very strange-looking creature to John, and at five foot eleven, with easily two hundred pounds of shredded muscle, it's rather imposing too. It stands shirtless, its skin a dark violet-purple color. Small horns curl out from the top of its head, and a long tail pokes out from a pair of burlap pants, coming to a sharp point.

John stops for only a moment—taking in the creature's appearance and its witty comment—before lunging toward it.

After planting its right leg, the creature flips over John, whipping him with its tail while in midair, tearing a slit in his flannel and leaving a gash along his back. John lets out a grunt as he hits the ground and takes in the full pain of the slashing.

"You sure you don't want to talk this out, buddy?" the creature asks.

John gets to his feet and squares up to the creature. "I'm not your buddy," he replies before throwing a right hook. The creature throws up its arm to block the punch, then counters with a swift kick just under John's rib cage.

As John lies on the ground wheezing with the wind knocked out of him, the creature snickers. "At least make this fun for me." It then snaps its fingers, and a long serrated knife appears in its hand. It throws the knife at John's feet and beckons him to get up.

John slowly curls his fingers around the hilt of the twelve-inch knife—even during a fight he can't help but admire the craftsmanship of the blade. He takes a deep breath and jumps to his feet, taking several swipes at the creature. The creature dodges the attacks with ease, almost looking uninterested.

Before John's frustration takes over, he changes things up. Faking as if he's going to attempt another stab at the creature, he simply tosses the knife into the air. The creature's eyes follow it for only a moment, giving John just enough time to land his left fist square into its jaw. As it stumbles backward, John catches the knife and brings it down for the kill. But just before he makes contact, the creature vanishes, leaving a purple cloud of powder in its wake.

John put so much power behind the knife strike that his momentum takes him directly into the purple cloud and straight to the ground. Coughing profusely and covered in purple residue, he gets to his feet and braces for another attack. But another attack never comes, only the creature's voice from atop the large tree.

"Alright, alright, I get it; you can fight. Now, would you put that knife down so I can explain why you're here?"

CHAPTER 4

As the creature drops down from the tree and walks toward John, his grip tightens around the knife. Trust issues are one thing John never quite conquered during his time in therapy.

"Alright, keep the knife, see if I care. But I've been instructed to guide you, and that's what I'm going to do. Even though this seems like a pointless endeavor," the creature remarks.

"Guide me? Guide me to what?" John snaps back.

"Finally, you start asking the right questions. Can I start from the beginning? You know what? I'm going to start at the beginning. Walk with me."

John follows a step behind, unsure of what to make of all of this.

"First off, you can call me Kaigen. And you are?"

John can't think of a good reason to lie, so he doesn't. "John."

"I'm assuming you found your way here by means of that Scottish fellow on the other side? Yeah, I've heard his story, and you know, he got it almost entirely right. Well, the beginning of it, anyway."

John perks up. "You know the guide? So you can go back. Take me back. Take me back now!"

"Look, John, I'm about to go on a monologue here that will cover a lot of your questions, so please . . . no more interruptions."

John grunts under his breath but says nothing.

"When Balloch first fell through that door, a group of farmers greeted him. A big, burly folk, most similar to humans if

I had to say. He was asked to return to his world, and when he would not, they brought him to the king, King Cavarus Umor, who lived near the top of that mountain range over there." Kaigen points to a mountaintop far off in the distance.

"Above that spot, the food and resources for survival are unparalleled and, more importantly, plentiful. We call it the 'Enchanted Lands,' and it is separated from below by a two-hundred-foot-wide path with sheer, thousand-foot drops on either side. Cavarus built a castle there to make sure that everyone got what they needed, and nobody was left without. He was a good king, a noble king . . ." A look of sadness washes over Kaigen's face before he quickly brushes it off.

"At first sight of this outsider, the king was skeptical, but eventually, he decided to allow him to stay, and even showed him how to travel back to his world. For there is a door leading back to his, and *your*, world. It is forever bonded with a tree, which is identical to the one you saw when you first arrived, and the only two trees of their kind.

"Balloch traveled between worlds for some time, bringing back other humans with him, and showing them our magical world. They built their own lives here, and for a while, everyone lived in peace—that is, until Balloch decided he fancied the throne. He felt it was his right, and many others agreed, for they thought the king had gone soft by allowing everyone to have access to the Enchanted Lands. So Balloch snuck into the king's chamber late one night, and with the very blade you hold in your hand, he slit the king's throat and assumed his place as the new ruler of Mhorelia.

"Chaos unfolded rather quickly after that. He and his followers torched villages that did not recognize his rule; they burned forests to the ground, and they built a wall with one massive gate, which separated the Enchanted Lands, including his castle, from everyone else. To add to that, Balloch uprooted the tree, and with it, the door allowing someone to go back to your world; and he moved it inside of his castle walls, making it impossible to leave without his permission. Since that day, things have never been the same, for Balloch holds all the resources for him and his followers, leaving very little for the rest of Mhorelia."

Kaigen pauses for a moment. "Any questions?"

"Yeah, about a thousand. First question, the guide said Balloch came here hundreds of years ago. So, why isn't he dead?"

"Ah yes, I should've mentioned, time moves a bit differently here. From what I have gathered from my years of traveling to and from your world, ten years here is about a hundred and fifty in your world."

John shakes his head, not believing any of this, but he forces himself to soldier on, because unfortunately, it appears he is not waking up from this dream.

"Fine, I'll go with that. Second question: why on earth am I here? And how the hell was I the only one that fell through that door back there?"

"That's technically two questions . . . But I thought you would've figured that out by now; you're the Chosen One. The one who has come to defeat the new king and bring back peace to this world, or at least give it a try. You see, the king had a magical creature place a seal on the door, stopping anyone from entering, unless they possess the skills and honor to defeat him."

"That's ridiculous. Why would anyone do that when they could just have the door sealed forever?"

"I've always assumed it was his narcissistic belief that no person is capable of defeating him."

"That checks out. So, all I have to do in order to get home is defeat a narcissistic sociopath who took over a mystical world that has been unreachable for the last few hundred years. Seems easy enough; take me to him."

"Unfortunately, John, this is where it gets complicated."

"Oh, *this* is where it gets complicated."

"As you may have noticed, I can teleport. But I can only teleport myself and small objects, and you are neither of those things. So, in order to reach him, you must make *The Ascent*. That involves traveling up these mountains in front of us, traversing winding and treacherous cliff ledges, sailing across massive lakes, and dealing with every different climate you can imagine. By the way, you might want these."

Kaigen snaps his fingers, and a leather pouch appears, filled with water. He snaps his fingers again, and a leather-strapped bag appears, filled with bread, wrapped meat, clothes, and shoes.

"You'll need the clothes to blend in; don't want anyone getting spooked if they see you in the ones you're wearing."

He snaps his fingers one more time, and a small glass vial appears.

"What's that?" John asks.

"Ointment."

"Why would I need ointment?"

"To clean up that nasty cut on your back. I wouldn't want it to get infected." Kaigen gives John a wink before adding, "It's also got some calming properties as an added benefit."

John rolls his eyes at the word 'calming'—one of his least favorite words used by snake oil salesmen.

"I've also included a belt for you to sheathe that dagger. No need for you to cut yourself any more than you already have."

"You cut me . . ."

Kaigen shrugs his shoulders. "On this journey, you will encounter a variety of species here, some of which you may be familiar with, others you most certainly will not. You'll come across the denaros, tall and feathered creatures that live in the forests and look similar to a creature you have in your world. I believe you call them owls. Then there are the climours, a real moody bunch; they may remind you of a gorilla, and like a gorilla, they'll tear you in half if provoked, so tread lightly if you meet one. Most importantly, there are the alterian, majestic creatures that look exactly like wolves from your world, only much, much larger. While their beauty and grace are unmatched, so is their power. If you come across one on your journey, do not try to reason with it, do not try to befriend it, just turn and run. They are the toughest and most ruthless creatures here, who trust very few, and I suggest you do the same.

"Others include the widaps, the centaurs, the brackoa, the stagglehorn, and so on, and so forth. I'm not going to stand here and name them all for you."

John is trying hard to take in all the information Kaigen is giving him, but it all seems so unreal to him. His life has always been filled with routine and logic, certainly not creatures and quests. Every fiber of his being is telling him to stop talking to this thing standing in front of him, that this is all some ridiculous coma dream from hitting his head too hard. But his curiosity—and maybe a bit of intrigue—keeps him asking questions.

"What's the deal with all your finger snapping?"

"Just another one of my many talents. I can snap my fingers and summon anything that I'd like, as long as it's right where I left it. I can also send objects anywhere I wish."

"As long as it's small enough," John says.

"Now you're getting it."

John holds up his new dagger. "Would this be about as big as you could go?"

"Oh, I could go bigger, but my limit would be somewhere around a full-length sword."

"Then, why didn't you give me a sword?"

"You're hard to please, John. Just be happy with that, would you?"

John eyes the dagger intently, and another thought pops into his head. "How do you know so much about the new king, and why do you have his knife?"

Kaigen takes a long pause and avoids eye contact with John. "I serve the king, and he has tasked me with keeping tabs on you as you make your way to him."

John stops walking abruptly. "What? You serve the man who has me locked in here? The man who burned villages to the ground?

The man who is starving all those who oppose him? I knew I had it right, pegging you as a coward the moment I saw you."

"Things aren't always as simple as they seem."

Excuses, excuses . . . John thinks. Anger and frustration drip off of John's words: "You really are a coward. Let me ask you one final question. You listed lots of different creatures and animals, but you never said anything about yourself. I don't know who or *what* you are, but please tell me there aren't any more of you around this place. Please tell me I won't encounter any spineless, traitorous, honorless *things* like you on my journey."

Kaigen's face goes completely blank, as if he had never felt an emotion before in his life. John meets his piercing stare, and there is a clear shift in his tone as Kaigen replies, "Like I said, I am here to keep track of you during this frivolous journey on which you will most likely fail . . . and that journey starts *now*."

Before John can reply, Kaigen turns away and vanishes, leaving John alone, staring at a shimmering purple cloud hanging in the air.

Chapter 5

When Kaigen saw the door to Earth start to glow—signifying someone had used the door to Mhorelia—his heart skipped a beat. He's waited a long time for someone to fall through that door, and John did not disappoint. He's an angry one—that's for sure—but maybe that's just what Mhorelia needs.

These thoughts envelop him as he stands in front of Balloch's Hall—an enormous building that sits inside the towering castle walls. The stone blocks used to construct it were laid so precisely that the walls appear to be a smooth surface scaling forty feet high. He takes a deep breath and proceeds up the sizable stone steps that lead to its entrance. He pauses for a moment before knocking, and as he does, the door slowly creaks open.

Once inside, he can smell the oil of the lamps burning along the walls, illuminating a long ornate carpet. The carpet ends at another set of steps, smaller than the first, but much more impressive, as they are laid with bronze. At the top of the steps sits a golden throne engulfed in the shadows of the castle walls.

As Kaigen walks toward the throne, his heart begins to race. He has served the king for a couple of years—albeit against his will—and if there is one thing he's learned, it's that the king has a temper. He stops suddenly as the voice of Balloch cuts through the darkness: "Well, what of him?"

Kaigen hesitates to respond as Balloch's deep voice echoes off of the castle walls.

Balloch does not appreciate the delay. "I said, *what of him?*"

Kaigen sheepishly answers, "Master, he is nothing but a man, who stands no chance against the mighty Balloch. Fear not—"

"*Fear!* I fear nothing!" Balloch interjects furiously.

Kaigen falls to one knee and drops his head. "Apologies, my king. I meant only to say that this man is not a threat, and he most certainly is *not* the Chosen One."

"Do not patronize me. We've not had a person come through that door in decades; he must be someone of value. After all, I did not force that denaro to put just any spell on that door; it was only to open for the most honorable fighter . . . *The Chosen One.*"

Kaigen again hesitates, never truly knowing how to speak to the king—him being such a volatile man. "This outsider goes by the name of John. He is a confident, strong man with excellent hand-to-hand combat skills. He even showed promise when I tossed him your knife, almost besting me. His resilience and relentless nature may prove to be his best qualities when it comes to his journey."

Balloch spits at Kaigen's feet. "*Relentless?* Oh, he'll relent. Many have attempted to usurp me, and not one has even come close. Something always gets in their way. Be it the cliffs, the storms, the cold, the heat, the stings of the brackoa, the venom of the widaps, or the ferocity of the climour; something will always stop them from reaching me. And if they make it to my gates, they will face the wrath of my army! And if one lucky soul slips through the cracks and finds themselves at my door"—Balloch unsheathes his sword—"they will face their greatest challenge yet, *Balloch MacNicol,* ruler of Mhorelia!"

CHAPTER 6

The first few miles of John's journey were neither perilous nor exciting. Compared to some of the other hikes he's done in his life—like the thirty-one mile march up the Cordillera Blanca mountain range in Peru, or the forty-five mile trek through the Atlas Mountains in Tunisia—this is a walk in the park.

After changing into the clothes Kaigen had given him, he quickly made his way through the fields of grain, picking a long piece to chew on as he walked. There were figures working far in the distance to either side of him—most likely the farmers that Kaigen had mentioned—and he opted to stay as far from them as he could, ducking down at times to avoid being seen. If all goes well, he hopes to complete most of this trip alone.

An hour of walking later and he now sits by a stream, washing off as much as he can of the purple coating that's left covering his body after his scuffle with Kaigen. As he finishes off his pouch of water, he thinks back to what Kaigen said: *"Things aren't always as simple as they seem." What could've possibly happened to make him side with a madman?*

He pushes past that thought and takes stock of his supplies. His pockets contain only his phone, cigar, lighter, and rental car keys. The phone was shattered during his fight with Kaigen, and the cigar comes out ruined as well—only worsening John's mood. Next, he rummages through the bag Kaigen gave him, hoping for some better luck. *At least he left me some food,* John thinks before taking a bite of the hardened bread. *Stale. Figures.* He then pulls out the corked vial of ointment and stares at it. "Why must everyone in my life be so naive?" he mutters before tossing it into the stream.

After filling up his pouch with water, he trudges on for another few miles. Slowly, the hill goes from a gradual to a steep incline, and John is loving it. A tough hike has always been a great way to clear his head. What he isn't loving is the fact that he's already gone through his food rations, and the scenery here is much more dismal than when he first arrived. At some point during the last five or so miles, the lush fields had turned to deciduous forests. He looks around, reminded of the time he spent a spring in rural Vermont, half expecting to hear birds start chirping. But there are no sounds to be heard. And with the sun getting lower in the sky, and the terrain getting rougher, he needs to find a place to sleep, and some food to go along with that.

Another mile goes by, and something catches his eye—a dense packing of raspberry bushes just up ahead. These raspberries— bright scarlet red and the size of his hand—are unlike anything John has ever seen. John can't believe his luck. He quickly rips one from a branch, cutting the top of his hand on a massive thorn hiding inside the bush.

"Oof." *At least it isn't too deep,* he thinks as only a small drop of blood drips down his hand. Taking a bite of the berry, he forgets about the pain from the thorn wounding him. *Sweet yet subtle, this would be amazing in a Thanksgiving pie.* He scarfs down two more berries and fills his pack with seven more.

Excited and energized, he decides to go a little farther before packing it in for the night. But as he walks along, a most peculiar thing happens. He can't be sure why, but an ear-to-ear grin forms on his face, and not long after that, he begins to laugh out loud as he walks. Everything is changing around him; the trees are a little bit brighter, the grass a little more green. He even starts to hear the most beautiful voices singing in the distance. It's like he's woken up in a whimsical fairy tale, and little blue birds might pick him up at any moment to carry him to his destination.

But then, before he can take it all in, everything changes. His feet feel heavy, as if someone had replaced them with cinder blocks, and he struggles with every step. The vibrant colors he loved just a moment ago suddenly shine too brightly for him, and his head begins to pulse. Nausea sets in as the objects in front of him start to blur. The whole world seems to be spinning around him, and he finds himself yelling the one word he had hoped he wouldn't need to utter on this journey: "Help!"

And just like that, the world goes dark.

CHAPTER 7

John's next memory is hazy, but it's one he won't soon forget. The sounds of whispers reverberate around him: "What should we do with him?"

"Who is he?"

"He could be a spy. End him."

"Quiet!" a comforting yet powerful voice says, cutting through the whispers, causing John to stir.

His senses come back to him in waves. He's propped up against what seems to be a large and jagged rock. He can feel the cold dirt beneath him and a warmth on his left cheek from what he assumes is a campfire. The savory smell of something cooking nearby touches his nose as his eyes slowly open.

At first, he isn't sure what to make of what he's looking at— as his eyes are still adjusting to the darkness around him, and his brain is still very much in a fog from whatever caused him to pass out. He can make out the shape of a person standing over him— a woman, fierce and stunning by the looks of her.

He notices her height first. At six foot two, she'd be imposing even if John were on his feet. Her long, silklike, curly red hair flows over her toned shoulders, coming to rest just above the small of her back. And her ripped physique easily shows through her all-leather getup, composed of a halter top, skintight pants, and sharp, pointed boots.

John is so busy admiring her figure—and is still in such a daze—that it takes him a moment to spot the three-foot-long blade she has pointed right at his throat. His eyes slowly widen as he stares blankly up at her. He is rarely at a loss for words.

She speaks first. "Would you look at that; he finally decides to wake from his slumber."

John remains silent, looking around, trying to make sense of his surroundings.

"You look a little confused, so let me clear things up for you. Next time you go wandering through the Badlands, try to be a bit less naive," she continues before taking a bite of one of the berries.

"Don't!" John blurts out as he lifts his body up. She steps on his chest and pushes him back to the ground.

"Relax. It wasn't the berries that did you in; it was the thorns." She pokes his hand—now bandaged—with her sword. "I figured even a woodsman like yourself would have known to be more cautious around these parts."

Woodsman? John thinks.

"And what are you doing this far east, anyway? Your people usually keep to themselves," she says as she presses the tip of her sword into his left pec, directly above his heart.

John pauses for a moment, unconfident that she'll believe his lie. "Traveling."

"Traveling …?" She gazes into his ocean-blue eyes, trying to get a read on him. "And does the name 'Lorena' mean anything to you?"

John shakes his head. *What is she going on about?*

"Really?" she presses.

"Should it?"

"I suppose not," she says before quickly sheathing her sword. "Well, I'm Lorena. Now get up and come sit by the fire; it gets cold at night around these parts. You can stay with us tonight, but after that, we leave you."

As John takes a seat by the fire, he eyes the three other people sitting around it, all of whom look unsettled. Two of them look a bit younger and are clearly brothers—with matching facial features and body types, they could even be twins. Their long, lustrous brown hair is half tied up into topknots while the other half falls down their backs. They are dressed head to toe in thin brown leather armor, with green cloaks to complete the ensemble.

While still tall and having the same pale skin as the rest, the third person looks much more ominous and menacing. Black leather armor covers the majority of her body, with a black hooded cloak up over her head. The firelight dances off her stoic face, and jet-black hair falls from her hood. While nobody looks particularly happy to have John in their presence, she looks downright angry.

"That's Melara, and those two are Killian and Darian, twins if you hadn't noticed. But we still don't know your name," says Lorena.

"John . . . John Atwater."

"Well, John, Melara just finished cooking up some stagglehorn if you'd like something to eat. We may even have a morsel of Elvish bread to spare."

John hides his surprise at the word "elvish" and examines the four of them again—this time noticing the pointed ears poking out of their elegant heads of hair, the quivers full of arrows strapped to their backs, and the bows lying at their feet. Maybe it's a side effect of the thorn pricking him, or maybe it's the fact that he has seen so many previously unreal things today, but he's surprised at how quickly he comes to terms with the fact that he's sitting around a fire with four elves. He smiles slightly, thinking about how proud Jayden would be.

But that nice thought is short-lived as Melara interjects. "Do not give him any of our Elvish bread; he doesn't deserve such pleasantries."

"Relax, we have no quarrel with the woodsmen, at least not *this* woodsman," Lorena states.

Melara's eyebrows raise, but she brushes off the odd phrasing. "That may be, but I am not convinced he is a woodsman. Why would a woodsman travel this far east? It is not in their nature. What if he's a spy?"

"Again with this? So, you're saying Balloch sent someone all the way down here just to see what we're up to?"

"I'm not talking about Balloch . . ."

"Ohhh . . . that's something I hadn't thought of, but just as unlikely." Lorena turns to John and continues, "You wouldn't be working for a creature named 'Kaigen,' would you?"

John's heart begins to pound, but he tries to play it cool. "A creature named . . . Kaigen?"

"A *foul* creature," Melara adds.

"He's not all bad, just misunderstood," says Lorena.

"Misunderstood? Why must you give that vile creature your sympathy? I don't care what he's been through."

"Melara . . . he has nobody."

Melara shrugs. "I don't really care. Ever since he came into our lives some seventeen years ago, he has been nothing but trouble. Spending his time spying on us for Balloch, all the while we suffered."

"Enough of this! He isn't a spy, and that's the last I'll hear of it. Let's just eat our food, get some rest, and we will send John back home in the morning," Lorena snaps.

A silent tension lingers in the air. John doesn't want to raise any suspicion, but he also has no plans to change his route. "Actually, I was thinking of heading up the mountain a little farther."

All eyes shift to John, and Lorena's demeanor shifts dramatically. "No, you are heading back home in the morning. Is that going to be an issue?"

John can feel his temper rising. He's in a place he doesn't want to be, surrounded by people—no, *elves*—he doesn't want to be with, and he's been done taking orders for a long time now. He knows he can't turn back, but he also knows he can't take all four elves by himself.

"I said, is that going to be a problem?" Lorena repeats and slaps him on the shoulder. Upon doing so, a small yet unmistakable bit of purple residue puffs off of John's collar.

Oh no . . .

All four of the elves jump to their feet. Melara knocks an arrow and simultaneously shoulders her bow. Before John can stand up, Lorena gives him a powerful kick right in his sternum. John tumbles backward, slamming into a thick tree trunk about ten feet from where he was sitting.

"I knew it! He's a spy!" shouts Melara. "Let me put an arrow right between his eyes."

John stumbles to his feet, attempting to speak, but nothing comes out. Excruciating pain follows every breath he takes. He tries again. "Wait, I can explain."

But Lorena doesn't want to give him the chance; looking toward Melara, she says, "Do it."

Melara releases the arrow without a second of hesitation, but right before it hits John, a purple blur careens into him, knocking both of them to the ground.

John looks up in shock. *Kaigen?*

Kaigen jumps to his feet. "Everyone, stop!"

"Not a chance," Melara whispers as she lets another arrow fly at Kaigen.

In a flash, he swats the arrow away with his tail and shakes his head in disappointment. "I was really hoping we could talk this out . . ." He leaps toward the twins and teleports himself into them, knocking both to the ground before they have any time to react. Melara removes a dagger from her boot and takes a swipe at Kaigen, but he teleports behind her and kicks her in the back. The blade never had a chance. In his final move, he teleports behind Lorena, holding John's dagger to her throat.

John pats his hip where he last saw the dagger, not even realizing Kaigen had taken it.

"Now . . . how about we try this again?" Kaigen says as everyone gets to their feet.

Lorena lets out a sigh, and surprisingly, she calmly responds, "Oh, Kaigen, it's been a while."

Kaigen removes the knife from Lorena's neck. "Think you can control these children while I do some enlightening, Lorena?" That comment gets him three sets of glaring eyes from the other elves. "Allow me to get straight to the point: John Atwater is the Chosen One."

"What?" the twins shout in unison.

Melara shakes her head, and Lorena's smirk quickly fades as she asks, "What did you just say?"

"Why is it I always end up repeating myself around you people? It is as if I am surrounded by inferior beings who lack the ability to—"

"Enough of your jokes!" snaps Lorena.

Any mutual respect that Lorena and Kaigen had for each other seems to have disappeared as she continues, "The Chosen One is a myth brought about by *your* master! It has no basis in truth and is merely a shallow attempt to convince himself that he has even a shred of honor."

"Is that so . . . John, why don't you inform these thankless elves how you arrived in Mhorelia, from the beginning."

All eyes turn to John. "Short story, really. I took a trip to Scotland for work, went on a hike on the Isle of Skye, fell through a door in a mountainside, and then I had the pleasure of meeting this bundle of joy," John explains as he gestures to Kaigen.

The elves look John up and down, and Melara clearly doesn't believe a word of it. "Lovely story; did you two practice that one together?"

Kaigen paces in frustration. John himself is at his wits' end. He's tired, hungry, and even after only five minutes with them, he's already sick of elves.

"You know what, I'm done with this! Do you think I want to be here? Do you think I want to be surrounded by elves, and poisonous brambles, and obnoxious, purple, whatever-the-hell he is? Do you think I want to hike to the top of a mountain to kill someone I don't even know, wearing these ridiculous clothes? No!"

John tears the shirt off his torso and throws it in the fire. As the shirt goes up in flames, the fire illuminates his muscular upper body. Everything becomes visible to the elves: his broad shoulders, the jagged scar through his otherwise flawless abs, the bullet hole scar still visible from his visit to Vietnam, and most importantly, *The Undesirables* tattooed across his left pec.

"No way," mouths Killian.

"It's really him," whispers Darian.

Kaigen grins. "I told you he's not from this world."

"This proves nothing. Just because he isn't from here doesn't make him the Chosen One," declares Lorena.

"Seriously? Look, I understand you thought it would be you who would slay the mighty Balloch—"

"I have spent the last twenty years trying to free us from his terror!" interrupts Lorena.

"And look how far you've gotten. Stuck at the bottom of the island to regroup, *again*, telling yourself that this time will be different. Well, maybe this time can be different, if you would just take this for the blessing that it is and let John help you," urges Kaigen.

John scoffs, "There's no way I'm helping them. I can do this alone."

"I am through with this foolishness! Am I the only one here with any sense?" yells Kaigen. "You all may have different reasons, but you have a common goal—to kill the king."

"And why are you so keen to help us kill the king? You're his servant, his puppet . . . *his pet*," says Melara.

Kaigen's brow furrows as his grip on the knife tightens. Lorena slowly wraps her fingers around the hilt of her sword. Melara flips the dagger in her hand and assumes a fighting stance. Just before all hell breaks loose, Killian shyly whispers, "The denaros."

"Excuse me?" Lorena responds.

"The denaros," Killian repeats, a bit more confidently this time. "What if we let the denaros decide? We do ourselves no favors by fighting each other, miles away from our true enemy."

"The boy has a point," Kaigen agrees.

"They did place the spell upon the door, and they are the wisest among us," adds Darian.

"And more importantly, they're unbiased," says Kaigen. "They have no reason to accept him as the Chosen One. They may even kill him for stepping foot on their sacred land."

"Works for me," says Melara.

Lorena thinks about it for a moment. "I don't like this idea."

"Unless you have a better one, I say we go with it, or I can leave you all how I found you," Kaigen says as he tosses his knife to John.

John observes Lorena intently as she ponders her options. Maybe it's the exhaustion, or maybe it's the exhilaration, but he finds himself curiously nervous. He's not nervous for a fight, no; he's always ready for a fight. He's nervous that his journey may end right here, and that is what's curious to him, because despite his previous outburst, he doesn't want it to.

Through gritted teeth, Lorena responds, "Fine. Show him the way."

CHAPTER 8

John and Kaigen walk silently along a thin, moss-covered path, through what seems like a never-ending forest. Well, it was a path when they started; now they're just zigzagging around towering trees in the darkness. Each one must be four stories tall, with not a branch on them until about thirty feet up.

John feels a bit more comfortable after changing back into the clothes he arrived in—his favorite buffalo plaid flannel bringing him a small sense of home in this strange world. However, the comfort stops there, for he has no clue what to think of Kaigen. He may have saved John's life, but he also threatened to leave him to fight to the death if Lorena chose Option B. And what is the deal with the two of them? They're acting like old college buddies, the way they jar back and forth with each other. Which is more than John can say about the other elves. The twins are shy and look relatively indifferent toward Kaigen, but Melara has a contempt for him that is almost tangible.

After about twenty minutes of walking, John decides to end the silence. "How did you find me back there? Do you have a tracker on me, or did you just make a lucky guess?"

"When I teleport, I can only go to locations I've been to before. Luckily for me, I've been almost everywhere, but unluckily for me, I had no idea where you were along your journey. So I started where I left you, then found my way to the elves' camp. And just in time, I might add." Kaigen looks back at John. "You're welcome, by the way."

"I had it under control."

"Is that so? Because from where I was standing, Melara almost sent an arrow right between those pretty blue eyes of yours."

"Hmph, she's a real charmer. How do you know them, anyway? They don't seem to be very fond of you."

"I've known them for a while now, Lorena for the longest. I met her close to nineteen years ago." Kaigen shakes his head and chuckles. "That's a fun story for another time."

Nineteen? Didn't Melara say seventeen . . .? John thinks, but doesn't interrupt. *Best to file that knowledge away for later.*

"Anyway, those elves were the first to try to make The Ascent to remove Balloch from the throne. Their first attempt came fifteen years ago, and they have failed many times since that day. The king has never paid much attention to them, but for the last few years, he has asked me to follow them and report on their progress. Never to assist, only to report. Unfortunately for them, they've never even come close. In fact, they rarely make it around the denaros' land, the land we're walking through at this very moment."

"Why don't they just do what we're doing, and cut through this forest?"

"The denaros don't take kindly to visitors. They prefer their solitude among the trees and the night sky."

"If they're so opposed to visitors, then what are they going to say when we show up?" asks John.

Kaigen stops abruptly and faces John. "That's a fair question, and if I'm being honest, I have no idea. But you'll be sure to let me know if it goes well, for you must do this next bit alone."

"What? You're not coming?" John is taken aback.

"Look, John, my relationship with the denaros is complicated at best. I will only hurt your appeal to them."

"You're unbelievable. You brag about saving me, and then drop me off into a situation where I could immediately be killed again. What's your endgame?"

"I have no endgame, John. I am merely here to guide you on your journey. And like I said, for this bit, you're better off without me."

John is yet again unsure of what to make of Kaigen. With every sentence he spits out, John feels he understands his motive even less. One minute he's helping him, and the next he's going on about how he can't assist in any way. The only thing John knows for sure is that he doesn't trust him.

"Fine, leave me. I don't need you anyway." John starts to walk away, but turns back after a step. "Let me ask you one more question. If you aren't supposed to assist me in *any way* . . . then why did you save me?"

"So you admit it! I did save you!"

John turns around, disgusted, and takes off.

"Wait! The truth is . . ." His voice trails off as if he's deep in thought. John stops in his tracks, but doesn't turn around. "The truth is, I felt bad for you. It would be embarrassing for your journey to end so quickly."

John briskly leaves without turning back, not wanting to give Kaigen the benefit of seeing his face flush with anger.

Before long, John finds himself at the edge of a large circular clearing, about a hundred yards in diameter. He surveys the clearing for any denaro, not really knowing what he's looking for. The only description he's been given is that they look like some sort of overgrown owl. After a minute of searching, he steps into the field of grass, each blade about eighteen inches tall and blowing in the cool night breeze. If the circumstances were different, this place would be a relaxing sanctuary for John to clear his head, but his mind is racing instead. *Where the hell are they?*

As he gets to the center of the field, the wind picks up. Shadows circle him on the ground, and he looks up to see huge silhouettes swirling around him in the moonlit sky. He feels a twinge of panic and clutches his knife as the figures surround him. One by one, they gracefully land, eight of the most majestic creatures John has ever seen.

Each stands at least twelve feet tall and is covered with shimmering feathers of varying hues. Their sharp talons grip the soft soil beneath them. They stand quietly for some time, their piercing eyes locked on John. The way they cock their heads slowly to the side, as if they are evaluating him, only increases John's restlessness.

Finally, one steps forward, a clear two feet taller than the rest. While the others have different shades of colored feathers covering their bodies, this one is charcoal black from top to bottom, making it all the more intimidating to John.

Her soft yet thunderous voice carries through the night as she speaks. "Who dares to enter our sacred land?"

Might as well get right to it . . . "My name is John Atwater . . . and I am the Chosen One."

"Hmmm . . . is that so? And what proof do you have of this?"

He sheathes his knife. "I come from another world. And today, I fell through the door to this world. Now all I want to do is get back home."

The towering creature looks toward another, this one much smaller than the rest. "What say you, Ellioch? It was you who placed the spell upon that door."

"That I did, Alura. And when I did, I made certain it would only open for an honorable fighter, one with courage and the inability to relent. As per Balloch's request."

John pipes up, "And here I am . . ."

Alura looks to John and ominously responds, "Hmmm, we shall see," before waving her wing in a flourish. Upon doing so, she knocks John over with a gust of wind, and with that gust appear three people in a full sprint, heading right for John.

John jumps to his feet and barely has time to register the first attacker, who swings a thick club directly at his head, missing by inches as John ducks down in the nick of time. Unfortunately, John doesn't see the second attacker coming; the assailant jumps into the air and drop-kicks him in the chest with both feet.

When John gets to his feet, he has a brief moment to compose himself as the two attackers gather their footing. He grunts and spits to the side.

"Alright, let's do this."

Another swing of the club grazes John's shoulder, but throws the attacker off balance, leaving John an opening to land two heavy punches to his rib cage. The second punch cracks two ribs, and the man cries out in pain.

Feeling the presence of the second attacker, John throws his arms up, but still catches a right hook to the side of his body, followed quickly by an uppercut to his jaw. John stumbles backward into the first attacker, who promptly puts him in a chokehold. He grasps at the attacker's massive arm as the breath is drained from his lungs. He can feel the world going black around him, and in one final attempt, he thrusts his foot backward with all the strength he has left, connecting with the attacker's kneecap and snapping his leg.

The man lets out a bloodcurdling scream and releases his grip, giving John the chance to unsheathe his knife, then, in one swift motion, spin around and slit his throat. As the blood drips from the knife, he stares down the other attacker, out of breath but never more confident. He's never lost a one-on-one fight before, and he isn't losing one today.

They both run at each other, and John tackles him with such ferocity that it slams the attacker's head into the ground, knocking him unconscious. In a fit of rage and still clutching his knife, he pounds on him until the life leaves his body.

As John gets up, standing above the man, he notices for the first time that there is a third attacker, patiently waiting about fifteen paces ahead of him with her bow drawn. The second they make eye contact, she lets the arrow fly, and it sticks halfway into John's shoulder.

Adrenaline still pumping and without so much as a wince, he looks at the arrow, and then back at the shooter. "Really?" he says before flipping his knife in the air, catching it by the blade, then hurling it into her chest. The bow falls from her hand as she drops to the ground, dead within seconds.

All that can be heard is John's heavy breathing as he looks around at the three bodies lying on the ground. As his breath slows, the bodies slowly vanish before his eyes, as well as the arrow lodged in his shoulder. Bewildered, he looks at the denaros, who haven't moved a feather since the fight began. Without an ounce of sympathy, Alura concludes what John has known his entire life. "Hmmm, it appears you can fight after all."

"Excuse me?" John replies.

"We had to be sure you were capable, and as it seems, you show promise to be the Chosen One."

"Promise? What do you mean, *promise?*"

"You are the first to set foot in this clearing in twenty years . . . and live." John picks up his knife as she continues, "Now begone, before I change my mind."

They move to fly away, and John calls out, "Wait! Does this mean we can pass through your land?"

"Hmmm, we do not condone what you're doing . . . but as long as you are in their company, the elves who sit at our doorstep can pass through."

Don't condone what I'm doing . . . unbelievable . . . And how did they know about the elves? "Fine, and what about my wound?" He points to his shoulder, now slowly oozing blood.

The denaros all take to the air with one big swoosh of their wings, and Alura yells back, "That is not our concern."

"Seriously?" John says aloud, to nobody but himself. He cuts a piece of flannel from his shirt and ties it around his wound to stop the bleeding, before making his way back to the group.

He slows his pace when he can see the fire through the trees, and using the moss to mask his footsteps, he creeps forward until he is just within earshot of the elves. They are still sitting around the fire with Kaigen, gossiping about John.

"He's dead. For sure, he's dead. Nobody trespasses on the denaros' land and lives to tell the tale," says Melara.

"Ye of little faith. I bet he is on his way back right now with not so much as a scratch on him," Kaigen says.

"Enough of this talk; he is not the Chosen One," says Lorena.

"But, Lorena . . ." Killian starts.

"His markings," finishes Darian.

"In his world, they call them tattoos," informs Kaigen.

"It doesn't matter what kind of markings he has—"

"*Tattoos*," Kaigen corrects.

"Whatever. A mark does not make you a warrior. I bet he didn't even visit the denaros. I bet he turned and ran like a coward," Lorena says.

At that moment, John can't take the belittling any longer, and he steps into the firelight. Startled, the elves jump to their feet.

"Bit jumpy, aren't we?" asks John.

Bloody, dirty, and covered in sweat . . . He's looked better.

"So much for 'not a scratch,'" jokes Kaigen. "What the hell happened?"

John sits down on a log by the fire. "Eh, it was nothing, really. Just met a couple of big owls, chitchatted for a little bit, and then killed three people . . ."

The elves remain speechless. He picks out a piece of Elvish bread from the bag next to Killian and takes a bite. "Anyway, they're going to let you all pass through their land." He can't help but smirk while he finishes speaking. "But only if I am there to accompany you."

Melara scowls. "You must be joking."

"Afraid not, lady. It appears I just may be the Chosen One, after all."

He still doesn't believe it himself, but he can see how much it bothers her, so he goes along with it. John also notices that the twins are desperately trying to hide their smiles. *Maybe not all of them hate me after all.*

Probably a smidge more confidently than he should, and with way too much sarcasm, he grabs a cup of liquid sitting by the fire and stands up abruptly. "So let's raise a glass to this new alliance, one that will forever be remembered as—"

"Enough!" shouts Lorena. "We do not need your mockery on this journey. We will have enough trouble as it is."

John doesn't respond. He just stands there, staring blankly back at her. He hears the words, but for some reason, he can't quite make sense of what she is saying.

"Well? What are you staring at?" Lorena asks.

John tries to speak, but words refuse to form. *What's happening to me?* His face goes pale, the cup falls from his hand, his left knee buckles, and he falls forward toward the fire. Kaigen teleports in front of him, catching him before he hits the flames, and lays him gently on the ground.

"What's wrong with him?" asks Lorena. Kaigen tears off the hastily made bandage from John's shoulder and removes his shirt, revealing dark purple lines branching from the wound.

Kaigen looks up toward Lorena and responds grimly with only one word, "Poison."

Chapter 9

John gasps for air and shields his eyes from the blinding light of the sun. His body shakes uncontrollably, and his breathing is rapid as he tries to get a grip on his surroundings. An elf runs to his side, and John grabs his arm forcefully. It's Darian, or maybe it's Killian. John couldn't tell them apart on the best of days, and given his current state, not a chance.

The elf yells to his brother, "Darian, get me some water!"

So this is Killian, John thinks as Darian tosses a pouch of water toward them. John loosens his grip on Killian's arm, allowing him to pour the water into his mouth.

"Breathe, John," Killian says calmly.

After a few long breaths, he looks down to see that his wound left by the arrow has been skillfully bandaged, as well as the slice on his back from his first encounter with Kaigen. *Kaigen.* John looks around but can't locate him.

"If you're looking for Kaigen, he left just before sunup. Not sure when he'll be back," says Killian.

Figures, John thinks, rolling his eyes—not so much bummed Kaigen left as he is annoyed that he left him alone with these elves. Although Killian seems nice enough.

"You should be thanking him," Killian adds, pulling out a vial from his bag. "If he had not had this ointment, you would most certainly have perished. While I am an excellent healer, the poison that entered your blood was starting to take over."

John recognizes the vial as the one he threw in the stream at the start of his journey. Kaigen must have found it when he was tracking John to the elves' encampment.

"This ointment is very rare; I have never seen this much of it in one place. It can cure almost any affliction, and it comes from the talons of a denaro. However, it can only be harvested upon their death. How Kaigen came about this much of it is unknown to me, but there is one dose left, so use it wisely," instructs Killian before placing it in John's bag.

"Thank you," John says, "and thanks for not leaving me to die."

"I am a healer, John. I would never leave someone to die." He leans in close and whispers, "Especially not the Chosen One."

John smirks and looks toward Melara and Lorena, who are packing up their camp rather impatiently. "Yeah, but they might."

"Ah yes . . . They'll come around; just give them time. Oh, and Kaigen told me to give you this." Killian hands John another shirt. "He said not to ruin this one."

Melara glances over at John and Killian. "Are you two done holding hands? We're already behind schedule as it is."

The group finishes packing and enters the forest one at a time. Melara takes the lead, followed by Killian and Darian. Before John can enter, Lorena places the flat side of her sword across his chest to stop him. "Listen up, we may be stuck together for now, but if you cross us at any point along this journey, you will not live to regret it."

As the two of them lock eyes, he wonders if they could ever coexist peacefully. Probably not. He steps into the forest without a word, having learned long ago that sometimes the best thing to say . . . is nothing at all.

John catches up to the twins—finding their company to be the least hostile. As they walk, he learns more about their lives over the last twenty years, more about the journey that awaits them, and more about Mhorelia itself.

Killian explains, "Mhorelia is essentially a circular island that stretches a few hundred miles from one side to the other. The landscape is flat around the edges of the island, with enough basic resources for the population to survive, *barely*. As you make your way toward the center of the island, the terrain steps upward in a series of large plateaus, each one far different than the last. These once well-populated plateaus leading to the Enchanted Lands are now home to only a few small encampments of people, who share the land with all sorts of dangerous creatures.

"After Balloch took over, many chose to join him, most notably the centaurs and the shape-shifters."

"Shape-shifters?" John says.

"Yes, like Kaigen. If he chooses, he can shape-shift back into a more human form, one of great strength. Why he never does is a mystery to us all."

"A mystery indeed. And what benefits does taking this current form have?" asks John.

"When Kaigen is purple, he has heightened skill in elusiveness, speed, and stealth."

"And they can all teleport like him?"

"No, not all of them. Some could teleport. Others had the ability to fly, or throw fire, or even the ability to become unseen to the eye. Naturally, Balloch decided these could all be of use to him, so he bribed their villages with resources from the Enchanted Lands, and in return, they would do his bidding. They *were* a magnificent species, but unfortunately, they were deadly under Balloch's rule."

"*Were?* Did something happen to them?"

"Well—" Killian starts before Darian shoots him a look. "That's a long story . . . one for a different time."

John rubs his forehead in thought, both puzzled and annoyed. Feeling constantly like he isn't being clued in on all the information he needs, information that may be vital to him in the future. This kind of leadership would never have been tolerated in The Undesirables . . . but these elves aren't The Undesirables.

Killian seamlessly picks up where he left off, acting as if nothing had been withheld. "The Mhorelians who did not join his army fled down the mountain and away from his terror. They now sit at the bottom of these mountains with very few resources to survive. Most have accepted the fact that this is what life is going to be from now on, but others have sworn to take back the throne and restore balance to this once great land. We are one of the few groups that still believe.

"Unfortunately, over the last twenty years, we have made little progress; something always sets us back. Most of the time, we run out of resources like food, water, or medical supplies, and we need to turn back to resupply. Sometimes, the weather makes parts of the island impassable. Other times, we have dealt with injuries that require more medical attention than Darian or I can provide."

"Do you always end up at the bottom of the island where I ran into you?" asks John.

"Not always—sometimes just the nearest safe haven. But when we need a long break, the lower we go, the better. Balloch and his forces would never travel this far from the Enchanted Lands."

John knows he shouldn't ask, but the question nags at him. "You have tried and failed so many times . . . Do you ever worry that this task may be impossible?"

"You're right, we have tried and failed time and time again, but we do not have the liberty to think that way. This is our home, and we need to fight for it. Besides, I have a feeling that this time will be different."

"And why is that?"

"Because this time, we have you," Darian says.

John considers this as they march through the forest. He hasn't had people counting on him in quite some time, and he has to admit to himself, it feels good. In fact, if these twins believe in him, maybe soon enough, the others will too. One thing still puzzles him, however. "If it is such a journey to get to the Enchanted Lands, how did food and resources make their way to all parts of the island?"

"Ah yes, I almost forgot. There are two long paths that jut out from the Enchanted Lands and circle down to the bottom of Mhorelia. They branch off at various points and lead to every major part of the island. We call these the 'Enchanted Paths.' Sadly, Balloch had them barricaded up shortly after he took over as king. His men built stone walls so high and thick that no one could ever take them down."

"Of course he did . . ." says John.

Deciding he's heard enough for the time being, he opts to walk in silence for a while. Soon, they step into the clearing where John fought the previous night; however, there are no signs that there ever was a fight. Instead, there's just tall grass blowing peacefully in the wind, making John feel once again at ease.

As they reach the center of the field, a denaro flies overhead. The elves quickly drop to their stomachs in an effort to conceal themselves. John stands tall and waves to the denaro— recognizing him as Ellioch from the night before. As the elves cautiously get up from the ground, John notices a look he hasn't seen before from Lorena. *Jealousy? Interesting,* he thinks, but chooses to say nothing.

"Whoa," says Darian.

"That's the one who placed the spell on the door to enter this place," John tells them.

"How do you know?" asks Killian.

"Because he told me."

"Unreal. I cannot believe you actually spoke to them," says Killian.

"Let's keep moving," says Lorena. "We've lost enough daylight already, and we need to cross the canyon before nightfall."

"The canyon? I thought we were going up," says John.

"You are correct, however, about ten years ago we had a shift in the ground that caused a deep canyon to form," says Darian.

Must've been an earthquake, John thinks. "Why do we have to cross before nightfall?"

"Creatures come out at night to feed in the canyon . . . Vile creatures," says Darian.

"Hard to kill," adds Killian.

"You heard Lorena, let's go!" yells Melara.

John stops talking and follows the elves at a brisk jog. He's briefly tempted to say a witty comment, but between the elves, Kaigen, and the denaros . . . he has seen enough creatures for one day.

The tall trees that engulf them slowly thin out until, eventually, they are walking through an open field, stepping through patches of dirt and grass as they make their way up the slope toward the canyon. The sun is low in the sky when they finally reach the edge.

John wasn't sure what to expect of the canyon, but he wasn't expecting this. It isn't too deep—maybe thirty feet at its deepest point—but the length has to be several hundred yards from one side to the other. Consisting mostly of big boulders and downed trees throughout, there doesn't seem to be much of a clear path either.

Lorena looks to the sky. "We've got maybe an hour of daylight left."

"We can make it if we hurry," says Melara.

John notices the twins glance sideways at each other.

"That's going to be close," Darian cautions.

"Is it really worth the risk?" asks Killian.

"The only other option is to head back through the forest to where we started. We cannot stay the night here; you know as well as I do that all sorts of creatures venture up to this side of the canyon in the darkness," Melara reminds him.

"Most of them are harmless," says Killian.

"Do you want to take that risk?"

All eyes turn to Lorena, who is grappling with the decision. "We cannot go back. Mind your footing and make haste; we need to hurry."

The twins lock arms. "Together till the end," they say in unison.

And with that, the elves start a rapid descent to the canyon floor, with John close behind. They jump from boulder to boulder, walking along the fallen trees when they can, stopping only to listen. John isn't exactly sure what they're listening for—besides the occasional rustling, the canyon is eerily silent.

He draws his dagger once after seeing a three-foot-long lizard peering at him, but Killian shakes his head, and they keep moving. As they advance atop the boulders, John looks down to see a long, semitranslucent casing, almost like a snake has molted its skin. *No way that's a snakeskin; it's got to be twenty feet long and almost a foot thick,* John thinks. But then he remembers the size of the denaros, and he picks up his pace.

As they near the end of the canyon, the boulders there are much smaller, but they're also more densely packed. It looks as if they'll make it across before sundown, but then Melara slips off one of the rocks, and another one shifts, pinning her leg. She cries out in pain.

"Melara!" yells Lorena.

Her calf is now sandwiched between two large boulders. It doesn't look like her leg is broken, but they won't know for sure until they can move the boulder . . . *if* they can move the boulder.

"Quick, everyone get a hold of something; we move on three," orders Lorena.

The twins get into position to pull from the back while John and Lorena squat down to push from the front. There isn't much room on the left side of the boulder, so Lorena and John are squished close together on the right side.

"One, two, three!" They all heave. The rock barely budges, and Melara cries out again. They try a few more times but get nowhere, only causing her more pain. Their hands keep slipping off the rock as they struggle to grip its smooth surface.

"Stop!" yells Lorena. "We need to find another way."

Just as she finishes speaking, the last bit of sunlight drops below the horizon. And that's when the noise starts. *Hsssss.*

The twins jump on top of nearby boulders and shoulder their bows as the hissing sound rapidly intensifies.

"What is that?" says John. And then he sees them: three giant snakes slithering atop the rocks, heading right for them.

Lorena wastes no time spitting out orders: "Darian, Killian, take those two! I've got the one on the left!" She looks at John. "You! Find a way to move that rock."

And then arrows start flying. Killian and Darian's first two arrows pierce the eyes of one of the snakes, killing it instantly. The other two snakes slide under the rocks and away from view.

"Where are they?" shouts Lorena.

John moves to get a better view of the boulder trapping Melara. It's slightly misshapen on the left side. *Maybe if I could get underneath it . . .* He starts to shift the adjacent boulder to allow himself more room to push.

Then Killian calls out, "Lorena, behind you!"

The snake moves to strike, and Lorena barely has enough time to dive out of the way, falling hard on her left shoulder. The twins shoot several arrows toward the snake. Most of them miss, but one lodges in its tail, and it slithers beneath the rocks once more.

Meanwhile, John has gotten underneath the neighboring boulder and is slowly rocking it forward. "What are you doing?" Melara demands. He continues to rock it until it gains enough momentum that he can roll it forward, leaving him just enough space to get under the rock that is trapping her.

***

Lorena gets to her feet and grabs her shoulder, feeling the dislocated bone. She walks to a nearby rock and throws herself against it, letting out a muffled grunt as the shoulder pops back into place. She'll be feeling that tomorrow, but for now, the pain will have to wait.

A *hiss* behind the twins causes them to jolt around and shoot arrows blindly into the canyon. The sound of two arrows bouncing off rocks shortly follows. With the twins distracted, the second snake sneaks up behind Lorena and wraps itself around her, leaving only her one arm free, gripping her sword.

The twins quickly take aim at the snake wrapping itself around her, but it's difficult to make out what is snake and what is elf in the darkness.

"Shoot!" she yells as she desperately flails her sword around, attempting to cut some part of the snake before she suffocates.

"It's too dark!" yells Darian.

"We don't have a clean shot!" adds Killian.

Just before the snake squeezes the life out of her, Lorena's sword catches the tip of its tail, cutting it clean off. It loosens its grip for only a second . . . but that's all the time Lorena needs. She spins the sword around and shoves the blade straight through the head of the snake, piercing its jaw shut. As the entangled pair falls to the ground, the twins run to her aid.

***

John is positioning himself underneath the boulder, trying to block out the rest of the action and focus only on Melara. He gets the best grip he can find on the bottom and meets her eyes. "Ready?" She nods.

He lifts once, slightly shifting the boulder. He tries again, moving it another inch. At first, he was worried he was going to hurt her, but she hasn't made a peep, her eyes trained on something behind John. Fear fills them as she whispers, "Snake."

The snake picks up speed as John makes one final attempt to free Melara. He puts his two-hundred-forty-pound frame underneath the boulder and lifts with all his might. The veins bulge out of his fully tensed, muscular forearms, and every sinew in his body strains in unison as he lets out a yell, giving the rock one last push. Mercifully, it moves just enough for Melara to fall into John's arms. She has only a split second to remove the knife from John's waist, and as the snake lunges for his neck, she plunges it into its head.

The two of them fall to the ground as the snake flops around wildly. The twins—having freed Lorena—appear just in time to sink their blades into the creature, ceasing its movement altogether.

And there they lie, panting, tired, injured, and in need of a moment of peace. Melara shifts to her side and lets out a muffled moan as pain shoots down her leg.

Lorena drops to her side. "Can you walk?"

She gets to her feet and attempts a step, immediately falling to the ground in agony. The silence in the canyon is cut short by the sound of something in the distance. John looks behind them, and as the last light fades away, he sees dozens of silhouetted heads coming straight for them.

"We need to go *now*!" John barks.

"She cannot walk!" Lorena snaps back.

"Fine, then I'll carry her."

"No chance!" yells Melara.

John looks back to see the snakes closing in fast on their position and grits his teeth. "We don't have time for this." He scoops up Melara before she can object. "Run."

They sprint toward the exit of the canyon with little regard for their own safety, smashing into rocks left and right; the canyon becomes a roar of grunts and cursing. As they near the opposite side of the canyon, the terrain rises and the rocks become scarcer. Most of the snakes have turned back at this point, but one snake refuses to give up its pursuit. With the extra weight of Melara, John is falling behind. He sees the elves go up and over the canyon wall one by one, first Darian, then Killian, and lastly Lorena, who looks back in horror at how close the snakes are to John. "Hurry!" she screams.

John can feel the fatigue in his muscles taking over as he ascends the canyon wall. His legs burn with every step, begging him to give in and fall to the ground beneath him. But John refuses to give up. He takes every last bit of strength and willpower left in his body and lunges up over the side of the canyon, with Melara still in his arms. As they fall to the dirt, the snake springs up and over the ledge toward them, but the elves are waiting.

The snake gets two arrows to the side of its body, and Lorena slices it in two with one effortless swing of her sword. Its head falls to the ground and rolls toward John, stopping inches from his face, eyes open and still filled with determination.

After a long exhale, he meets Melara's gaze, expecting her eyes to be filled with relief, admiration, or, at the very least, thanks. But he finds them filled with another emotion instead, one that catches him off guard.

Anger.

CHAPTER 10

"How dare you," Melara snarls at John. "How dare you!" she yells again and kicks John in the side, leaving her wincing in pain from her injury.

"Melara! Enough!" says Lorena as she steps in between them.

"He had no right!"

"Killian, find a way to help with Melara's leg. Darian, get a fire going," Lorena says before bending down to Melara until she's face-to-face with her. "It's going to be alright."

"He had no right," Melara whispers again.

Killian and Lorena lift Melara and help her to a nearby rock, where they prop her up, looking away from John—who's left baffled by her outburst. Lorena then offers John her hand. "Come with me. We need some firewood."

After the two of them are out of earshot from the others, John breaks the silence. "What on earth was all that?"

"You did well today, John Atwater. You displayed courage, strength, and you did not freeze up when we needed you most. Maybe I misjudged you."

Is she complimenting me? That's a big step forward for the woman who almost had me killed not twenty-four hours ago, John thinks.

"And as for Melara, although I would never say it in front of her, you did the right thing. She is a proud fighter and will refuse help from everyone, but today she needed it.

"In her early years, before Melara and I met, she spent her days competing with three brothers, always vying for attention from her father and always coming up short. I truly believe those circumstances made her the fierce woman she is today. She has fought for everything her entire life, so forgive her lack of gratitude. Melara may never admit it to you, but she knows you are the reason she is alive today. You might not even get a thank you, at least not with words, but she may show you, in her own way. Just give her time."

"You know . . . I can understand that. I can even respect that. I've never liked relying on others. It makes me feel vulnerable, and I hate that feeling."

Lorena chuckles. "That, John, we both have in common."

"With that being said . . . thank you," says John.

"For what?"

"I'm not the only one who saved a life today. If you hadn't chopped that snake's head off, there'd be two fangs stuck in my chest right now."

"That was nothing, really. Killian and Darian's arrows would've killed that snake. I just struck it for good measure," she responds, avoiding his gaze.

John knows full well those arrows were hardly a pinprick to that monstrous snake, but he doesn't want to push his luck. "Well, I guess I'll have to thank them as well. They make a great team, those two. Reminds me of some friends I had back home."

"*Had?*"

A wave of sorrow washes over John. "They died about a year ago."

Lorena places her hand on John's shoulder. "I'm sorry to hear that, John. That must've been hard."

John nods. "It was."

"I cannot imagine losing Killian or Darian, and I hope the day never comes. But if it ever does, I know for certain that they will be by each other's side. '*Together till the end,*' as they always say."

"Is that their motto?" asks John. "I heard them say it right before we entered the canyon."

"They've been saying that forever. Usually only when times get tough, though . . . so pretty often," she jokes.

John laughs unexpectedly. Nothing like a good joke to lift one's spirits, although he never pegged Lorena to have a sense of humor.

They proceed to gather firewood in silence for the next hour—simply enjoying each other's company—before returning to camp, where they find Melara asleep with a splint around her leg. Killian and Darian are sitting by the fire.

"That was fast. How'd you make that fire so quickly?" asks John.

Killian holds up a thin stick and a small log with a crevice dug into it. "We spin this stick until it creates enough heat to light a small amount of tinder. It's actually quite simple. I could teach you if you'd like?"

John pulls the lighter from his pocket. "I appreciate that, but I prefer to use this." He strikes the spark wheel, and a flame appears, prompting gasps from the elves.

"Is this a device from your world?" asks Darian.

"Indeed it is. Go ahead, try it out." They each take turns creating a flame and lighting bits of grass on fire until John eventually makes them stop. "We don't want to use all of its fuel."

"Fuel?" says Darian. "Oh, like the fuel from a Tree of Light."

"Tree of light?" John asks.

"Across Mhorelia, there are large trees that contain an oil which can be extracted by tapping a hole into the tree," Darian explains. "However, the oil is very explosive, so we must plug up the hole when we're done. I'll point one out to you if we come across one. But for now, let's rest."

As they sit by the crackling fire, all thoughts turn to Melara.

"How bad is her leg?" asks Lorena.

"Badly bruised, but nothing is broken," says Killian. "With the splint and the herbal rub I used to reduce the swelling, she should be back to normal in a few days."

"We also gave her a mild sedative to help her sleep and dull the pain," says Darian.

"Ah yes, Ethereal Root. Take even the smallest dose, and you'll be out for hours. How much do we have left?" asks Lorena.

Darian holds up a small pouch. "Quite a bit. With all the injuries we had on our last journey, I wasn't taking any chances. How's your shoulder?"

Lorena rubs her shoulder, still sore from the dislocation. "It's seen better days. Some Ethereal Root tea should do the trick. What about you, John?"

John is sore—he can't deny that—but compared to Lorena and Melara's injuries, he can't complain. He also never cared for sedatives; he knows it's better to keep a clear head. "I'm all set." They sit in silence under the stars for a couple of minutes before John speaks up: "How many times have you attempted this journey?"

Killian responds, "It's been so long, I have lost count. Over the last twenty years, it must be close to—"

"One hundred and seventeen times," Lorena interrupts grimly. "Our first attempt was fifteen years ago, when the twins turned eighteen. Sometimes we travel for months; other times, we last only a few days before turning back."

"How far have you gotten?" John asks.

"We've made good progress in the past," Lorena says defensively.

John backs off. "I didn't mean to offend you. It just seems like such a daunting journey. After all, it's only been two days and I've already been shot, poisoned, and attacked by snakes."

Lorena doesn't apologize, just softens her tone a bit. "It's not all bad. Some parts would even be enjoyable if the stakes weren't so high and we really were just . . . '*traveling*.'"

John can't stop his grin. "I thought it was a good lie."

"Well, tomorrow we can take things a little slower. We need to heal, especially Melara, and we need to stock up on food for the journey. A short walk ahead is a forest full of stagglehorn. A perfect spot to hunt without fear of being attacked."

"How can you be sure we won't be attacked?" asks John.

"There are no predators that live in these parts of Mhorelia, and Balloch's forces would never travel this far from the Enchanted Lands," Lorena assures him.

"And what of the snakes?"

"They will keep to the canyon, and any that choose to venture outside of it will be deterred by the fire."

Good, John thinks, feeling certain he never wants to see another snake in his lifetime. Lorena drinks her tea, and they sit in silence for a while around the campfire. This brings back a fond memory for John from high school—the time he spent sitting by a fire with friends all around him, enjoying an ice-cold beer and the smell of his cherry cigar lingering in the air. What he wouldn't do for an ice-cold beer and a cigar right now . . .

One by one, the elves fall asleep around him—the Ethereal Root tea taking them into a deep slumber. Eventually, John closes his eyes and drifts off, hoping to dream about that peaceful memory from over two decades ago.

Unfortunately, the dream that follows is anything but peaceful.

John exhales softly, his breath forming a small cloud in the cold Siberian air. He's covered from head to toe in white tactical gear, lying perfectly still on the snow-blanketed ground. Carl—a massive human being and the team's leader—is lying next to John. Behind them are Jenny and Lucy—twin sisters recruited right out of college, and not to be trifled with. Finishing off the group is the oldest, Ben, who's beginning to show his age. He's been a part of this team for the last thirty years, and it's taken its toll.

The Undesirables received intel that an American diplomat was being held hostage somewhere along the mountain range they've been ascending for the last five days. Exhausted, hungry, and frigid . . . the team is hurting. And as John stares ahead at the thin, rickety bridge that spans before him and his team, a thought nags at him. *Something isn't right.*

"No movement up ahead. You take point. We're right behind you," Carl whispers to John.

John ignores his own instincts, slowly gets up, and makes his way forward. The thin wooden boards creak underneath the team's feet as they step onto the bridge. The wind has died down, and it's become eerily quiet as they make their way across, the only sound coming from the ice-cold water rushing twenty feet below. At the halfway point, John raises his fist, and the team stops. He slowly pans his head around and notices there are only three bodies behind him. *Where the hell is Ben?*

"Contact front!" is all Carl can get out before bullets start zipping past them. On the opposite side of the bridge, three men come running out from the cover of the trees. Jenny and Lucy—the sharpshooters of the group—quickly take them out with deadly accuracy. Two rounds to the chest for each of them. Carl and John open fire on the enemies still hiding in the forest. For what seems like an eternity, bullets fly in both directions. Carl takes a bullet in his left thigh and writhes in pain. Another bullet tears through Jenny's collarbone, and she falls to the boards beneath her feet. John looks around at his team in horror, knowing they're sitting ducks, and it's only a matter of time before they're all down.

Then the shooting just stops. But the air is still for only a moment before the bridge begins to shake. It abruptly falls out from under him, and his body is twisted around in midair. He looks up to see the silhouette of Ben standing at the end of the bridge, holding the knife that just sealed his team's fate. That's when his body hits the water.

John jolts awake, his muscles tense and sweat covering his entire body—a way he's woken up many times before. He scans the elves. *Good, I didn't wake them.* As he rolls back over, he slowly closes his eyes, hoping more than anything that he won't end up in Siberia again.

CHAPTER 11

"What?" booms Balloch. Kaigen kneels and looks away, the frustration in Balloch's voice sending a chill down his spine. The king sits at the end of a long wooden table in his personal dining hall, clutching a glass of red wine. An ornate tablecloth extends the length of the table, colored with beautiful reds and golds, and there are pewter candelabras placed every five feet. The room is normally meant for hosting elegant parties . . . but not today.

"They've been at it for only two days, and they're already past the canyon! How is this possible?"

"Well . . ." Kaigen pauses, knowing he needs to choose his words wisely. "The denaros, they let them pass through their land."

The king's glare intensifies. "They did what . . .? Those creatures are supposed to be neutral in this war, and yet, they defy me like this."

"Well, technically they didn't . . . They made sure not to endorse their journey—"

"And yet," the king interrupts, "they allow them to pass? Seems like an endorsement to me."

"They did injure him, sending an arrow right through his shoulder."

"And has he recovered?"

"He's on his way, the elves being such excellent healers and all. They also had some oint—" He stops himself, pausing to think of other wording. "Some healing herbs that seem to be working. But mark my words, it will slow them down."

"Hmm, healing herbs . . ." ponders the king.

"The women are banged up pretty badly as well. Those snakes did quite a lot of damage in the canyon," Kaigen blurts out.

"Good!" says the king happily. "But it may not be enough . . . Do we have any troops in that area?"

"Troops? For what? You aren't worried about them, are you?" Kaigen says.

"Worried! No. But they won't be expecting any excitement after the canyon, so I'd like to give them some."

Kaigen pretends to think to himself about the troops, but his mind is elsewhere. The king has never tried to intervene with the elves before. He's never even shown the least bit of worry, but something has changed. Clearly, John being with the elves is causing him some unease, but sending troops—that seems like overkill. He's right, though. They won't be expecting it, and that worries Kaigen.

"We may have some centaurs a few miles farther up the mountain, but do you really think that is necessary, master?"

"What is necessary is none of your concern! Go find them and alert them to the elves. I want them dealt with."

Sensing that he may be pressing a bit too much, Kaigen replies, "Yes, master, it will be done."

Kaigen stands, but before he can walk away, the king grabs his arm. "You'd better not be helping those elves . . . for you know the consequences for disobeying me."

Kaigen's mind is filled with a flurry of anger, fear, and a touch of sadness, but he keeps it all inside, just nodding to the king instead, his mouth unable to form words. The king releases his grasp, and Kaigen turns away in a flourish, walking at a fast pace toward the door. Before he can exit, the king yells out one last demand: "I want an update by tomorrow . . . or else!"

Kaigen's emotions are on the verge of bubbling over, so he vanishes in a purple cloud, teleporting himself as far from civilization as he can . . . where nobody can hear his screams.

***

After having concluded his outburst, Kaigen now sits on the edge of a pond, staring at his own reflection. The purple face that looks back disgusts him, even though he knows that isn't fair. He'd love to turn back to his normal self, but if anyone were to see . . . It's just not worth it. Balloch's rule was simple and clear: "You can only turn back on Earth, in order to blend in while bringing me scotch and information of my old home, and if you ever shift back into your natural form while in Mhorelia . . ." In truth, the "information" he feeds Balloch is more like misinformation, as Kaigen would never tell him how advanced Earth has become. He clenches his knuckles, not wanting to think about the consequences.

There will come a day, though, when he will shift back. And when that happens, there will be hell to pay.

CHAPTER 12

John rises around midmorning, and for the first time since he arrived in Mhorelia, he's well rested. Still sore, admittedly, but a good night's sleep has put him in much better spirits. The same can't be said of Melara. While she may have slept well, the frustration is evident on her face from the moment John opens his eyes. She wants to run, to hunt, and to be of some use to the group, but she's forced to sit by the smoldering campfire instead, aggressively plucking blades of grass. John actually feels bad for her, remembering a time he broke his collarbone back when he played high school lacrosse and had to miss the final three games of the season. He had to sit on the sidelines, watching as his team lost, knowing there was nothing he could do.

Killian and Darian are seated nearby counting their arrows, and Lorena has changed into a green, hooded cloak, which seems like an odd choice, considering it must already be close to seventy-five degrees.

"How many have we got?" she asks the twins.

"Forty-five left between the four of us," says Darian.

"We'll make as many as we can while you're out hunting," adds Killian.

So that's what the cloak is for, John thinks.

"You shouldn't go alone," Melara advises.

"Balloch may have troops stationed around most of Mhorelia, but he wouldn't have anyone this low on the island. There is nothing to worry about. I'll be back before lunch with a fresh stagglehorn, and I'll need you to cook it up for us," says Lorena.

"Even so, it's best to have someone with you," says Melara.

Killian examines her leg. "You are in no condition to travel, Melara."

"I'll go with you," John offers.

"What . . .?" Melara says distastefully. "Can you even hunt?"

"I used to go out hunting when I was a kid with my uncle. I nabbed my first deer when I was thirteen." Although not technically a lie, he used a rifle to kill that deer . . . not a bow. "Anyway, you'll probably want some help with carrying it back to camp, right? I assume stagglehorn are pretty heavy animals."

"Fine," mutters Melara.

"Here, you can borrow my bow," Killian says.

"We'd better get on with it. It's only going to get hotter," says Lorena.

John scarfs down a few pieces of dried meat and bread, along with two more berries. It's all he has left, and it barely fixes his hunger—they really need to find some food. He then fills his water pouch in a nearby stream, grabs Killian's bow, and the two head for the woods.

These woods are similar to the ones John encountered earlier in his journey, and although the trees may be different, they look very similar to the ones back home. Birch, oak, maple—John picks them all out as they walk. However, one tree they pass by is unlike anything he has seen in Alabama—a Tree of Light. It towers above them, standing at least a hundred feet tall; it conjures up images of the ever-climbing redwoods in Northern California.

"Magnificent," he says aloud.

"Yes, and thankfully this one has already been tapped, otherwise we would be here for hours trying to get through the thick bark," says Lorena, pointing to a plug in the side of the trunk. They quickly pull the plug, draining just enough oil to fill a small pouch on Lorena's belt, and then continue with their hunt.

Both Lorena and John are well hidden, cloaked from head to toe in green. Thankfully, the trees provide much-needed cover from the sunlight, allowing them to creep through undetected and a bit cooler.

After about ten minutes of walking, John whispers to Lorena, "So, what exactly does a stagglehorn look like?"

"It stands about four to six feet tall, on four legs, and has brown-colored fur and large horns coming out of its head."

"Large horns . . . I thought you said we weren't in any danger?"

"We aren't. They're very skittish creatures. I imagine if many were running at you, then you might be in danger, but they usually run away at the sight of us."

"If you say so."

"You say you killed your first animal when you were thirteen; that's impressive. What type of bow did you use?"

"Well . . . it was similar to this one," John says while holding up Killian's bow. "Maybe a little smaller."

"Let's see who's a better shot. Do you see that tree over there?" Lorena says, pointing to a felled oak about fifty feet away.

"There's like twenty trees over there. Which one are you talking about?"

"That one," Lorena says as she knocks her arrow, shoulders her bow, and shoots the tree dead center in one fluid motion.

John's eyes widen as he knocks an arrow. "It's been a while, so I probably won't be able to shoot quite that well." He pulls back the drawstring and looks down the length of the arrow, hands shaking. He lets it fly and misses wide left, sinking into the dirt about fifteen feet past the tree.

Lorena shakes her head. "You've never used a bow, have you?"

"Technically, I have, although I was five, and it had a suction cup tip."

"Suction cup?" she says.

"It's like a rubber tip that sticks to . . . You know what? It doesn't matter. I'll just go fetch the arrows."

"Good idea."

They walk another half hour, seeing only birds flutter by and the occasional squirrel scurry up a tree. At least John thinks they're squirrels. Some animals here are identical to the ones back home, but some others are quite literally from a different world. After another ten minutes of walking, they decide to sit still and wait for a stagglehorn to come to them, and it doesn't take long.

Lorena taps John on the shoulder and puts her finger to her lips. She points behind him into a small clearing of trees where the sun is shining in. John is blown away by what he sees. By Lorena's description, he was expecting some sort of big, weird, moose-looking creature, but the creature he's staring at is utterly magnificent. Its horns are easily three feet long, slightly curved, and are as thick as a flagpole at their base. The way the sunlight causes its fur to shimmer is so mesmerizing, John almost doesn't want to kill it. But then a pang of hunger hits, and he steadies his bow.

Lorena whispers into his ear: "Slow your breathing, aim about a foot above its spine, and let it fly. My arrow will be right behind yours."

Following her orders, he points the arrow at the animal and raises it ever so slightly to compensate for the distance. But as he steadies his aim, his eyes fixate on something in the distance beyond the stagglehorn. Lorena sees it, too, and quickly pulls John behind a bush, covering his mouth before he can produce even the faintest sound. The fear in her eyes confuses John. He got only a small glimpse of it, but what could it possibly be to make her so alarmed? Without making a sound, she mouths something: "Centaur."

John gently moves a branch of the bush to get another look. Just as he does, a spear travels straight through the stagglehorn. It's dead before it hits the ground.

"Nice shot, Eldar!" says one of the centaurs.

"Do I ever miss?" Eldar boasts as he rips the spear from the corpse.

"What shall we do with it?"

"Leave it; we've got business to attend to," Eldar says before trotting away arrogantly. The other three centaurs with him follow without question.

"Savages," Lorena says under her breath.

After they deem it is safe—about twenty minutes later—Lorena and John kneel by the stagglehorn's side. She softly closes its eyes and whispers, "I will kill him for this," before turning to John. "There is nothing I hate more on this island than centaurs. They kill without purpose or remorse. It's a sport for them."

"So, they're our enemy?" asks John.

She nods. "Without question. Every last one of them sided with Balloch when he claimed the throne."

"Wait, I thought you said this was a safe place to be, that there was nothing that could harm us here?"

"I thought it was. Centaurs have no reason to travel this far south. It doesn't make sense. There is nothing down here they would want unless . . ."

"Unless what?"

Her eyes go cold. "Unless they are here for us."

They immediately break into a full sprint, heading back to the camp. With the centaurs having a twenty-minute head start, they have little chance of making it in time. And even if they do, the centaurs will have had the element of surprise against a banged-up group of elves.

As they get closer, a scream rings out through the forest, followed by silence. John and Lorena stop dead in their tracks. "Melara," they say in unison before taking off again.

Just as they are coming up on the camp, John grabs Lorena's arm. "Wait!"

"What are you doing?" she spits as she yanks her arm away.

"We need to think about this. You know we can't take all four of them by ourselves."

Distraught and angry, she snaps back at him, "And what do you suppose we do, John?"

"We go in slow, survey the situation. They don't know we're here, and the second they do, we're done."

She thinks about it for a moment before begrudgingly agreeing. And so they creep, ever so quietly, toward the camp. As the trees become sparser, they witness a commotion unfolding.

"Where is he?" Eldar demands as he presses his foot into Melara's leg, causing her to scream again.

"Stop!" Darian yells before getting hit in the back with the butt end of a spear, sending him to the ground.

John grabs Lorena's shoulder—in case she's thinking about running to them. But, surprisingly, she doesn't move. She just stares at them with a look of abject horror mixed with a ferocious hatred.

"I said, where is he? I will not ask you again," says Eldar.

"He died. He died in the canyon," says Melara.

"Really? The Chosen One died from being bitten by the fangs of a measly snake . . ."

For a moment, nobody says a word as Eldar ponders this. Clearly the leader of this pack, he is the one the others look to for direction.

"Ha! Ha! Ha!" he bellows. "I guess he was *chosen* for dinner!"

The other centaurs break out into hysterical laughter. John just shakes his head and whispers under his breath, "Wow."

After the laughter subsides, another centaur speaks up, "So, let's kill them."

Lorena's body tightens. She lifts her bow and points an arrow right between Eldar's eyes, but before she shoots, Eldar speaks. "No! We need to bring them to Kaigen. That was our directive."

Kaigen? What is he up to . . .? John thinks. He exchanges a glance with Lorena—who's clearly thinking the same thing.

Once the coast is clear, they step out from the trees with two very contrasting mindsets. Lorena furiously paces back and forth, mumbling threats under her breath.

"I'll kill them! I'll kill them all!"

It's clear to John that this is going to be a big problem, and Lorena confirms his notion when she unsheathes her sword and starts after the centaurs. He tackles her, getting a hold of her briefly, but she wriggles violently in his arms, cursing his name.

"Let me go! Let me go now! I need to save them!"

"Stop! You're not thinking," John yells before getting an elbow to the nose. He releases her and grabs his face. "Fine! Go get yourself killed; see if I care."

She immediately runs off in the direction they left, then stops abruptly. And after taking a few short, vicious breaths, she turns her sword around and stabs it into the ground with a loud grunt. As the wave of emotion leaves her, she sits down on a nearby log, head in hands. John can't tell if she's hiding fear, anger, or sadness . . . or maybe all of the above.

"John, I was only a girl when Balloch took the throne, turning eighteen the week before. I lived just a few miles from the Enchanted Lands. My family didn't have much, just a small home next to a shallow pond, but I loved that pond. I used to spend hours exploring the lightly wooded area around it. It was a happy place, a tranquil place.

"I was off exploring on the day he ordered the elves to vacate *his* land. Can you believe that? *His* land. Well, my parents refused, along with many other families in the area. And while I was out gallivanting around, he murdered them, then burned our house to the ground. I returned home to a pile of ash, the only sound in the forest coming from the charred wood crackling— that is, until I heard hooves approaching."

"Centaurs?" asks John.

"Lots of them. I thought I was going to die. But suddenly, I heard a peculiar noise, and someone was grabbing me. They put a bag over my head and threw me over their shoulder. I was bouncing on that shoulder for what felt like hours. I tried to scream, but nothing would come out. Finally, we stopped, and they gracefully placed me on a wooden floor, miles from any danger. And when I ripped the bag off of my head and looked down, my entire body was covered in a purple residue."

John's eyebrows shoot up. "Kaigen?"

"I never saw him, and he denies it to this day, but I have no other logical conclusion to draw. Kaigen saved my life, although I didn't know it at the time. It wasn't until a year later that I officially met him and found out about his purple vanishing act. But soon after he saved me, I descended farther down the mountain and met my new family. You have to understand, John. Melara, Killian, Darian . . . they're all I have left. And I will do anything I can to protect them."

This is a side of Lorena John hasn't seen yet, a caring and surprisingly vulnerable side. And after learning that she, too, lost her family at an early age—and knowing the pain that brings— he wants desperately to comfort her, but he resists the urge, thinking that might set her off. Instead, he asks, "So, if Kaigen doesn't want to kill us, then why did he tell the centaurs where we set up camp?"

"I don't know, John. Kaigen has always been an enigma to me. As Killian mentioned earlier, the shape-shifters joined Balloch soon after he took over. But throughout the years, some of them would help our cause in secret, aiding us in small ways as we attempted to make The Ascent. Balloch caught wind of this and decided it was time for their alliance to part ways. So, on the sixteenth anniversary of his crowning, he invited them all to a feast at his castle, thousands of them. He told them they were toasting to another year of 'peace and prosperity.' But what they were really toasting to was their demise, for he'd laced every drink with poison."

"Except Kaigen's?"

"Except Kaigen's. I don't know why the king spared his life, or why he still serves him. Perhaps it is out of fear."

John thinks back to what Kaigen said to him when he first got here: *"Things aren't always as simple as they seem." Makes a bit more sense now, I suppose.* But his mind is still filled with so many unanswered questions. He decides to ask Lorena the most pressing question on his mind: "Do you trust him?"

"I think I do. Melara might think that he is a spy for the king, but what she doesn't know is that every time he has visited us on our journeys, he has helped us in some way: slipping us crucial information about a route we were about to take, warning us of an ambush, or giving us a bit of food that we so desperately needed."

"Why don't the others know of this?"

"He would only help under one condition: I wasn't to tell another elf."

"Should you be telling *me*?"

Lorena flashes a smile, saying, "You're not an elf," but then it quickly fades from her face. "His motivation may be unclear to me, but he always seems to come through for us when we need him. And now it is my turn, even if that means battling four centaurs *alone*."

John can no longer resist the urge to comfort her, so he gently places his hand on her knee. "But you're not alone."

She places her hand on top of his. "Then come with me and help me save my family."

"No. That plan is still too dangerous," he says as he looks around the campsite. "But I think I know another way . . ."

Chapter 13

"This is risky," Lorena says as John steps out from behind a tree, wearing the clothes Kaigen gave him to blend in.

John shrugs. "They think I'm dead, thanks to Melara. And you said it yourself, I can pass as a woodsman."

"You do look remarkably similar, but they still might kill you anyway. Look what they did to that stagglehorn."

"I guess that's a risk I'll have to take," John says as he gathers up all of the supplies he will need for his plan to work.

"We should be able to cut them off if we head through those woods. It appears they took the long way around," Lorena says.

"Why would they do that?"

"Probably to make Melara have to walk farther on her hurt leg . . ." A wave of anger shoots across Lorena's face.

"Well, then, we've got no time to waste."

The two trudge through the woods, slowed by the extra weight of the others' gear. While the centaurs took all of their weapons, they left everything else at the camp.

They stop only once, allowing Lorena to harvest as much of the stagglehorn as possible, letting John know the importance of using every bit she can. He is amazed at the speed and surgical precision with which she cuts into the animal; they're done and moving again in less than five minutes.

Before long, they come to the other side of the woods, to the edge of a well-traveled path, lined with tall, thick bushes—perfect for hiding. There's a wealthy man who lives near John back in Alabama, his driveway lined with tall and well-manicured shrubs, similar to these. John feels a sense of longing as he stares at them. It's funny how the littlest thing can transport him back home in his mind, if only for a moment.

Lorena's voice snaps him back to reality. "No fresh tracks; looks like we made it here before them."

"Yes, but only just," John replies as they hear the loud voices of the centaurs in the distance. Lorena hands John his water pouch, full to the brim.

"Remember, woodsmen are arrogant, so in order to convince them, you've got to act as such. Do you think you can do that?"

"Arrogant? Oh, I can be arrogant. I'll just pretend I'm talking to a bunch of elves."

Lorena squints her eyes in subtle disdain, saying, "Time to go," and pushes him through the bushes. He's only in the open for a minute before the centaurs spot him and draw their weapons.

"You! Who are you? What are you doing here?" says Eldar, his spear cocked back and ready to throw.

"What am *I* doing here? What are *you* doing here? And why have you got three elves tied up behind you?" says John.

"That is none of your concern. Now answer the question. *Who. Are. You?*"

The elves respond with looks of confusion until he replies, "Hmph, are you blind? I'm a woodsman."

Eldar's eyes narrow, his grip tightens on his spear, and he audibly grunts. For a moment, John thinks he may have overplayed the arrogance and that he's about to end up with a spear through his chest. "A woodsman, you say . . . And what would a woodsman be doing this far from home?" mutters Eldar.

"Searching," John says bluntly.

"For what?"

"For this." John holds up his water pouch.

"And what is that?" asks Eldar, becoming increasingly annoyed with John.

Might as well play up the arrogance. "Hmph, I figured someone of your *stature* would know what resides in these woods."

"You woodsmen have no respect. Tell me, or else," Eldar demands.

"Respect?" John rolls his eyes. "If you must know, the trees in this forest produce a liquid that is very valuable. One that improves strength and stamina. How else do you suppose we woodsmen are such a force?"

"Strength and stamina?" says Eldar.

"Lies!" yells another centaur. "We've never heard of such a thing."

"Not surprising . . ." John says.

Eldar finally loses his temper and throws his spear into the ground by John's feet. "Give it here! On behalf of the king."

"On behalf of the king? We have no opposition to the king, but still you steal from me?"

Eldar slowly moves forward until they are only a foot apart. "Let's just say you gave it to us out of the goodness of your heart. That is, unless you want a spear through that precious heart of yours."

"Fine," John says through gritted teeth, "but you will regret this." He hands Eldar the water pouch.

"Wait!" yells another centaur. "What if it's a trick? What if it's poison?"

John rips the pouch from Eldar's hand, saying, "Fools," then takes a swig.

Eldar rips the pouch forcefully from John's hands and, satisfied it isn't poison, takes a drink. He grimaces and spits it out. "Awful!"

"I figured it might be a little harsh for someone like you," John says with a wink.

"How dare you," Eldar growls as he chugs three mouthfuls of the liquid, puffing out his chest with a sense of pride and hubris.

John sarcastically claps three times, pausing in between each one. "Well, congratulations; look how tough you are." Just as he finishes speaking, he knows he's gone too far. Eldar spins around and kicks him in the chest, sending him flying backward.

"Maybe that'll teach you to have some respect."

As John rolls on the ground wheezing, Eldar picks up his spear, and they walk away, as if nothing had just occurred.

Lorena runs to John's aid the minute the group is out of sight. She lightly feels around his chest, and although it's very painful, he doesn't think anything is broken.

"You really took what I said to heart about being arrogant, John."

He chuckles. "Worked like a charm."

"How much did you drink?"

"Only a sip. I had too."

"We better get going, then. Let's just hope they drink the rest of it, and quickly," she says before helping John to his feet.

They follow the centaurs from a safe distance, sticking to the tree line in case they need to hide. At one point, the centaurs' voices rise unexpectedly, and they're certain they've been made; but after a series of remarks at John's expense and an eruption of laughter, it's clear they're just mocking him.

After walking for about twenty minutes, John realizes he can't feel his feet, but says nothing. A short while later, he notices his body feels looser, and he decides it might be worth mentioning. The thought is clear and concise in his head, but what comes out is slurred and slow: "H-Hey, Lorena . . . I'm feeling a, a, a bit . . . different."

"Oh, no . . . We need to keep moving. Come this way and keep your voice down." He shuts his mouth, realizing he probably was much louder than he set out to be, sort of like when someone is getting drunk and doesn't realize their voice has gone up fifty decibels.

Although they don't pick up their pace at all, John and Lorena find themselves right next to the group of centaurs in minutes, only separated by a row of shrubbery. They drop to their knees and wait as the voices of the centaurs become slurred as well, and much louder than before.

"What is going on?" one of them yells.

"Shut your mouth. You're yelling," says another.

"Eldar . . . Eldar, something is wrong," says the first as he drops to the ground.

John peers through the bushes to see Eldar spin around, looking first to his companions, and then to the water pouch in his hand. At least John is fairly certain that's what he sees; his vision is starting to blur.

"It's a trick! Kill the elves!" screams Eldar. Then, in less than a second, arrows pierce the necks of two of the centaurs. Lorena's speed is breathtaking as she knocks a third arrow, but she won't be fast enough. John bursts through the bushes and Eldar throws his spear, only missing due to John's clumsiness as he trips over a root and face-plants on the ground.

He rolls over just in time to see another centaur fall, courtesy of Lorena's third arrow. The only one left is Eldar, and although he's larger than the rest, and clearly tougher, he drops to one knee as the dizziness kicks in. Lorena emerges from the bushes, arrow drawn back, ready to end him. But then she stops, places the arrow back in her quiver, and slings the bow around her back.

"Eldar, is it?" she says as she bends down and picks up his spear. "You walk around like you're invincible, preying on the weak and leaving nothing but destruction in your path."

He looks up at her, and although he's almost keeled over, his voice sounds as lucid as ever: "Spare me your lecture and get this over with, *Elf.* But know this, you will never make it . . . You will die screaming, just like your parents."

At the mention of her family, the world seems to stop altogether. The wind ceases, the birds stop chirping, and John watches Lorena as years of anger, hatred, and loneliness bubble up inside her all at once. The last sound John hears before he passes out is the spear traveling straight through Eldar's body and penetrating the path behind him.

***

When John opens his eyes, he's unsure how long he's been out. *I've gotta stop waking up like this,* he thinks, this being the third time in as many days that he's passed out unwillingly. He must've been out a while because the world has gone dark and stars blanket the sky. The elves sit around a crackling fire, laughing and eating what looks to be the meat that Lorena got earlier in the day. Seeing Lorena happy is a pleasant change, considering the last memory he has of her is her blank face after such a ruthless kill. Not that the kill wasn't necessary; it was just so personal. But after learning about her history, who could blame her?

Their eyes meet, and John realizes he's been staring at her for quite some time. "Well, when were you going to mention you had rejoined us?" she asks.

John blinks his eyes a few times, still groggy from his unexpected nap. "Man, that Ethereal Root tea really is some powerful stuff. Best sleep I've had in years."

Killian laughs. "That was brilliant! How did you come up with that idea?"

John points to Lorena. "First, I had to convince this one not to run after you and fight all four centaurs by herself . . . and all it cost me was my nose."

Lorena shrugs her shoulders and smirks. "At least I didn't break it."

"Jury's still out on that," John says before he moves his nose around and exaggerates how painful it is with a dramatic, "Owww." The twins break out into laughter, and John can't be certain, but he's pretty sure he sees Melara trying to hide a smile.

"But how did I come up with that plan? To answer that, I need to go back a ways . . .

"I was undercover, posing as a worker for a group that I won't go into detail about, but suffice it to say, they were some really bad people. Once I got what I needed out of them, I was told to leave in the middle of the night and let my organization take care of the rest. But these people . . . they had done some really, really bad things, and I just couldn't let it go. So, that night, I put a massive dose of sedative in the pitcher of beer they were passing around at dinner. They were big drinkers, so I knew they'd all have a few drinks. One by one, they went back to their rooms, and when the last one was gone . . . I dealt with them myself."

An uncomfortable silence lingers, and John fears he may have overshared. But then, Melara speaks up, calming his uneasiness: "Maybe you won't be such a bad addition to our group after all."

Darian playfully throws a piece of Elvish bread at Melara. "Don't get all sentimental on us now, Melara. You're supposed to be the tough one."

A wave of relief passes through John as the elves erupt in laughter once more. Lorena passes John a piece of cooked stagglehorn. "I bet you're starving. Try some of this; you've earned it."

As he grabs it, Melara extends her hand and adds, "You should try it with some Elvish bread; it's much better that way."

As John grabs the bread and thanks Melara, he steals a glance at Lorena, who discreetly nods in approval and whispers, "I told you."

CHAPTER 14

Kaigen watches from afar as the centaurs approach the last hill standing between him and them, and he still doesn't have a clue what he'll do when they get to him. The elves were supposed to die by Eldar's spear; that was Balloch's directive. Why did he lie to them when there's so much at stake? Maybe he's starting to believe John can pull this off. Maybe he's starting to believe he really is the Chosen One, after all. But this is reckless, even for Kaigen.

As he continues to watch the centaurs, he notices something isn't quite right. They're walking in a curious manner, zigzagging across the path. *What the hell are they doing?* Then the first two drop to the ground. He can't quite see what caused them to fall—being too far away to see the arrows—but he gets a better idea when John comes stumbling out of the bushes next to them. Eldar's spear narrowly misses John after he drops to the ground, or maybe he fell. Yup, something is off, and Kaigen can't quite place it. But after the third centaur falls and Lorena steps confidently out from the bushes, a wave of relief hits Kaigen. And Eldar dying next—courtesy of a *ferocious* spear throw—well, that really brings Kaigen joy.

But his relief is short-lived as panic sets in when John falls to the ground. *He's dead,* Kaigen thinks. But it looks as if they are picking him up. *They wouldn't be carrying him if he were dead; they'd just leave him.* None of this makes any sense, but Kaigen has little time to worry. Now he must figure out how to tell

Balloch. Yes, he should head straight to Balloch and inform him of Eldar's death, but first he must travel elsewhere. Things are getting too close for comfort, and if this group is going to stand a chance, they may need some help . . .

He closes his eyes and vanishes.

When Kaigen opens his eyes, he's kneeling in the grassy field on the denaros' land. As usual, this place should be a sanctuary for relaxation, with the soft wind blowing and the sun shining bright, but Kaigen's mind is filled with fear.

Alura drops to the ground in front of Kaigen, having moved so swiftly and quietly that he has no time to react. "Do you remember what I told you when you last stood in this very spot?" she says, speaking so calmly it makes Kaigen's skin crawl.

Kaigen slowly raises his head to meet her piercing stare. "You shall never return . . . or . . ."

"Or what?" she snaps.

Kaigen shudders. "Or I will kill you myself."

"Hmmm, so you do remember. Then this next part will not be a surprise to you, will it?" Alura raises both of her wings in the air to attack.

"Wait!" he pleads. "I'm here for a good reason!"

Alura sends a gust of wind toward Kaigen, knocking him back. "Last time you were here, you stole something that did not belong to you. Those talons were not yours to take," she howls.

He struggles to get up and stutters, "L-Look, I-I—"

"You desecrated a sacred burial ground to make a potion, and now you defy my order never to return here!" she interrupts, sending another gust at Kaigen.

He gathers himself onto one knee. "I had to. I had no choice."

"You always have a choice," Alura says before raising her wings one final time. "And now you will pay for that choice."

"He has my son!"

There is a shift in the wind as Alura lowers her wings ever so slowly, cocking her head at Kaigen. "Your son? I did not know you had a son."

"Not many do. The boy was barely two when the king took him from me. And I was told never to mention it to anyone, *or else*."

"Hmmm, so that's why you do the king's bidding."

"Yes . . . and that's why I stole those talons. And for my son, I'd do it again."

"Hmmm, well, consider the act of sparing your life as a token of my forgiveness. There is nothing I would not do for my children. However, if you come here again . . . I *will* kill you. Now begone."

She turns around, but before she can fly away, Kaigen blurts out, "Will you not help us?"

Her body remains stationary as she spins her head around. "No. I am sorry about your son, but that does not change our position. We will not choose a side."

Kaigen resists the urge to yell after her as she flies away. To tell her how easy it is not to take a side when you aren't affected. How they could do so much good if they chose to help. It may be risky, but in the end, it's worth it. It's worth the sacrifice.

But no, he says none of that. Instead, he just sits there in the field, thinking about his son. Thinking about how he is going to do everything he can to protect him, no matter the cost. And if he has to do it without the denaros, so be it. With that, he teleports to the king's palace.

First, he checks the Great Hall, nothing. The dining hall, nothing. He then tries the king's living quarters . . . still nothing. But as he stands in the king's quarters, he hears the distinct sound of swords clashing together, followed by the king's voice barking orders.

Kaigen peers out the window that overlooks the training grounds, situated at the back of the castle. These training grounds were used on a daily basis when Balloch took over; he was always obsessed with having the most efficient killers in Mhorelia. But for the last few years, they have been all but abandoned. Used mainly for bored archers to wager who's a better shot, or for lovers to meet up in secret where they know they will not be disturbed. The archery targets and human dummies were dilapidated only one week prior—having not been properly replaced for some time now—and the ground was a grotesque mix of sod, mud, hay, and stone.

This makes the sight Kaigen witnesses even more surprising as he gazes down upon the grounds. A fresh layer of dirt has been packed down across the entire area. All unnecessary debris has been removed and discarded. New weapon racks have been assembled, and on them stand what look to be freshly forged weapons. Ropes have been strung up to signify archery lanes, with every lane having a line of archers formed behind it, and a target peppered with arrows at the other end. There are brand new dummies, made of wooden stumps and straw, with fresh cuts from the swordsmen who attack them from every angle. And at the center of it all stands Balloch MacNicol, yelling at two men who are fighting in the middle of a perfectly drawn circle on the ground.

"Mind your footing, lads! Strike with ferocity!" Balloch yells. One of the swordsmen blocks the other's blow, and as their swords are held together, he kicks him out of the ring and onto his back. "Alright, next two, you're up!"

Kaigen decides to walk down to the grounds instead of teleporting. He needs the extra time to work through what he's just observed, and to figure out how to break the news of Eldar. *Why has he brought back the grounds? He must be worried. Maybe he has already heard of Eldar's demise,* Kaigen thinks as he proceeds down the stairs.

Sooner than he'd like, he finds himself standing next to Balloch. "My king—"

"He's dead, isn't he?" Balloch whispers into Kaigen's ear.

"Yes."

"I figured as much when you hadn't returned. Was it at the hands of the newcomer? Or the elves?"

"The elves, Your Majesty."

Balloch grits his teeth. "Don't let the others know. I don't want them to get any ideas, or start any rumors. They know he has arrived, but they don't yet know what he can do."

"And you, are you worried, master? With the training grounds being restored—"

"They should never have fallen into this state!" Balloch interrupts as he glares back at Kaigen. He begins to pace around a man who has found himself in the fighting circle. "Our soldiers have become too content, too fat, too happy. They haven't seen battle in so long, they forget what it looks like!" He rips the sword out of the man's hands, kicks him to the ground, and raises it to strike.

Kaigen unsheathes the sword of the man standing closest to him and slides underneath Balloch, blocking the blow before it slices through the fallen soldier. By now, every soldier on the grounds has gathered around them.

Kaigen stares into the king's eyes, which are now filled with an untethered rage. "What are you doing?" he says to the king.

"You should ask yourself the same question," Balloch says as he pulls his sword away and throws it to the ground. "I am Balloch MacNicol, ruler of Mhorelia . . . I don't have to explain or justify anything I do. But you . . . you are just a measly little shape-shifter who has forgotten his place in this kingdom."

Now it's Kaigen's turn to be filled with rage. He has done everything asked of him, no matter the cost. Suddenly, his mind is filled with vengeful thoughts: stabbing the king through the heart with the sword he now holds in his hands, removing the king's head with one swing of his blade, or choking the life out of the king while all the others watch.

Balloch interrupts his murderous thoughts, saying, "In fact, I think it is long overdue for you to prove your worth to me. To prove to me that you are worth keeping around."

Kaigen's grip tightens on the sword. *Prove my worth? I'll prove my worth . . .*

"You five," Balloch yells, pointing to five men standing across from Kaigen, "subdue this creature! Everyone else, step back!"

Five men hesitantly step forward, and for a solid fifteen seconds, they stand motionless. While Kaigen despises the king, these five men have done nothing to him specifically, although they are certainly not without sin. He doesn't want to fight them . . . but he doesn't have a choice.

"Get on with it!" the king yells as he kicks a soldier toward Kaigen. The man barely has enough time to raise his sword before Kaigen kicks him in the stomach. He drops to one knee, and his sword falls from his hands. As he looks up, Kaigen's fist connects with his jaw, knocking him unconscious.

One down, four to go.

Two more men run at Kaigen from either side. He teleports to the closest one, shoulder first, and knocks him to the ground, then turns and raises his sword to block a blow from the other. They clash swords three more times in quick succession before Kaigen drops to the ground and spin kicks the soldier's legs from under him.

An overzealous third attacker comes from behind and swings his sword at Kaigen. *Idiot.* He easily swats the sword away and punches the man to the ground with his left hand.

Two down, two staggered, and one hanging back. He steals a quick glance at the king, who looks uninterested at best, which only makes Kaigen angrier.

Let's end this.

In a matter of seconds, he teleports behind each of the two injured soldiers, giving one three quick punches to the back, and the other a stiff kick in the side of his kneecap. The final soldier runs at him, but Kaigen teleports behind him, slams him to the ground by the collar of his shirt, jumps on top of him, and knocks him out with his first punch.

But he doesn't stop there.

He punches the man again. And again. And again. Rendering his face bloodied and broken. Then he lets out a barbaric scream, raises his sword, and stabs it into the ground . . . inches from the man's head.

Clap, clap, clap . . . The king slowly claps his hands together. "My greatest warrior; you truly never disappoint me," says Balloch. "Now go clean yourself up. We have business to attend to." Kaigen exits the grounds aggressively, without a word. All those who've gathered give him ample space as he makes his way through the crowd, afraid of being his next victim.

***

An hour or so later, Kaigen finds himself alone in his room, deep in thought. Well, technically it's his room, although he rarely spends any time in it. Given to him a few years ago by the king, it is yet another reminder that he is being held hostage here.

Ten years earlier, Kaigen had met a woman—a shape-shifter just like him—named Marion. This was not a love story that developed over time; he fell for her the moment he laid eyes on her. After three years of living with one another, they decided it was time to have a child. It took some trying, but a year later, Isaiah was born. He came into the world on a cool summer night, marking the best, and the worst, day of Kaigen's life. Due to an awful twist of fate, Kaigen's beloved Marion died in childbirth.

She meant everything to him, and he was left a broken shell of himself. As he held his son in his arms, tears streaming down his face, he vowed to do everything in his power to keep him safe. But two years later came the night of the big feast. The feast where Balloch decided he would end the entire shape-shifter race, save for two, Kaigen and his son. He didn't poison Kaigen like the rest of them, no; he drugged him instead. Kaigen's last memory from the night of the feast was sharing a cup of ale with the king, after which they walked down a hallway in silence until he stumbled, fell to the floor, and blacked out.

He woke the next morning tied to a chair, sitting opposite the king. Balloch's next words haunt Kaigen to this day: "We have your son. Everyone else is dead."

He teleported across the room and grabbed Balloch by the throat. "You thought those binds could hold me?"

"No . . . But if you do not remove your hand from my neck, do you want to know what will happen to your son?" Balloch asks flatly.

Kaigen has been his servant ever since.

His thoughts are interrupted by Balloch entering the room, followed by Kaigen's son. Kaigen jumps to his feet. "Isaiah!" he says, looking at his son, before shifting his eyes to the king. "Why have you brought him?"

"Easy there," says the king, holding up a sword to stop Kaigen. "You seemed a bit tense out on the grounds today. I wanted to make sure you didn't do anything irrational. Also, I thought it was about time you saw your boy again. After all, it has been a while."

"You have kept him from me for over a week! And you expect me to remain rational?"

"I could not have your mind preoccupied while you were assisting Eldar. But after what you did today, you deserve a little time with the young lad," says Balloch, motioning to Isaiah.

Kaigen embraces his son with open arms, squeezing him tighter than he ever has before.

"Have they hurt you?" he whispers in Isaiah's ear.

"I'm okay," Isaiah whispers back.

They hold their embrace for a little while longer. Kaigen would love for their hug to last forever, but he slowly releases his grasp and turns his attention back to the king. "What do you need me to do?"

"Now that's the spirit. I have humored this group of traitors for long enough, and now their little quest will come to an end. They will be arriving at a small town that sits on the edge of

Brackoa Lake in a few days' time. From there, they will have two options: take the river that parallels the lake, or attempt to cross the lake and risk being attacked by the brackoa. If they have any sense, they will take the river . . . and we will be waiting for them.

"I want you to inform every troop we have stationed in that area to pull out and regroup along the river's edge. Tell them to hide in the dense undergrowth of the woods that line the river, and when the elves come through, their journey is over."

"Why don't you just have the troops ambush them in the town? It seems risky to have them wait along the river," says Kaigen.

"I do not want to give any credibility to their cause. If people see my troops gathering to fight, it may garner a following for this 'Chosen One,' and I won't have it. This is to remain a secret until they are all dead."

"Understood, and what would you like me to do once I've delivered this message?"

Balloch gives Kaigen a wry smile. "Isn't it obvious? You're leading the ambush."

PART II

THE LAKE

CHAPTER 15

John is beyond grateful for Lorena's decision to take a few much-needed days to recover before they continue their journey. He hasn't bathed or washed his clothes since he arrived, and although a stream isn't the ideal place to do either, it certainly gets the job done. And he must admit, being naked in the wilderness is rather thrilling.

Melara's leg is healing up nicely, thanks to some rigorous rehabilitation techniques provided by Darian, and some sort of salve that Killian rubs on it three times a day. The twins' fighting abilities are not lost on John, but it's clear that their specialties lie in the art of healing.

Killian can name every plant they pass by on their journey, noting each one's medicinal properties and what you can make with them. Whether it's a salve to reduce inflammation, a tea to help you sleep, or a deadly poison that they can dip their arrows into—everything has a purpose.

Then there's Darian. He, too, has a gift for crafting and applying medicine, but his unique skill is knowing everything there is to know about how the body works. He talks about how massaging your shoulders can relieve headaches, how stretching your hamstrings can relieve back pain, and shows John multiple pressure points that help reduce stress. John can't help but think how easily he would excel as an athletic trainer for the Crimson Tide back home.

Lorena and John spend a considerable amount of time hunting to stock up on supplies before they head to their next location: Brackoa Lake. She teaches him how to slow his breathing before he shoots—which he's already well-versed in from his time in the military—and how to steady his arms so his arrow flies true, something he definitely needs to work on. They don't run into any stagglehorn. However, they take down enough small game animals for a sizable meal, with lots to spare.

During this short time, they're all genuinely enjoying themselves for once. It's funny, the difference a few days can make. John was ready to fight these elves to the death when he first arrived, and now he's sharing laughs with them. That being said, the thought of home never strays too far in John's mind.

Once Melara's leg has healed and they feel they have a sufficient amount of food for the journey, they head for Brackoa Lake. It's not a long journey, taking them only a day and a half to reach the town bordering the lake. Small wooden huts line the streets, the smell of fresh fish lingers in the air from a nearby market, and boats of every size line the beach. There are men and women fishing from docks that reach out like fingers into the still lake. To John, this seems like a pleasant scene, but to Lorena, something is off.

"Where are all of Balloch's people?" she asks.

"Probably hiding in the shadows," says Melara. "Keep your guard up."

A flock of small birds flies overhead, squawking as they go. Killian points to them. "Look!"

"Is it that time already?" Darian asks.

"Yes indeed. The whitewings are making their descent south," says Killian.

John raises an eyebrow. "Whitewings?"

"They're elegant birds that bring luck to all who they pass over," informs Killian. "They also happen to be my favorite animal on this island. So peaceful in nature, and so beautiful."

"Looks like we don't have to worry, after all," Darian says.

John can't tell if he's kidding or not; the twins genuinely seem to admire these birds. It's no matter, though. John is eyeing everyone with suspicion as they walk through the market. But nothing looks wrong to him. There's a man droning on about his unbreakable fishing line, a patron is haggling over the price of netting at a nearby hut, and two dogs are begging for food at a booth to his right. A ripple of sadness hits John as these sights conjure up memories of his market back home.

As if sensing John needs it, a puppy walks up to John and rubs up against his leg. He drops to one knee and gets face-to-face with the pup, scratching it behind the ears. He laughs as the pup licks his face repeatedly. *"No matter where you are in your life, take time to enjoy the little things,"* he can hear his therapist say.

"I said, keep your guard up," says Melara sternly.

"Oh, sorry, I forgot to vet him." John grabs the puppy playfully by the ears. "Are you a spy, little guy? If you're a spy, you know you have to tell me."

Melara rolls her eyes. "We should ask around the market, see if they know anything about Balloch and his troops."

"Good plan," agrees Lorena.

The first hut they come to is run by an older man, probably in his late sixties, with a long gray beard. He's selling blue tentacles, about five feet long, with two rows of suckers going up the side of them.

"Brackoa tentacles? How'd you manage to get your hands on these?" Lorena asks the man.

"Washed up on shore yesterday, still fresh. How much would you like?"

"Brackoa has always been a bit tough for my liking, but the twins like it. Do you mind cutting one in half for us?"

"Not a problem," he says, before taking a cleaver and chopping the tentacle in two. "I'll wrap it for your journey."

"Journey? How did you . . .?" Lorena trails off.

"I've seen you come through here at least a dozen times over the years. We don't get many elves this way. It would be tough to forget a group like yourselves," the man says as he wraps the severed tentacle in cloth and ties it up. "However, that one looks new to me." His eyes point to John.

"Ah yes, he's a woodsman," she lies. "He joined our journey a while back."

"Is that right . . .?" he says, clearly not convinced. "No need to worry; you'll get no trouble here today."

"I can see that . . . Where did all of his men go?" she asks quietly.

"No need to whisper. They all left a day ago, headed up the river. Packed pretty light for such a long journey, but there's plenty of game to be hunted past the lake."

This last comment leaves John unsettled. If there is one thing he knows from his past: You pack for the journey ahead of you, and you leave nothing to chance.

Lorena thanks the man and gives him a piece of Elvish bread in return for the brackoa tentacle. Knowing how much they glorify Elvish bread, that tentacle must be worth a lot.

"Why would Balloch's men just up and leave?" John asks.

"Unclear, but it doesn't matter. We need to find someone who will bring us upriver and past this lake," says Lorena.

"Can we go around?" John says.

"Impossible. There are dense forests with thick swamps for miles on either side of the lake; it's impassable," says Lorena.

"Why don't we just sail across the lake? Seems like it would be faster that way."

Melara shrugs. "That's a great idea . . . if you want a quick death."

John shakes his head. "Glad to see you're back to normal."

"She's right, though; the brackoa that inhabit this lake would see us dead in a day. Those tentacles the man was selling were actually from a baby. Full grown, they are much larger and much deadlier," says Lorena.

Figures, John thinks as he lets out a long and obvious sigh. "Alright, let's get on with it."

"You go on ahead. Darian and I are going to look around the market for supplies," says Killian.

Lorena nods. "Okay, meet us at the docks in ten minutes. It's at least a four-day journey along the rivers, and I want to get going as soon as possible."

The twins head off toward a hut that's engulfed with dried plants, hanging from every rafter of its structure. Meanwhile, John, Lorena, and Melara head to the docks. They move past a few sizable boats—close to fifty feet long—outfitted with harpoons on the sides and massive white sails. Lorena explains that these are for fishing in the center of the lake, and the harpoons are there for defense against the brackoa. There are several cutouts along the side of the boats, so if wind isn't present, the crew can use oars to paddle back to shore.

Then they pass a few smaller boats—thirty feet in length—used for fishing in the shallower waters of the lake. These boats also have sails, but they have multiple oar holes as a backup as well. Finally, they arrive at a twenty-foot-long boat, with one lone mast pointing toward the sky, and a sail strung high upon it. The walls of this boat are markedly shorter than the rest, and two oars sit inside. A man sits casually on the dock next to it, staring down at his feet dangling in the water.

"This is the boat you're choosing? It's so small," John whispers to Lorena.

She waves him off dismissively. "Excuse me, sir, are you for hire?"

"For a price," the man responds without looking up.

"In exchange for a trip up the river, how does ten pounds of stagglehorn sound? We could even throw in some of our medicines, known all throughout Mhorelia," says Lorena.

"I do not trade like those folks in the market. It will take more than stagglehorn to get me to make that journey," says the man, still not making eye contact.

"It's a fair price," says Lorena.

He gestures to the empty docks. "Well, by all means, if you see anyone else willing to accept that price, you can ask them. But I think you'll find that they've all gone home for the day."

"We'll throw in two loaves of Elvish bread," she counters.

He scoffs, "You elves and your bread."

Melara's face turns red with anger, and the whites of her knuckles start to show as she squeezes the hilt of her knife. But as she takes a half step forward, Lorena raises her arm slightly to block her way. They exchange a look, and Lorena removes a pouch that hangs from her belt. "How's twenty silver coins sound . . . and you lose that attitude?"

His eyes jolt up. "Well, why didn't you say so sooner! Climb aboard!" As she tosses him the pouch, John realizes it's the first time he's seen any sort of currency since he arrived—later finding out it's mostly used in the North. They pile in their gear just as Killian and Darian arrive.

"Is this the boat?" asks Killian.

"A little small," Darian points out.

"Thank you!" John says emphatically.

"Would you three shut up," scolds Melara. "This boat is the only one nimble enough to make it up the river, so unless you want to swim, I suggest you get in."

When Melara looks away, Killian turns to John and raises his eyebrows, prompting a stifled laugh. Melara spins her head back around quickly and stares at them both with narrowed eyes. As John spends more time with Killian, he's finding it impossible not to admire him. The elf is deadly with a bow; he cares deeply, and every once in a while, he displays a slightly juvenile behavior that would make even the most cynical man grin.

Shortly after boarding, they head upriver. Calling it a river is really giving it too much credit; it moves so slowly that it's almost impossible to tell which way the water is even flowing. Luckily for them, it's a windy day, so they take off without any issues.

As John paces the boat, he finds it a tad more spacious than he had originally thought. About ten feet wide at the midpoint, and slowly curving into points at both ends, it provides enough room for everyone to sit comfortably.

The guide—who reveals his name to be Dano—stands at the back of the boat, holding a long wooden rod that he moves back and forth to steer the boat. He opens up immediately once they are on the water, probably in an effort to earn some additional coin along the way. He talks about the history of the river and how it branches off and connects with the lake at various points along the way. And how it was man-made a thousand years ago to avoid coming up against the brackoa on open water.

It all seems far-fetched to John, but then again, so does everything he's encountered on this journey. Once he's done giving a history lesson, he talks at length about his boat. About how he built it by hand and how he can remember the exact location of every tree he cut down to construct it. He even shares that the oars are made of a lighter wood, so it's less strenuous to paddle, if needed. And he is especially proud of the steering mechanism at the back, designed to change the direction of the boat with the slightest movement from side to side. He demonstrates this by quickly jarring it back and forth, causing the boat to rock wildly.

"Would you knock that off!" yells Melara.

"Uh-oh . . . does somebody get a little seasick?" Dano teases.

Melara looks away in disgust, trying to mask the fact that he's right, her face turning a shade paler. Dano laughs it off and steadies the boat. "Alright, I'll behave myself, but we've got at least a four-day journey ahead of us, so you'd best get comfortable."

"We're well aware of the journey ahead," says Lorena.

"Ah, so you've made this trip before?" Dano asks.

"Many times."

"Must we make small talk with this man?" says Melara, loudly enough for Dano to hear.

"You'd better play nice, or I'll rock the boat again," says Dano.

"If you rock this boat again, I'll slit your throat while you sleep," Melara replies flatly.

"Okay, everybody, let's not lose our heads before the journey has even started," John cuts in.

And with that, they proceed in silence for many hours—the only occasional sounds coming from Killian and Darian talking quietly among themselves, or Lorena sharpening her sword with a small stone. Melara has shut her eyes, probably to try to quell the seasickness. They aren't rocking badly, but every time they make a turn, John can see her face cringe.

As they float along, John spends his time watching the tree line to his left. Every hundred feet or so, the river branches off, and he can just catch a glimpse of the lake where it connects. He whispers to Dano, "So, how often does this river feed into the lake?"

"It depends. Toward the end of the river, quite a lot, as you've probably noticed. But as we get farther along, it becomes less frequent. In fact, in about another five minutes, we'll reach the last branch for miles."

"You know these waters well."

"That I do. I've been traveling along them for years, carrying passengers who are willing to pay."

"Are there others?"

"Oh yes, I am one of many who travel these rivers."

John eyes him with suspicion. "Really . . . I don't remember seeing any others at the docks."

Dano replies, "Don't you remember? They'd all packed it in for the day."

John looks around at the beautiful day, the sun shining and not a cloud in the sky. Then his eyes meet Lorena's, whose gaze is already locked on his. She drops the rock she was using for sharpening and points her sword at Dano. "Where were the others today?"

"I don't know. I'm not their mother. I don't keep track of all of them."

"Where were they?" she repeats, a little louder, rousing Melara and alerting the twins.

He goes silent, and John's eyes instinctively sweep the tree line. Nothing looks amiss, just tall trees, thick bushes, and . . . Wait. He looks down in the water and notices a small amount of purple residue floating past the boat. *Kaigen.*

"It's a trap," says John.

Melara eagerly shoulders her bow and points an arrow directly at Dano.

"Whoa, whoa, whoa. Let's slow down for a second. If you shoot me, you're all dead as well," says Dano.

Lorena stands and faces Dano. "What did you do?"

"Look, the deal was I bring you up the river, and Balloch's troops take you in. That's it. Everyone goes home alive. But if you shoot me, you die. That was the deal."

"You know what's funny . . ." says Lorena. "You actually believe that."

At that moment, John sees a dozen men rise from the bushes, arrows poised to shoot.

"Get down!"

Lorena drops to the deck of the boat, and the others lie flat, just before the arrows fly. Most whiz past them, but a few hit the side of the boat; and one beautifully shot arrow flies directly into Dano's neck, killing him instantly.

"What do we do?" yells Killian.

"Shoot back!" yells Melara, who gets up on one knee and fires an arrow into the woods. The other elves follow suit and fire at the trees, before dropping back to the deck when another round of arrows comes their way. John remains on his back, peering over the edge every chance he gets so he can see what's going on. Without a bow, he feels useless—not that he'd be that helpful even if he had one.

"Keep shooting!" yells Lorena.

The elves fire again, and John sees two of the men fall to the ground. Another round of arrows peppers the side of the boat.

"We're sitting ducks out here!" John warns.

"We can take them," says Melara.

But as the elves prepare to fire another round of arrows, the men have vanished.

"They've retreated," says Killian, and he stands to get a better look. Just then, six men step out from behind the trees and point their arrows, tipped with fire, at the boat.

"Get down!" Melara yells before tackling Killian toward the front of the boat, narrowly avoiding a flaming arrow to the chest. His head slams against the deck, knocking him out cold. The other five arrows stick into the side of the boat, and a steady flame begins to rise.

Darian crawls to Killian's side and shakes him. "Killian! Killian!" But Killian is unresponsive. The arrows are flying in rapid bursts now, pinning them down, unable to fire back. *They must be staggering their shots,* John thinks.

"Lorena, what do we do?" shouts Melara.

Just then, the wind picks up and they begin to cruise down the river. "It appears luck is on our side," she says. "Stay low and let the wind take us far away from here."

But John takes one look ahead and sees they are nowhere near safety. There is one final branch of the river heading toward the lake on his left, and past that . . . there must be at least fifty men on both sides of the river. He waits for another round of arrows to hit the side and then sprints toward the end of the boat.

"What are you doing?" yells Lorena.

He jumps and slams the steering rod to one side, forcing the boat to veer sharply to the left. They turn just in time to take the last river branch heading toward the lake, scraping the side of the boat along the muddy bank.

"Why did you do that?" she repeats. But her question is quickly answered as a barrage of arrows, fired from farther ahead, splashes harmlessly into the water behind them.

Lorena peers over the edge, and seeing no one, she rises to her feet and starts giving orders: "Melara! Help me put out this fire. We cannot let it reach the sail. John, get us to the lake and keep us close to the bank. Darian, how is your brother?"

"He's breathing, but he won't respond to me."

"Prop him up. We will tend to him shortly."

Lorena and Melara proceed to douse the fire with river water as John guides the boat. They remove all the arrows from the side of the boat and toss them in the center.

"None of them went through, so we should be alright," says Lorena. Just as she finishes speaking, the wind forces them out of the narrow river and onto the open lake, its vastness leaving them in awe.

John looks around, seeing water in every direction. *Oh yeah, we're alright . . . for now.*

Chapter 16

Once the boat is deemed seaworthy, the attention turns to Killian as Lorena and Darian assess his condition. He's breathing, but the deep gash in his forehead needs to be patched up. Darian cleans the wound thoroughly and applies an ointment before wrapping a cloth around Killian's head. While they tend to Killian, Melara sits in the center of the boat, meticulously scanning the arrows they recovered. Her actions may have saved Killian's life, but she no doubt feels responsible for his current condition.

"How many did we get?" John says.

"Eighteen that are usable, but the flaming arrows are no good."

"Decent haul."

"We'll need all we can get," says Lorena, joining Melara on the deck.

"How is Killian?" John asks.

"He's alive for now, just unconscious. No telling when he'll return to us," says Darian. He kneels and places his hand on Melara's shoulder, startling her. "Melara . . . thank you."

"What? I-I caused this," she responds.

Darian shakes his head. "If you had not done what you did, he would no longer be with us."

Melara leans her shoulder against Darian, showing an unexpected display of vulnerability that John has not seen from her before. It's a touching scene. *They've been through so much together,* John thinks, and instantly, he feels like an outsider again.

Brushing that aside, he turns his attention to Dano, still slumped over with an arrow protruding from his neck. "So, what should we do with him?"

"Let's throw him over," says Melara, her vulnerable moment over as quickly as it came.

"Agreed," says Darian. He and John hoist Dano up and move to throw him overboard.

"Wait!" says Melara, then rushes to their side. She rips the arrow from his neck and smiles. "Nineteen."

They continue along the edge of the lake for hours, doing not much of anything. Lorena goes back to sharpening her sword. Melara cleans the arrows and splits them among the four quivers, and Darian sits next to Killian, preparing food for the group. He's deeply focused as he separates the small game they cooked earlier in the day, but John can see the look in Darian's eyes, a look of mourning. His brother's condition is weighing on him.

He saw a similar look many years ago in the eyes of his old teammate, Jenny, after a mission in Southern China went horribly wrong. The Undesirables were all set to pull out and go home when a banded krait—an extremely venomous snake—bit her twin sister, Lucy, in the calf. Fortunately, there was an evac waiting close by. She was promptly rushed to the hospital and administered an antivenom. Unfortunately, by the time she was admitted, she was experiencing full-body paralysis. She was intubated and put on a ventilator immediately. Jenny stayed with her for two weeks, reading to her, listening to music with her, and sleeping on a cot next to her hospital bed. She never left her side, not once. That was the day John realized the bond between twins is like no other.

John's eyes start to well up as he looks at Darian, but he quickly wipes away the tears. *This is no time to get sentimental.*

After another hour, the sun sets on yet another day in Mhorelia, and John can only wonder how many more days until he'll be home again . . . If he ever does get home. "You said this is a four-day journey, right?"

"Yes, four days. But we've never taken the lake before. Should still be about four days if we stick to the shoreline," says Lorena.

"Shouldn't we be worried about another ambush, traveling this close to the shore?" says John.

"I'll take a fight with a thousand men over a duel with a brackoa in the open water."

"Are they really that dangerous?"

"Very few people have tangled with them and lived to tell the tale. Some of them are so strong they can pull boats to the depths of the lake. But mostly, they'll attack with their legs, swinging them wildly to knock you into the water. Then they'll pull you to the bottom, never to be heard from again."

John guides the boat inland and clears his throat. "Very well, then, the shoreline it is."

They steer the boat in shifts throughout the night, taking turns keeping watch for an attack. John hands over the reins to Melara around midnight, when the moon is high in the sky. He uses his pack as a pillow and pulls a large wool cloth over him as a blanket. The temperature has dropped substantially over the last couple of hours, chilling John to the bone and giving him a constant reminder of how much he misses the Alabama heat. Darian is huddled next to Killian, providing him with some much-needed warmth as they sleep. John looks over at Lorena—sleeping alone—and a thought comes and goes in his mind before he even has the chance to wonder.

***

The following morning, John squeezes his blanket closer to his chest and rolls onto his side. He managed to sleep fairly well—despite the uncomfortable floorboards, the low temperature, and the constant rocking from side to side. The sun rises over a faraway mountain peak and showers the boat with light. Aside from Melara, everyone else remains asleep, and they marvel at the sight together. The horizon has transformed into a spectacular display of reds and oranges. The colors reflect off of the still water in front of them as the softest of breezes push them along. All around hangs a calming silence, a peaceful silence.

"Isn't it beautiful?" Melara says softly.

"It is."

"It's moments like these that could make you forget what we're doing . . . Forget we're at war."

Darian and Lorena sit up slowly and take in the scene. "Too bad it won't last," says Lorena. "A red sun like this . . . it's not a good time to be on the water."

Red sky at night, sailors' delight. Red sky at morning, sailors take warning . . . John thinks. *I thought that was just an old wives' tale.*

"I guess all we can do is enjoy it while it lasts," says Darian. "Who wants breakfast?"

They gorge on nearly all of their remaining food: a couple of squirrels, a few more pieces of stagglehorn, and some bread with butter that Darian got in town before they set off. All that's left when they're finished is the brackoa tentacle, one more loaf of bread, and a few berries. Luckily, the lake water is drinkable, so they'll have an endless supply of that, but food is going to be a problem.

Lorena and Melara have a solution, though, directing John to lead the boat into the open water and keep it as steady as he can. They break off a few pieces of bread and drop them into the lake. Then they stand like statues, staring into the water, waiting. They wait for about ten minutes, not moving a muscle. John is about to speak, but before he can get the words out, they both quickly raise their bows and shoot into the lake. Two long fish float to the surface; they're blue with red stripes down the side of them.

"Alright! Stripers!" cheers Darian. "A lake delicacy."

They shoot another twenty fish as they float along—which should suffice for the next couple of days. Cooking them, however, is another story. With no way of making a fire on the boat, they'll have to be eaten raw. John is initially opposed to the idea, but once

Darian has filleted them, they don't look half bad. He bites into one hesitantly, but he's relieved at the taste. *Just like sashimi.*

After they've eaten lunch, John recounts the days in his head, trying to determine how long he's been in Mhorelia. *Seven? Maybe eight days?* It's all been so hectic; it's hard for him to keep track of the time. Suddenly, he has an urge to learn more about what lies ahead, in order to be prepared, if nothing else.

"So, you've said that most people chose to head down the mountain after Balloch took over, in fear that his troops would find them. But this island seems so vast, are there any people we might encounter along the way that have managed to stay hidden? People who could help us?"

"Truth be told, we don't know much about who stayed behind after Balloch took over," Lorena admits. "It was all chaos. We assumed that if you didn't make it down, you didn't make it. The town we left yesterday is the last known inhabited town before the summit."

"So, it's safe to assume that anyone else we meet along the way is an enemy?" asks John.

"Not necessarily; there are rumors of groups who stayed behind. Groups that live their lives in the shadows," says Lorena.

"Like the Cliff Elves of the North. A striking group of elves who hunt Balloch's scouts under the cover of darkness," says Melara with pride.

Lorena looks at Melara, and her eyes soften. "It's been a long time since we've heard any word of them, Melara."

Melara glares back at Lorena. "They're out there!" she says. "I'm sure of it . . ." Her voice wavers. She walks to the front of the boat, looking out longingly into the distance.

"What was all that about?" whispers John.

"She's a Cliff Elf, just like those she speaks of. But while they chose to stay in the North and fight, she chose to help others escape down the mountain. Others that could not fend for themselves. It was a hard choice, for she left her love in the North that day, promising to return . . . But that was a long time ago."

They sit in somber silence for a moment until Darian cheerfully pipes up, "Don't forget about Leon!"

"Who's Leon?" John asks.

"He's the best cousin a couple of brothers like us could ask for," Darian says as he pats Killian on the shoulder. "He lives somewhere on this ascent we're taking, but we don't know where. Last we saw him, he was picking flowers on the other side of Brackoa Lake."

"Something was off about him that day; his mind was elsewhere," says Lorena.

"Yeah, he's always been an interesting elf . . ." Darian says, smiling wistfully. "That must've been five years ago."

"Wait, how did he make it all the way down the mountain? And didn't he help you when you came across his path?" asks John.

"He has never gotten in our way, even aiding us in the past. But the last time we saw him, something was different. It was as if he didn't want anything to do with our cause," says Lorena.

"Never really understood why. He was always a great warrior, even if he was a little strange," says Darian.

"Yes, a great fighter indeed," says Lorena. "But now he spends his time hiding away somewhere, speaking with his stagglehorn."

"What?" John says in surprise.

"That is how he travels such great distances with ease. He rides the stagglehorn and uses them to avoid Balloch's forces," says Darian.

"Stagglehorn can speak?" John says.

"Well . . . he can speak with them," says Lorena.

Darian shrugs. "Like I said, he's an interesting man."

"Well, I hope I get to meet him. I'd love to see someone ride one of those animals," John says.

"You may just get that chance," says Darian.

From the front of the boat, Melara interrupts their conversation. "I wouldn't count on it."

John looks ahead, seeing a gloomy sight bearing down upon them. The sky has darkened, and storm clouds have gathered. With those clouds comes an unmistakable wall of rain that threatens to hit the boat at any moment. Whitecaps form in the distance, making the boat rock back and forth. *Crack!* Lightning strikes the sky, followed by an onslaught of thunder, punctuating the severity of the storm—and the little time they have left to prepare for it.

"We need to get back to shore. Now," says Melara.

"Oh, brother," Darian's eyes focus on Killian, "together till the end."

The wind picks up, causing the boat to rock uncontrollably and spin away from the shore. John unties and removes the boat's sail from its mast. "Quick, tie down everything you can!" he yells.

"We need to get back to shore!" Melara repeats.

"We don't have time!" John argues as he throws them the rope that was holding up the sail. Another bolt of lightning strikes the lake just ahead of them.

"He's right; we're too late. Start by securing Killian!" shouts Lorena.

Just as the rain starts to pelt them, John grabs the steering rod and points the boat directly into the storm. "Hold on!" he yells as a wave barrels toward them.

They get Killian secured, shoving their packs underneath his body, just as the wave hits. The boat jumps up into the air on impact, knocking them off balance and sending all of their fish flying off into the lake—the same fish that they risked coming out this far into the lake to catch.

Killian's body bounces about, but the ties used to secure him hold strong. As they all attempt to steady themselves, another wave crashes into the boat, flinging the elves violently backward. Lorena crashes into the mast, and Melara falls into John, knocking him sideways and whipping the boat around. John gets up quickly and rights the boat, but as he looks around frantically, he notices someone is missing . . . *Where's Darian?*

"Help!" comes a faint voice from somewhere in front of John. The rain is coming down so hard, he can barely see three feet in front of him. "Help!" the voice calls again. He grabs Melara's arm, hoists her up, and passes her the steering rod.

"Hold us steady," he says. They hit a couple of smaller waves as John crawls forward, searching for Darian on his hands and knees. The wind is gusting faster and louder now, and it's becoming nearly impossible for John to hear anything. A wave hits the side of the boat without warning, causing him to crash into Lorena and smash his jaw on the side of the mast in the process. Blood instantly streams down the side of his face. Everything in his body is telling him to grab hold of the mast and hold on for dear life, but then he hears it one more time.

"Help!"

There. It's faint, but through the rain, John can just make out Darian's hand perilously gripping the side of the boat as he's being dragged through the water. Without hesitation, John leaps toward Darian, grabs his arm, and yanks him into the boat. He wraps his arms tightly around him as he shakes uncontrollably.

Melara is gripping the steering rod with everything she's got as John, Lorena, and Darian lie on the boat floor, clutching whatever they can while this small fishing boat braves the vicious storm for another five minutes. And then, without warning, the storm ceases. It's gone as quickly as it came. In fact, it all happens so fast, none of them loosen their grip for another few minutes, sure that they would have to endure another round of the storm's thrashing.

What finally makes them release their grasp is the faint sound of someone coughing up water. They look around curiously at each other, but no one is making a sound. Coming to the same conclusion all at once, they jump to their feet and run to Killian's side. He must have swallowed half a gallon of lake water during the storm and is retching violently. Darian kneels at his side as John unties him from the boat. One look at the paleness in his face and John can tell that he is not well, probably still a bit concussed too.

Despite his condition, he opens his mouth to speak, but no sound comes out on his first attempt. His eyes struggle to stay open as he mouths something to Darian.

"What is it?" Darian asks. "Do you want water? Food? What do you need, brother?"

"Bro-oh-oh," Killian mumbles.

"What's that, brother? I'm not sure I understand."

Killian's eyes open wide as he raises his hand and points behind the four of them. A large shadow looms across Killian's face as he gets out one more word: "Brackoa."

Chapter 17

Time stops. The only sound comes from the water dripping off of the ten-foot-long tentacle sprouting from the lake. At its base, it must be at least a foot thick. The sun peeks out from behind a fleeting storm cloud and shines upon the slimy, rough skin that makes up the tentacle. Its two rows of suckers pulsate as the tentacle slowly curves toward the boat.

The elves seem to be in shock, standing in stunned silence as the tentacle cocks backward. John's hand instinctively grabs his sole weapon—the small dagger still dangling from his belt. *That won't do.* His eyes dart to Lorena just as the brackoa forcefully thrusts its tentacle downward. He pulls her sword from her belt, and in one fluid motion, he chops the tentacle clean off. It falls into the boat and wriggles around wildly, with a green liquid oozing from its severed end.

That marks the end of the silence.

A muffled scream emanates from below the surface, and the water erupts around them. Tentacles pop out on every side and start taking swipes at the boat. These seem to be a bit smaller than the first, but still just as frightening. One smashes into Melara—who still hasn't moved—sending her flat on her back. The rest of them duck down just as a tentacle swings in from the right, narrowly avoiding it. But it tears through the boat's mast like a paper straw.

Once the shock wears off, everyone finds their footing and gets to work—except for Killian, who's in no condition to fight.

John tosses Lorena her sword and pulls out his dagger. He looks on in amazement at the elves' choreography as they fight. It feels like he's witnessing a deadly dance as they flip and roll around each other, shooting arrows in every direction.

John is so entranced by their fighting style, he barely has enough time to raise his dagger upward and pierce an oncoming tentacle that comes crashing down on top of him. The suckers grab his arm as he buries the knife deeper and rips it sideways, covering his body with its blood and slime.

As he wipes the brackoa's insides off his face, another tentacle grips the boat's edge and jerks it sideways. John crawls to the side of the boat and repeatedly stabs at it until it releases its grasp.

"This isn't working!" yells Lorena. "We need it to surface!" Just as she finishes speaking, a pointed, dark purple head protrudes from the water with one giant yellow eye.

"There!" yells Melara. The elves take aim to shoot just as a tentacle crashes into the side of the boat. All three arrows miss their mark and ricochet off of the tough shell that encases its head. The head darts back under the surface, and they undergo another round of flailing tentacles—only this time, they take on much more damage. Darian's legs are swept from under him, dropping him hard on the deck. Lorena takes a tentacle to the head, and Melara takes another to the chest.

Through the chaos, John notices a smaller tentacle slowly creeping up the side of the boat . . . right next to Killian. Before John can yell a warning, the tentacle seizes Killian's leg and attempts to pull him overboard. John abandons his dagger and runs to Killian, grabbing him underneath each arm as he cries out. John only just gets his footing when the brackoa really starts to pull, almost taking the two of them overboard together. It looks as if Killian's leg will be torn clean off any second as he cries out once more in agony.

"Lorena!" John calls out.

She has just regained her footing, but she's still in a daze from getting knocked in the head. *She'll be no help,* John thinks. But he is mistaken . . . Her eyes stare straight ahead—still glazed—as she sheathes her sword, grabs an arrow, and shoulders her bow in seconds. The arrow flies true, penetrating the tentacle just below Killian's leg. A perfect shot.

The tentacle instantly retracts, and both John and Killian fall backward onto the boat in a heap. Lorena is at their side in an instant, looking much more lucid as she checks on Killian.

John gets to his feet as the tentacles all slowly withdraw into the lake. Darian and Melara are up now as well, looking battered but pleased. "We did it!" says Darian. "We vanquished the brackoa."

But behind him, the brackoa's head ominously rises from the depths and gradually opens its large, leering eye. *Not quite.*

The brackoa lifts all of its tentacles at once. Some have been severed, some have been punctured, but all of them are about to crash down upon the boat. "Get down!" John yells, grabbing Lorena's sword from her belt once more as he sprints the length of the boat. Four long bounds and he's leaping directly for the head. He flips the sword around in midair and stabs the brackoa square in the eye. The sword cuts straight through the back of its head, and it lets out one final shriek as its tentacles fall lifeless to the lake surface.

John plants his foot firmly on the brackoa's head and yanks the sword free. He swims to the boat as the departed creature sinks to the bottom of the lake. Darian and Melara hoist him aboard, and they all allow their legs to give out. John lies on the deck, his head propped up against the wall of the boat. Soaking wet, body aching, and in a state of shock, he stares up into the sky and recounts the last few minutes, with Melara and Darian sitting by his side. Lorena and Killian follow suit, and a well-deserved calm ensues.

Lorena breaks the silence, saying, "We did it," still not fully believing it herself. John feels her gaze as she grabs his arm.

"When you first got here, I had my doubts . . . I said some things to you that—"

"Stop," says John. "It's okay. I wouldn't have trusted me either . . . I'm just a guy from Alabama who's trying to get home."

Her eyes soften. "Whoever you are, you're one of us now."

John is overtaken with elation in that moment. He looks to his left, then back to his right. *I've got a team again.*

"I have to say, John, you are very skillful with a sword. And considering your inability to shoot an arrow, I'm quite surprised," Lorena points out.

John's grin widens. "Back home, I'm not just a fighter. I'm an engineer as well. Mostly, I fix complicated machines that I doubt you'd have here in Mhorelia. I was taught at a university, and although I was a skilled student, sometimes the stress would get to me. On one particularly stressful day, I took a walk down the road to clear my head, and I ended up passing an academy that specialized in swordsmanship. When I walked inside, there were two men dueling while a group sat and watched. The grace and power these two men possessed as they battled was mesmerizing to witness. I signed up without another thought and ended up practicing there three times a week for the next two years."

"Lucky for us you did," says Melara.

"So, when can I get one of my own?" he says as he holds up Lorena's sword. "I'd hate to keep stealing yours."

Lorena laughs. "We'll see what we can do, but until then, that dagger of yours will have to suffice." She takes the sword from his hand. "This is a family heirloom. I simply cannot part with it."

"Fair enough."

As she takes the sword from him, he is suddenly aware of an intense burning feeling on his arm. Amidst the chaos of the battle, he hadn't noticed the aftermath of what the brackoa had done. The skin where the suckers previously latched on has now turned a bright pinkish-red. It's hot to the touch and burns like crazy.

The adrenaline must be wearing off because the elves are noticing their wounds as well. Lorena has a patch on her neck with the same type of coloration as John's arm. Killian's leg and Melara's chest have similar afflictions as well. This realization sends John and the women into a panic.

"What is this!" yells Melara, ripping off most of her top as the burning intensifies.

"Killian! Tell me you still have it," Darian says.

Killian—still not at a hundred percent—points to his pack at the front of the boat. Darian worriedly paws through it, relief flooding across his face as he pulls out a glass jar, full of some sort of lotion. "It's unbroken!" he says aloud, then opens the jar. The rancid smell that emerges causes John and Melara to gag instantly.

"What is that stuff?" she says. "It reeks."

"We acquired it in town at the market while you were off getting us a 'safe passage' across the lake . . ." says Darian jokingly.

She glares at him and takes a big scoop of the lotion in her hand. "Let's see how well you did." She lathers it on her wounds, and the instant relief makes her moan, "Ohhh," in a blissful, satisfied tone.

Darian hands the jar to Lorena, but before she treats her own wounds, she rubs John's arm with the lotion. The pain drifts away in seconds, followed by a cooling sensation that feels like his arm has been filled with menthol. "Thank you," he lets out, a bit more suggestive than he had meant it. She smiles and hands John the jar.

"Your turn."

He brushes her red curls to one side and rubs a handful of lotion onto her wounds. Without thinking, John slowly begins to massage her neck and shoulders, causing her to moan ever so softly. Her shoulders tense up immediately after realizing what she's done. His eyes dart up, hoping nobody has noticed. Melara is still entranced by the lotion, and Darian is taking stock of their supplies. But as his gaze makes its way to Killian, he's certain that his eyes quickly shut, pretending not to have noticed.

"Much better," she says as she stands and turns away to hide her embarrassment. "Now we must deal with the problem at hand."

Melara sits atop the stump where the mast used to stand. The air is still around her. "If we cannot use the wind, it appears our only option is to row. We can use the sun as a guide to get us back to the shore."

"That's a long way to row," says Darian.

"Then we'd better get started," says Lorena.

John offers to row first, taking the oars and placing them on either side of the boat in carved rings. Dano was right: The paddles are much lighter than John had expected, and they cut through the water with ease.

While he hastily paddles back to shore—hoping to avoid another brackoa attack—the others figure out the food situation. All of the fish they had caught are now floating somewhere in the center of the lake, never to be eaten. In Killian's pack, they recover what is left of the bread loaf, and a few berries—although the berries were mostly crushed during the storm. That, and the tentacle that John sliced off to start the battle with the brackoa, are all that remain.

"We'll have to ration this out until we can find something else to eat," says Lorena, "with most of it going to Killian."

"And we must find a way to cook this brackoa. Unlike the fish, we cannot eat it raw," Darian adds.

"We can try to find something useful when we reach the shore," says Melara. "John, make haste."

"I'm working on it . . ." John says through his teeth as he quickens his pace.

After paddling for another hour, they mercifully reach the shore—if you can call it that—consisting of hundreds of trees surrounded by marshland. By then, John's arms are burning, not only from fatigue but also from the brackoa stings. Melara uses some rope to tie up the boat to a tree near the shoreline as they all reapply the lotion to their injuries. Unable to leave the boat, they get close enough to cut a few branches from the tree— hoping to find a spot farther up the lake to build a fire. What John wouldn't give to step back on land for a few moments. Melara seems to be doing a lot better on the water, though, probably due to all the deadly distractions they've had.

After gathering enough firewood, they set off again, but the wind still refuses to return. So they go back to rowing, taking shifts until the sun is low in the sky. A few more whitewings fly overhead, and John chuckles to himself, thinking about how "lucky" they've been. His stomach rumbles once, and then again. He's never been one to skip a meal, and the small slice of bread he had for dinner just isn't cutting it. When it's his turn to row again, night is upon them and the elves all lie down to rest, beat from their arduous day.

Between the sun, the storm, the fight, and the lack of food, John is ready to call it quits. Deep down, however, it's clear to him that giving up is not an option. So, he uses a tool he learned in therapy for when his thoughts get too negative: John goes to his happy place. He imagines being in his one-bedroom apartment, standing at his cooking island, all of the ingredients for a lasagna laid out in front of him. His hands are cutting, mixing, and spreading in a flash. Many smells waft into his nose: ground beef purchased from a butcher down the street, tomatoes he's bought at the local market, and herbs that grow in the planter that hangs from his windowsill. He imagines sitting down on his couch to watch his favorite show and then taking a bite of the meal he's prepared.

Outside his imagination, his mouth begins to water, and he is transported back to the lake. This thought of home propels him. He must get back. No matter what. His arms take on a robotic stroke as he presses on into the night.

As the sun rises once more in the east, Killian lets out a big stretch and rolls onto his side. John watches as his eyes flutter open and land on him, still rowing, wearing only his boxers. His shirt and jeans lie next to him, drying in the heat. Despite the first night on the lake being frigid, John found himself drenched in sweat last night. He rowed through the darkness, not wanting to wake the elves, just wanting to get home. His arms are trembling, his breathing heavy, and judging by Killian's face—his eyes wide in astonishment—he probably doesn't look that great either.

"John, why didn't you wake me?" says Killian. "I was supposed to row for half of the night."

An oar slips out of John's grasp, exhaustion finally setting in. "You just looked so peaceful, I didn't want to wake you."

"Very funny. Give me the oars."

John relinquishes the oars without any dispute. The rest of the elves have risen by this point, forcing John to rest. Again, John doesn't argue. He lies with his head propped up on a pack, still barely clothed.

"The trees have changed," says Lorena. "We must be halfway across the lake by now."

"That's not possible. He would've had to row the entire night," says Melara.

John tries to raise his arm to give them a thumbs up, but it's so worn out, he can't even lift it off the deck. He manages to raise his thumb and smile as Lorena kneels beside him, placing her hand on his bare chest.

"John . . . you've done well. Now it's your turn to rest." John's eyes are shut before she finishes her sentence.

***

When he wakes, the sun has crossed the midway point in the sky, and the smell of cooking meat fills his nostrils. He notices an odd sight unfolding in front of him when he sits up. The brackoa tentacle has rope tied around it about every twelve inches, and smoke is seeping out of a slit down the center. "What is that?" he says.

"This, John, is my stroke of genius," says Killian. "You see, we cannot eat this without cooking it, and we cannot start a fire on the boat. So, what do you suppose we do?"

"Enlighten me."

Killian removes the rope ties from the tentacle, and a cloud of smoke pours out. John's mouth waters immediately. The tentacle has been slightly hollowed out, and hot branches lie inside it.

"I have trapped the heat inside the tentacle, and it cooks from the inside out."

John's eyebrows raise. "That really is genius. Hey, did you take my lighter?"

Killian smirks and tosses John the lighter. "I never could've cooked this without it."

John eyes it with surprise. "I'm shocked this little thing still works after my dip in the water."

"Must mean our luck's changing," says Killian.

"Must be," John says as he places the lighter into his pack. Upon doing so, he notices his rental car keys at the bottom, waterlogged and battered. John picks them up and shakes his head. *They won't be happy about this,* he thinks before tossing them overboard.

Another wave of the savory aroma of Killian's cooking hits John's nose. "Not to sound too eager, but when will this meal be ready?"

"Lucky for you, it's just about finished."

Everyone is so hungry, manners go out the window. John cuts a piece free with his dagger and shoves it into his mouth. A smile bursts across his face as the flavor hits his tongue. The taste is somewhere between a squid and a chicken. *Delicious.* They eat their fill, laughing at times for no reason at all. There is something about flavorful food when you're starving that can really put you into a state of euphoria.

Unfortunately, the euphoria is short-lived. Even with the added energy the brackoa provides, and all five of them rowing in shifts, they are making very little progress. The elves head to sleep with sore arms and low spirits. John promises Killian that he'll wake him up this time around, and he means it. Another round of rowing through the night might kill him.

As the moon rises over the lake, a cool breeze comes in from behind them, causing the hair on the back of John's neck to stand on end. He has to stop and rest, but he isn't ready to wake Killian just yet—needing a bit more time in solitude. John's got nothing against Killian; he just wants some time to think. After all, he does his best thinking when he's alone.

The breeze intensifies, almost taunting him. *If only we had a way to prop up that sail.* John looks down at the oars, and then at the sail. *That could work.*

He starts by removing the oars and threading a separate rope through each of the rings where the oars were stationed, and he ties those ropes to the bottom corners of the square sail. He then takes his dagger and carves a slit into the ends of each oar. After attaching separate ropes into each slit, he attaches the other ends to the top corners of each sail. Once everything is fastened tightly, he raises the oars high into the air, allowing the sail to spread wide and take the full force of the wind.

Almost immediately, the boat starts to creep forward. *Engineering at its finest.* Another minute goes by, and the boat is really picking up speed now.

Killian rolls over and looks at John. "What in the name of Mhorelia are you doing?"

"Hop on up. I need your assistance," John replies.

Killian jumps up, and John hands him an oar. With the two of them together, they can spread the sail even farther to each side, catching more of the wind. When the others wake a few minutes later, the wind is really gusting, and John is struggling to hold the oar while steering. Darian quickly comes to his aid, skillfully maneuvering the boat so they can glide over the top of the water with ease.

Lorena and Melara both jolt to their feet. "What the hell is going on?" yells Melara.

"Just getting us there a little faster!" John yells back, the wind quickly making it harder for them to hear. Lorena and Melara struggle to keep their balance as they make their way to the back of the boat.

"This is mad!" says Lorena.

"Yesterday, I stabbed a forty-foot lake monster through the eye with a broadsword that was given to me by an elf . . . I think you'll be alright," John says, a playful smile forming on his face.

Killian laughs hysterically and turns to Darian. "Can you believe this, brother? We are flying!" Darian returns the laugh as they cruise along. The only elf not enjoying the ride—not surprisingly—is Melara. She lies on the deck with her eyes closed, muttering something to herself. Her face looks a shade paler, maybe even a little green.

With the wind rushing at their backs, they make up all the lost time. After switching off who holds the oars a few times, the other side of the lake comes into focus, and Melara yells something unintelligible at John.

"What?" he says.

"Would you stop this madness already!" she screams before turning and throwing up over the side of the boat. Killian and John lower the sail at once, and the boat slows to a crawl. Lorena runs to her side and softly rubs her back as she continues to vomit.

"I didn't realize she was that seasick," John says to Killian.

"We may have gotten a bit carried away," Killian replies.

Darian leans in and whispers in both their ears, "That was a lot of fun, though." The three hold back laughter as Melara splashes lake water onto her face. She sits back against the side of the boat and closes her eyes.

"I hate you all," she says flatly.

Lorena turns to the three in the back. "Maybe we row the rest of the way."

***

After docking the boat on the shore, they set up camp and prepare for bed. There are a few more hours until sunrise, and they could all use some sleep to recover. The march that lies ahead of them is long, but Lorena has assured John that it will be much easier than what they've just endured.

Right . . . he thinks as he lays his head against his pack, propped up on the muddy soil beneath it. A stick pokes into his back and a rock juts into his thigh as he tries to get comfortable. He thinks enviously of the plush queen bed in his bedroom at home, imagining pulling the soft linen sheet up over his face as he drifts off to sleep.

CHAPTER 18

Kaigen sits atop a tree on the far side of the lake, watching John and the elves fall into a slumber. The last few days have been a rollercoaster of emotions, starting with the conflicting feelings he felt when arriving at Brackoa Lake. His orders were to make sure there was only one possible boat left to take John and the elves up the river, and to bribe, or threaten, the captain of that boat to lead them slowly into the ambush.

The thought of killing John and the elves was weighing heavily on him. John has grown on him since his arrival in Mhorelia, and he's the best shot at taking down Balloch that Kaigen has seen in some time. And then there are the elves. Acting as a sort of dysfunctional family to Kaigen over the years—although they probably don't see it that way—he's not sure he could kill them either, especially not Lorena.

He's had to remind himself at least a hundred times that this is all for his son, and he needs to do anything and everything to ensure his son's safety. His son is his entire life, but what kind of life are they living . . .?

A few days earlier, as he sat under the cover of the tree line on the edge of the river, surrounded by a group of Balloch's soldiers, he kept asking himself that question over and over. Knowing deep down that the group heading toward them—the group about to be surely killed—provided the best possibility of a normal life for Kaigen and his son. *I must give them a fighting chance,* he thought, then moved to act.

"I'll be right back," he told the soldiers.

"Where are you going?" said one of them in return.

"You may not know this, but shape-shifters have to relieve themselves as well," Kaigen responded snarkily.

"Hmph . . . well, hurry back. They'll be here soon."

Once Kaigen was out of the eyeline of the soldiers, he teleported twenty feet above the river. But before he hit the water, he teleported back to the trees, leaving a cloud of purple in his wake to float lazily down the river.

The soldiers were so preoccupied with who was going to kill John that they hadn't even noticed the residue floating down the river when they started shooting. Kaigen watched as arrow after arrow flew toward the boat, knowing any one of them could end John's life, and the hope for Kaigen to live a normal one. He watched as Dano fell, as a couple of unlucky soldiers fell, and as the flaming arrows hit the side of the boat.

But still the boat continued onward.

Have some sense, John; the lake is your only hope, he thought, just as John leaped for the steering rod. A wave of relief poured over Kaigen as the boat turned toward the lake, but he hid it well, going on a tirade against the soldiers to save face. "Have you ever shot an arrow in your miserable lives!" he yelled. "The great and mighty Balloch entrusted you to defeat his enemies, and all you did was fell a lowly boat captain. You all should be ashamed of yourselves." For good measure, he kicked a soldier in the chest before teleporting to a faraway treetop where they couldn't see his happiness.

He followed the group for some time, staying out of sight. If Balloch had spies in the trees, he had to make sure he wasn't seen helping the group. He watched as they paddled into the center of the lake—losing them in the distance—and felt his stomach drop when the storm rolled in. *Surely they could not have survived that,* he thought.

Unable to find them for the rest of the day, he decided to teleport to the end of the lake and wait. He spent the next day looking out over the water, knowing he could be there for weeks without any luck. But as the moon was high in the sky, that's when he saw it. The white sail was moving ever closer to the water's edge. He could hear someone yelling—Melara maybe—and the sail was dropped. They rowed slowly ashore as she retched over the side of the boat.

It wasn't a pretty sight, but they had done it.

A feeling of happiness had enveloped Kaigen as he watched them step onto the land. But that feeling was only temporary, quickly replaced by a new emotion, the same one he now feels as he watches them sleep. Dread. For now, he must travel back to Balloch and deliver the most unwelcome news that his plan didn't work, and that is sure to be met with anger, and most likely skepticism.

Kaigen estimates he has at least one more day before Balloch becomes suspicious and decides to sleep on it. But his sleep is filled with nightmares, all involving his son and the horrible things that the king will do to him if he suspects Kaigen has shown any allegiance to John or the elves. He awakens covered in sweat as the sun emerges over the horizon. *Let's get this over with*, he thinks before teleporting to the king's fortress.

He expects to find Balloch eating breakfast alone, as he often does. But when he arrives at the king's personal dining hall, he is surprised to find at least a dozen men huddled around a map at the head of the table, deep in discussion. As the door closes behind Kaigen, no one so much as glances in his direction.

"What is the meaning of this?" says Kaigen. Still, no one pays him any mind. "Balloch!" he yells.

Balloch slowly turns to face him. "This is a private council meeting. What do you need?"

"Private council? For what?"

Balloch looks to his advisors, saying, "Give me a minute," and they all take their seats. By this point, Kaigen is standing right next to Balloch at the head of the table. Balloch peers into his eyes and replies, "After a few days had passed, it became obvious that the ambush did not go as planned. So I have hatched another plan. And this plan . . . does not involve you."

"I . . . I am part of your council," says Kaigen.

"Not anymore, for something else has recently come to my attention. A conclusion I should have come to a long time ago . . . You have been helping the elves."

Kaigen's heart pounds in his chest. He quickly turns to anger in an attempt to mask his deceit. "How dare you! I would never help those scummy elves. It was your good-for-nothing soldiers that screwed up. You should be blaming *them*, not me! They had a perfect shot at John. A child could have hit him at that distance. But they forced him to the lake instead, away from certain death."

"I don't believe you . . . And to think you did this knowing your son would suffer—"

Kaigen's anger consumes him as he grabs the king by his collar and gets within an inch of his face. "Don't you lay a finger on him!" The men all jump from their seats and draw their swords.

Balloch doesn't even flinch. "Easy, Kaigen. He's alive . . . for now."

Kaigen's mind is racing as he looks around the room, twelve swords ready to strike. He could take them all if he wanted, but his son wouldn't live to see another day. He slows his thoughts, trying to think of some way to convince the king of his loyalty. That's when it comes to him, the only thing he knows will work. He lets out a sigh and releases the king's collar.

"If only you would've sent me," says Kaigen.

"Excuse me?" says the king.

"You send brainless centaurs and tactless soldiers to do your bidding, yet I am truly your best weapon, and you seldom use me as such. I could slip into their camp while they sleep, and slit every one of their throats. It would be so easy."

"And you would do this?"

"For my son . . . I would do anything."

Balloch ponders this, looking at his advisors, then at his map, before returning his gaze to Kaigen. A smile comes across his face as he laughs softly. "And what would my people think of me if I sent you? Your people fight—or should I say, *fought*—with no honor . . . I still have some." Kaigen's face becomes hot with rage as Balloch continues, "I do not need you, nor do I want you in my presence. Leave me at once, and do not come back until you have something good to report."

"But . . . my son?"

"Consider this time away from him as a merciful punishment on my part. I could do much worse." The two lock eyes, neither wanting to be the first to look away, but Kaigen knows he must. While Balloch has his son, he will forever do what he says. He closes his eyes painfully, then vanishes.

CHAPTER 19

John watches closely as Lorena raises her bow, pointing an arrow at a large, hairy creature about fifty feet in front of them. A bomma—that's what she called it. However, to John, it looks something like a cross between a bison and a Highland cow, with its small horns, massive body, and shaggy fur. She has shot and killed four over the last seven days, with a fifth in her sights. Not for their meat—although that is an added benefit—but for the warmth that their fur will provide.

John has been getting impatient over the last few days, itching to keep going, but the twins have assured him that the fur will be necessary for the next part of their journey. A cold and snowy region is how they described it. All that being said, he has enjoyed hunting with Lorena, and the alone time that comes with it. Underneath the disciplined leader that stands before him, there is a caring soul with what can almost be described as a sense of humor. Couple that with her beauty, and John's mind can't help but wonder . . .

She lets the arrow fly, piercing the throat of the bomma just below its ear—the same spot she hit the first four. It immediately flees, taking off at great speed for such a big creature. But it won't get far. They track it for about a quarter mile, following the trail of blood it leaves behind, until they find it lying dead on its side. John helps her remove the hide and cuts slabs of meat for them to carry back to camp.

Killian urges everyone to apply one more coat of lotion to their brackoa wounds, even though they are just about healed by now. Darian cuts the meat up to roast over a campfire that has been burning all morning—mostly due to the oil they took from the Tree of Light, which seems to burn forever. And Melara helps Lorena with the fur, removing any traces of the bomma internals, washing it, and hanging it up to dry in the sun. As it dries, the two of them go back to fashioning arrows—something they've been doing every chance they get—seeing as all four quivers were nearly empty after they tangled with the brackoa. It's been like this for the last week: hunt, prep, eat, heal, sleep, repeat.

Lorena and the twins seem to be enjoying this, but Melara shares John's anxiety to keep going. She hasn't said anything in particular, but John can sense it. The quickness with which she takes on new tasks, rarely taking a beat to have a laugh or contemplate . . . She's raring to go, just like John, but why? That remains a mystery.

The skin takes only an hour to dry as the hot midday sun shines down upon it. Once it's dry, it doesn't take long for Lorena to fashion it into a nice fur coat, just as she did with the other four. It fits perfectly over John's newly washed and dried clothes—another benefit of spending the week by a lake. Then, with everything set for the journey, they're off, bags packed, coats thrown over their shoulders, and weapons at the ready.

Over the first few hours, they make very little progress. The terrain is similar to what John experienced in the denaros' land. Tall trees surround them as the hill steadily rises. Roots and large rocks block their way, forcing them to take a winding upward approach. The sun peeks through and lights up the forest floor every so often as gaps in the foliage appear. But around dinnertime, this all changes. The trees thin out, the roots disappear, and John can feel the temperature drop substantially.

They stop to make camp when the sun is low in the sky, despite Melara's urge to keep pushing forward. "We'll need our strength for the next bit; that's where the snow comes," Darian says. After they make a fire and cook some food, they all turn in for some much-needed rest. Well, everyone except John. Once again on this journey, he feels as if he's out of the loop on certain things. He needs to know what is going on with Melara, what is causing her angst.

When he is certain the others are asleep, he crawls to Lorena and gently shakes her arm. She opens her eyes and turns to him. "We're supposed to be sleeping, John."

"There's just something I need to know. What is the deal with Melara? Something is different about her since we left the lake."

She glances over at Melara, making sure she is in fact asleep, before whispering to John, "We are nearing her home, where the Cliff Elves reside. Or at least where they used to . . . We haven't ever made it that far, and there is no telling what remains of them. The closer we get to the top of the mountain, the more impact Balloch and his forces have had on the lands."

"So, she is hoping to reunite with her loved one, and you're afraid of what we'll find."

"I do not wish to get anyone's hopes up as we near the cliffs. It is harder for her; she has not seen her loved one in so long, but she has never lost hope."

"These cliffs . . . What are they like?" asks John.

"Magnificent, thanks in part to the Cliff Elves being such skilled builders. They created caverns in the side of the cliffs, hundreds of feet up, with huts placed on the edges that overlook the drop. These huts are connected by tunnels within the mountain, and long wooden staircases on the outside. It is truly a sight to behold."

John imagines this in his mind for a moment. "I'd really like to see these cliffs."

"As would I, but first we must get there, and that requires us to be well rested," Lorena says, smiling afterward and closing her eyes ever so slowly.

***

At first light, they eat a short breakfast and continue their ascent, making slow progress as the terrain becomes even steeper. The temperature continues to drop as they arrive at the top of the hill they've been climbing. That's when they see the snow, not so far off in the distance, coating the land in a blanket of white. The snow goes on for miles before disappearing into what John can only assume is yet another false summit.

He puts on his bomma coat and they continue onward. The wind picks up almost immediately, cold and blustery, sending shivers down John's spine. The fur is a nice addition, but it does next to nothing for the rest of his body. Soon, his hands start to shake, and he shoves them deeper into his armpits as they trudge along. His jeans offer little protection, and his legs stiffen up after only a few miles. His boots are holding up nicely, though, and the hood that Lorena attached to his coat is doing wonders for his ears.

Spending most of the time looking down at the ground to avoid the wind, he follows in the elves' footsteps to make sure he's on the right course. When he finally does steal a glance up, he panics.

Everyone is gone.

There are no signs of the elves anywhere. He can hardly see two feet in front of him as the wind and snow swirl wildly. He unsheathes his dagger with what little grip strength he has left in his almost certainly frostbitten hands. "Lorena! Killian! Darian! Melara!" He runs forward and spins around, unable to locate the tracks that were at his feet just a second earlier. He starts to yell again, "Lore—"

Before he can get her name out, hands grip his sides and hurl him backward, slamming him into the hard, icy ground. He rolls over quickly and finds his back against a wall. The wind has ceased, the snow no longer nips at his face, and four elves are standing over him. He's now in an igloo of sorts, only much taller and wider. A soft light shines through the tunneled door he was pulled through, as well as the small hole carved into the roof. As his panic fades, he surveys the dimly lit room with curiosity. "What is this place?"

"A safe haven, built long ago as a way to take refuge from the cold. It is one of only three built . . . We were lucky to find it," Lorena says.

"So, you've been here before?" asks John.

"Only once. This place symbolizes the farthest we've ever gotten on this journey."

Killian's head drops. "That seems so long ago."

"It was," says Darian. "But this time, we are much better off."

"I thought for sure we were all going to die that day," Melara says bleakly.

John thinks back over the last year of his mundane and somewhat boring life. He'd taken it for granted. It was the first time in almost a decade and a half that he didn't have to worry if he, or someone close to him, was at risk of dying. These elves have never had the luxury of feeling that, not for the last twenty years.

"No use dredging up the past; let's get a fire going," Lorena says, changing the subject abruptly.

In no time at all—again, thanks to John's trusty lighter—a small fire is filling the cavern with warmth, positioned directly under the hole in the roof. After a quick dinner consisting of only bomma jerky, they decide to turn in, hoping to get a restful sleep . . .

John exhales softly, his breath forming a small cloud in the cold Siberian air. He's back again. No matter how much time passes, he always finds his way back. Running, shooting, watching his friends die, and finally . . . falling. Falling to what he knows will be an icy river below him.

But something is different this time. He feels his body shake, and someone calls to him in a loud whisper: "John . . . John!" *Who is that? That voice sounds so familiar.* Right before he hits the water, his body shakes again, only this time, it's back to reality.

His eyes fly open, and he's face-to-face with Lorena. She clutches his body tightly and stares down at his drenched face. Even in the cold, he can't escape the sweat that accompanies this nightmare. "John, what's wrong?"

"Nothing, I'm fine," he says, deflecting instinctively.

"John, you were shaking so violently. And you muttered something, something I couldn't quite make out. It sounded like a name."

He stares up into her eyes, hoping she'll look away but knowing she won't. He's never told anyone about this dream, not even his therapist. This dream is his weakness; it represents his vulnerability. Still, she won't look away. "Ben," he says.

"What?"

"Ben . . . It's the name I was saying, wasn't it?"

"Maybe. Who is Ben?"

He hesitates again, feeling the urge to shut down. To stop talking. To roll over and say nothing more. He doesn't owe her this story. And yet . . .

Before he can stop himself, he spills everything to her. The betrayal, the mourning, the pain, the anxieties, and the dream that never seems to leave him. The only thing he keeps to himself is his revenge—that's a tale for another time. Once he's done, he waits in the still silence of the cavern, staring back at her as she kneels by his side. He hasn't felt this vulnerable in a long time. Wait, no . . . He's *never* felt this vulnerable. But as she processes his words, another feeling comes to the surface. Relief. Like a weight has been lifted off of his chest.

An endearing smile forms on Lorena's face. "You've been through so much, John, but you've got nothing to fear. We all have burdens we carry," she says as she gestures to Melara, Killian, and Darian. "And now . . . you no longer have to carry yours alone."

She wraps her arms around John, and his arms do the same. He buries his head in her shoulder, her red curls tickling his face as he feels a tear slide down his cheek. As they embrace one another, she whispers into his ear, "I think I'd better sleep with you tonight, in case your dream returns. Would that be okay?"

John simply nods, and she nestles in front of him. He lays one arm under her head, and the other over her body to find her hand. Their fingers intertwine. He tries to remember the last time he held a woman like this, feeling her warmth as they lie still. It's been far too long. He feels a profound peacefulness settle within him the moment his eyelids fall. His mind wanders as he drifts off—only this time, he doesn't find himself in Siberia. No, this time, he's sitting in a rocking chair on a porch in Alabama, sipping sweet tea as the sun rises in the distance.

The next morning, John's eyes lazily open as he lets his body wake gracefully, still relaxed from the comfort of Lorena. His lips curl into a smile as he lets go of her hand and runs his fingers up her arm, stopping at her shoulder and giving it a gentle squeeze.

Taking extra care not to wake her, he removes his arm from beneath her and gently rests her head down on the cavern floor. As he's crawling backward silently, he meets Melara's watchful eyes, studying him as she spins an arrow in her hands. Feeling like he should say something, he opens his mouth to speak. But before he can, Melara stops him.

"No need to explain yourself," she says. "I know she would never do anything that might jeopardize our goal." She then shifts her gaze to the arrow, still twirling in her hands. "Besides, we all have someone we long for . . ."

John starts a fire as the elves wake, one by one. First the twins, and then Lorena. Despite the fact that they've slept in an igloo, with subfreezing winds flurrying outside, and the impending climb that faces them, everyone looks alright.

They wolf down a breakfast and finish what's left of their water. John savors the last drops as they spill out onto his tongue, knowing it might be another full day before he can quench his thirst again.

The next half of the winter climb is grueling, no doubt, but it seems easier to John somehow. Maybe it's because he's well rested. Maybe he's well nourished. Or maybe it's the sparks of something growing inside of him that he doesn't want to admit exists, but also doesn't want to be extinguished.

After the first four hours pass, the snowstorm subsides. An hour later, a bead of sweat makes its way along John's neck and down his back. Could it be? Are they nearing the end? Thirty minutes later, relief hits John as they crest the next hill, and the snow becomes noticeably less thick. *Finally,* he thinks, saying a silent vow that once he returns home, he'll never visit a cold climate again.

Rock formations have been erected along the path they now walk. Although it's impossible to tell with the snow, it actually looks like *a path.* Perfectly lined and leading to a gap between two large rock faces that stretch for miles on both sides. They are no longer haphazardly meandering around in the snow; they are finally back on track.

As they emerge through the gap in the rock faces, the sight that lies in front of them is like nothing John has ever seen, or is it? The rocky hills still go for miles on either side of them, but thirty feet ahead, the ground simply disappears. John peers over the edge of the cliff, where clouds have formed below, unable to tell how far the fall would be. A bridge spans at least fifty feet between them and the other side. As he looks across, a feeling of unease passes through his body, but he can't seem to place why.

He loses his train of thought when he notices the elves staring at Melara, her eyes devoid of emotion. "It's all gone," she says. That's when John sees it. Multiple holes cut into the mountainside across the gap, staircases barely hanging on, huts with roofs that have been violently ripped to shreds. This is Melara's home. And her home is no longer.

She drops to her knees. Her eyes well up, but no tears form as her sadness quickly turns to anger. "Balloch will pay for this," she growls. "Him and all of his men . . . They will all die for this!" Her voice echoes off of the cliffs and rings in their ears: "*Die for this. Die for this. Die for this.*" The sound of Melara's cry is followed by a buzzing sound in the distance. It starts out soft, but grows quickly. John looks around in confusion, and his unease grows with the sound of the buzzing.

The elves draw their weapons just as the first few creatures fly up from below, their two sets of translucent wings beating vigorously, with trails of clouds following in their wake.

"Widaps," says Melara.

And that's when it hits John. His sense of unease. He suddenly knows where it's coming from. The bridge, the snow, the mountains, the ambush . . .

He's back in Siberia again . . . Only this time, it's real.

Chapter 20

Before John can form a thought, all four elves have lined the edge of the cliff with their bows drawn. "Aim for the heads!" Lorena yells as four arrows fly. John is trying desperately to focus, to get a grip on his surroundings as the creatures grow nearer. They look like bugs with their long, cylindrical bodies covered almost entirely in iridescent scales, all except for their heads. Five fly toward them. No, four. One just took an arrow through each of its large, protruding eyes. Green blood sprays from its wounds as it plummets below the clouds and out of sight.

John pulls his dagger from its sheath and braces for a fight. He stares at the dagger, and at his own hand, both shaking uncontrollably. He tries to steady the shaking, but it only grows. His arms and legs become like stone pillars as he falls to the ground, the dagger still clenched in his hand. John's heart pounds the inside of his chest while his conscious mind seems to slip away as he watches the battle unfold in front of him. Arrows sail through the air, widaps fly toward them, and an elf runs toward him. *An elf . . .* John thinks, unable to remember his name.

It's been a while since John has had a panic attack incapacitate him . . . He almost forgot how ruthless they can be.

The elf is yelling at him: "John! Get up! We need you!"

John tries to slow his breathing. He tries to find some way to stop his muscles from tensing up—*Killian!*—the elf's name suddenly surfaces in John's brain.

"What is wrong with him?" Lorena shouts as she narrowly dodges an attack from a diving widap.

"I don't know!" Killian yells back.

"Can he fight?" she asks.

"Not a chance," Killian replies.

John again tries to stand, with no luck. He needs to help, but he can't get to his feet. He is struggling just to slow his breathing. So there he sits, unable to move, only able to watch. And that's when Lorena shows how fearless she can be.

She drops her bow and unsheathes her sword as a widap dives toward John and Killian. With one twisting motion of her body, the sword splits the widap in two, each half crashing into the mountain on either side of them. The last of the first wave has been killed, but the buzzing has not yet ended. Melara and Darian aim their bows off the edge of the cliff, shooting arrow after arrow at the oncoming attack. Missing to the left, missing to the right. The widaps are dodging everything. Then, John's heart skips a beat . . .

Lorena has just jumped off the cliff.

Still in shock, John just sits there. Five grueling seconds later, a widap shoots into his line of vision, with Lorena's legs wrapped around its back. It spins wildly, trying to throw her off as she brings her sword down through its head. As it drops, another comes in to take her out . . . but it's too slow. She flips off of the one she's riding and grabs ahold of the other's wing, running her sword through its back and releasing it to its death.

She lands in the center of the bridge as two more widaps fall beside her. Distracted by her deadly acrobatics, they never saw the arrows coming as Darian and Melara struck them down.

Now there is only silence as the buzzing ceases.

John watches painfully as the elves walk toward him. His muscles mercifully unclench as the fear leaves his body. He lets go of Killian's shoulder, not realizing he'd been squeezing the life out of it. "John, what happened?" says Killian.

Maybe it's his pride, but John has always felt a sense of embarrassment after a panic attack. Only moments ago, it felt as if the world were ending. And now, suddenly, he's fine.

"It's complicated," he says to Killian.

Everyone has a look of concern or confusion on their face. Everyone except Lorena.

"No, it isn't," she says.

"What?" says John.

"It isn't complicated. You froze," she replies.

There it is, lying on the surface of John's emotions and always ready to pounce—anger. "It's not that simple," he says as he gets to his feet.

"You froze! When we needed you most!" she blurts out.

"You have no idea what I just went th—"

"I don't care!" she snaps back and kicks him in the chest. Melara throws her arms around Lorena to restrain her as John smashes into the rocks behind him. "You are not the Chosen One . . ." she says, her voice wavering ever so slightly.

"Lorena," Killian pleads, "we are in this together."

"Not anymore," she says flatly. "Grab your things; we're leaving." The elves hesitate, their eyes darting from Lorena to John—even Melara looks reluctant.

"Now!" she screams, prompting them to grab their packs and head toward the bridge.

John can see the doubt plastered on their faces as they follow Lorena, but no one speaks up, not even Killian. Before they cross, she turns one last time to John. "We are heading east over the bridge. Do not attempt to follow us."

As she turns her back to him, he replies coldly, "Looks like I'll be carrying this burden alone."

John sits with his back against the mountain. He doesn't move until long after the elves have disappeared into the distance, all the while thinking about how he got here. The trip to Scotland that he just *had to take*, the arrogant guide on his hike, meeting Kaigen and this group of elves after falling into Mhorelia, the cold, the hot, giant snakes, giant birds, giant bugs, the fighting, the killing, falling unconscious, falling unconscious again, and again . . . This whole endeavor has been one hellish experience after another. But for some reason, this is the worst he's felt so far.

He leans over and vomits. His body feels numb, and the pit in his stomach is bottomless. He knows what he needs to do. He needs to push this down and move on; that is what his training dictates. *But why is it so hard?*

As John takes stock of his supplies, he notices the extra food in his bag. *Killian.* The pit in his stomach grows deeper as he shoulders the pack and sheathes his dagger. When he's halfway across the bridge, his eyes dart to the holes in the side of the cliff. John keeps his gaze on them, feeling certain there was movement. He grips the bridge as the wind picks up and it starts to sway. The thought of falling from a bridge—again—is enough for him to lose interest. *Must've imagined something; better keep moving.*

Before long, he comes to a fork in the path. The elves went east, so he's going west. Why they went east is none of his concern, but it does provoke his thoughts. West seems to be a more direct path up the mountain. *Is it quicker? Less dangerous? Or maybe this is a dead end.* It doesn't matter, really, so he shoves those thoughts aside and keeps moving forward. The farther he travels, however, the more he questions the elves' decision. The path must be five feet wide at its narrowest point, and at some points, it feels like it could even be considered a road. Trees shade him from the sun, and a soft breeze keeps him cool.

But then the path just stops, with no warning whatsoever. A wall of trees that stretches as far as he can see stands before him. A nagging sensation to turn back surfaces inside of him, telling him to return to the elves at once. But then he remembers what Lorena said, *"You are not the Chosen One."* It shouldn't bother him. After all, he spent the majority of this journey agreeing with her, but for some reason, it bothers him. It's not as if she hurt his feelings, but if he isn't the Chosen One, then he's just a man trapped in an unknown world, with no hope of escaping.

No, he can't go back. He must move forward. The only way out is to keep moving forward.

"I am the Chosen One," he says aloud, hoping to convince himself, before stepping into the trees. The next few hours are slow going, but not all that bad. Branches break under his feet as he weaves through the forest. Birds sing in the trees all around him. Sunlight blots the ground as it finds its way through the canopies from high above. He stops once to eat what is left of the food—if Killian hadn't slipped him that extra bread and jerky, he'd be much worse off. That being said, he's seen no sign of water since he entered the woods, so that becomes his next priority.

After a few more hours of walking, he's still found nothing. Not a pond, not a river, not even a puddle. Seemingly out of nowhere, the heat starts to rise, as if Balloch has turned up the thermostat on this entire island. His mouth becomes drier and drier as time goes on. His lips crack, and he can feel beads of sweat seeping from every pore on his body. It is becoming unbearable, soaking through his shirt, stinging his eyes, and causing his jeans to stick to his thighs. He needs to find water, and fast.

He can't see it through the foliage, but the sun must be getting low in the sky by now. Unfortunately, this has no effect on the temperature. *Could it be even hotter at night?* he thinks as he plants his back against a tree trunk and slowly slides down to the forest floor. *This must be why the elves went east . . .* But then he hears something: *Crack!* A tree branch breaks under the weight of something in the distance. He jumps to his feet to get a closer look. A stagglehorn. *If a stagglehorn can live here, then there must be water nearby.* He follows the creature from a distance, making sure not to alert it of his presence, until finally, he hears it. The glorious sound of a stream. Elation fills his being as he picks up his pace, but as he gets closer, he slows, opting for a quieter approach. Water would be great, but water and a stagglehorn? He wouldn't need to find food for a week.

He hides behind a tree trunk that must be at least four feet in diameter, easily the biggest one he's seen for miles. Fifteen feet in front of him, the stagglehorn bends its neck to drink from the stream. Most people would've alerted it by now, but John is not most people. He knows how to keep quiet, how to stalk. He slowly unsheathes his knife as he inches closer to the creature. Twelve feet, eight feet, five feet. He spins the knife around and gets ready to pounce. That's when he feels the blade press up against his neck.

It appears he's not the only one with talents in stealth.

John freezes, unsure of what to do. He slowly raises the dagger out to his side.

"Easy now . . . How about you drop that knife," the man says, causing the stagglehorn to turn quickly and face them. But it doesn't run. In fact, it slowly walks toward John as the dagger falls from his hand. It comes within inches of his face, sniffing him curiously. "Don't worry," says the man as he steps in front of John and places a hand on the stagglehorn's head. "He won't harm you."

John looks him up and down. He's tall, wears a full-length black cloak, and has long dark hair and pointed ears. Another elf. *Figures.* Although this man does look noticeably older than the others.

The man removes the blade from John's neck. "And who might you be?" he says. "You couldn't be from around these parts, or else you wouldn't have tried to kill my friend here."

A friend of a stagglehorn . . .

"Leon?" John blurts out.

The man quickly raises his blade back to John's neck. "How'd you know that?" he says defensively.

John sighs. "It's a long story."

"A long story . . . Well, then, come with me. I've got all the time in the world."

His constant shift in tone is unsettling to John, the way he goes from aggressive to jovial in an instant. Then again, Darian did say he was rather strange.

Leon must've lived in this forest for a while, because he knows every turn to take in order to make their journey a quick one.

Moving left to avoid denser areas of the woods, taking a circuitous route to avoid an area of the forest with stinging wasps, and at one point, even taking to the trees to get across a sinkhole that spans nearly fifty feet wide and is unnoticeable to the naked eye. These choices also happen to be the exact opposite of the ones John would've made on his own. *Probably another reason the elves went east.* As he walks, his mind travels back to everything the elves told him about Leon. *He's a great warrior, who's very strange, can speak with stagglehorn, and who stopped believing in their cause.* This is all John knows, but he is determined to learn more.

"How long have you lived here?" he asks.

"In Mhorelia? Or in these forests?"

"Both, I guess."

"I have not lived in this particular forest for very long, but this year marks my seventy-fifth on Mhorelia."

Seventy-five? John thinks, throwing him for a loop. Leon is unlike any seventy-five-year-old John has ever seen, but then again, he's never met a seventy-five-year-old elf.

"I know," Leon says, interrupting John's thoughts, "pretty spry for an older elf, aren't I?"

John's lip curls, hiding a smile as he tries to figure Leon out. "I thought elves were immortal?"

"Immortal? No. I hope to live at least another hundred years, though." Leon's eyes narrow. "You really aren't from around here."

And just like that, John has a sneaking suspicion that Leon has already figured him out.

For the next twenty minutes, they walk in silence until John steps out of the forest and into an oasis. A lush field of grass spans in front of him, surrounded by trees that reach for the skyline. A river runs through the field, and John can see fish of every color swimming beneath its surface. A small arched bridge extends over the river, and in the distance stands a small house—ten feet by twenty feet and made entirely of wood, except for a stone chimney on one side. Smoke pours from the chimney, and the mouthwatering smell of a home-cooked meal steadily wafts into John's nose.

Without warning, Leon's blade is at his throat again. "Before we go forward, I need your word that you won't do anything foolish."

There it is again, the shift in tone that makes John's skin crawl. He meets Leon's unwavering stare and notices something. Not something superficial, but something most people might miss under his charming facade. *This man wouldn't hesitate to kill.* He hides it well, but there is something in his voice, in the way he carries himself. He's not to be trifled with. "You treat me with respect, and I'll do the same," says John.

Leon waits a few seconds and lowers his blade. "Fair enough." He hands John his dagger back. "Respect is rare around these parts."

When they reach the house, Leon informs John that he must wait outside for a moment. As he waits, he takes in his surroundings—the land is a quaint, well-kept, secluded, and very peaceful piece of property. This place is John's dream. What he wouldn't give to light up a cigar as the half-full moon shines down upon him. "Come on in, John!" Leon yells, bringing him back to the present.

The warmth of Leon's home fills John with a sense of calm. A stew is prepared on a table in front of him, a fire is burning past a hearth to his right, and Leon stands beside a tall, dark-haired elf. "My life partner, Gwyen."

"Pleasure to meet you. I'm John."

"Have a seat," she says kindly.

"Yes, John, have a seat. And while we eat, why don't you share with us that story you promised," says Leon.

No sense in making up any stories now; it's clear Leon knows he's an outsider. John retells the events of the last few weeks, sparing no details. How he arrived, when he met the elves, that Killian and Darian thought he was the Chosen One, the fights they went through, and even the episode with the widaps. When he's finished, Leon sits for a minute, thinking to himself. "Killian and Darian . . . I miss those crazy cousins."

"That's what you took out of all of that? You have no qualms about my story? Leon, you don't have any issues with the fact that I'm from a different world, that I may be the Chosen One, that I fought all those creatures, or with the elves parting ways with me? You believe all that . . . without question?"

"It's an interesting story, no doubt. And I certainly have questions. But when it comes down to whether or not I believe you, I have to ask myself only one question. Why would you lie?"

"And do you believe I am the Chosen One?" asks John. Half of him is genuinely curious about what Leon thinks, and the other half needs the validation to keep going.

"Well, I only just met you, John—although I am getting a sense of who you are."

"Okay, but do you believe there could even be a Chosen One?"

There's a long silence as Leon thinks this over. Only the sound of the crackling fire can be heard bouncing off of the walls. "I believe that Balloch's reign will not last forever, *but* I do not believe it will end because of one person. The Chosen One may exist, and it may even be you, but nobody accomplishes anything on their own. It will take the efforts of many to usurp that man."

John gets the feeling that Leon would've been a perfect fit for The Undesirables. His demeanor, his critical way of thinking, his stealth, and if the twins are right, his capability as a fighter. This feeling John has, it gets him thinking. "If you believe it is possible, and you know your friends are getting closer, and if you believe the story I just told you . . . then why don't you join them?"

"Five years ago, if you had sat before me and told me the same story, a thousand centaurs could not have kept me from joining the cause. But my circumstances have changed."

A door creaks open behind John, and he turns around in a flash, reaching for his knife. But he stops short of unsheathing it. A lock of brown hair becomes visible in the doorway, followed by a set of curious blue eyes peering around the door.

"Come on out, Alina," says Gwyen.

A girl, no older than five, comes running and latches onto Gwyen's leg. She looks up at John with curious eyes and then buries her face in her mother's dress.

"You have a daughter," John says. His mind starts piecing everything together. "When you last saw the other elves, was that—"

"About a day before she was born," Leon finishes.

"But that journey took us many grueling days to complete."

"On foot, yes. But by stagglehorn, and with the right supplies, that journey takes less than a day."

"Even through the snow?" John asks.

"Even through the snow," Leon answers, "thanks to a stagglehorn's excellent sense of direction."

"Is that so? Wait, why were you down there to begin with?"

"I had made the trip down to the lake to gather a plant that only grows along its shore; it's called *Cinda*. When the sun hits them, a large orange petal flowers from each plant. That petal is an excellent pain reliever when eaten. And that day, Gwyen was in unbearable pain."

"With Gwyen's pain and a child fast approaching, I guess that explains why they said your mind was '*elsewhere.*'"

"Ha! That it was," Leon admits. "And not long after, came the greatest day of my life."

It's clear from the look Leon gives Gwyen that he's not exaggerating in the slightest. Taking a sip of water, he looks at the three of them, a truly happy family. "There's just one thing I don't understand. If you know how bad Balloch is for Mhorelia, don't you want to do something about him? For your family?"

Leon grabs Gwyen's hand and looks deep into her eyes before turning to John. "I've lost too much as it is. The best thing

I can do for my family is stay here and look after them. Try to find some peace in this life."

John feels a little guilty as anger bubbles up inside him. "But what makes you think Balloch will stop with what he has? What's stopping him from taking over this sanctuary of yours?" As his voice rises, Alina hides behind Gwyen and grips her dress in fear. "I'm sorry," John says, "I didn't mean to scare her." Gwyen picks up Alina and walks her to her room.

"If you ever have a child, you will understand why I must stay here," says Leon. Although John still isn't convinced, he can see Leon isn't about to change his mind. "It's getting late, John. I wish we had a better arrangement for you, but we rarely get visitors around these parts." He points to a fur rug near the fire. John chuckles, thinking back to the places he's slept over the last two weeks. A boat, an igloo, the rocky ground . . .

"This will do just fine."

"Oh, and before you go tomorrow, I have a gift for my cousins that I would like you to bring to them. It may come in handy on your journey."

"Okay, but did you listen to my story at all? I may never see them again. And even if I do, they may want nothing to do with me."

"You're a smart man, John. You and I both know your journey with them is not yet finished."

***

Early the next morning, John opens the door of Leon's home to another sight that will stay ingrained in his mind forever. A stagglehorn, easily two feet taller than the one from the night before, stands in front of Leon as he runs his hand across its fur. John listens quietly as he speaks with it. After Leon speaks, the stagglehorn grunts back to him and rubs its face across Leon's.

"Come on over!" Leon yells, sensing John's presence.

John is only a few feet from them when the creature takes a quick step in his direction, causing John to flinch. It sniffs the air in front of John a few times and then turns back to Leon.

"Sundane likes you," says Leon.

"Sundane? You name them?" John says.

"Not all of them, but he was the first to speak to me. He found me when I was in a dark place. And since then, we've gone on countless adventures together. Some good"—he runs his hand over a scar on Sundane's neck—"some bad."

"How do you do it? How do you speak to them?"

"It's not something I was taught, nor something I can teach. It's simply a feeling I have when I am around them. Their sounds and movements do not become words in my mind, and yet, I can understand them."

Leon grabs John's hand and places it on Sundane's back. John runs his hand down the side of the creature, feeling the power residing just underneath its thin coat of fur. The heat, the muscles, the rise and fall of its chest with every breath. It brings back flashes of Eldar's spear piercing a helpless stagglehorn. By the time he's made his way around the creature, a new sense of vigor has awakened inside of him.

"Leon, show me the way to Balloch."

Chapter 21

Another day of hiking, another day of silence for the elves. That's how it's been for the last twenty-four hours of their journey, and it appears that today will be no different. They march up a wide path, with woods on either side of them that stretch for miles in the distance. Lorena has shut down almost completely, only speaking in short, matter-of-fact sentences. *"Pass me the bread. Let's rest for a while. Follow me."* It's starting to weigh on the other elves as they shoot each other glances of disdain or confusion when Lorena isn't looking.

Finally, having seen his brother emotionally torn for long enough, Darian breaks the silence. "Alright, I'll say it . . . What the hell are we doing?"

"We are going to kill Balloch and take back our land," says Lorena, staring straight ahead.

Darian's brow furrows. "You know that's not what I meant. Why did you react that way to John? Why cast him aside after all he's done?"

"My decision is final, not another word about this. We're losing daylight as it is," she says flatly.

Killian stops in his tracks and drops his pack on the ground. "No."

Lorena slowly twists around. "What did you just say?"

Killian conjures up a look of confidence as he raises his voice: "I said, *no*. John was one of us, *is* one of us. He didn't ask to come here, and despite that fact, he has fought alongside us every step of the way. He vouched for us with the denaros, he bled for us, and he has saved every one of us. He deserves to be here, and I will not walk another step until we have discussed this."

Lorena snaps, "There's nothing to discuss! He let us down when we needed him most. I trusted him, and when the widaps came, he crumbled. We don't need him, and we won't get any farther with him by our side."

"We have never made it this far! Without him, *we* crumble. We always have," says Killian.

"Killian, he will only slow us down. You saw him on the bridge. He was not fit for battle."

A look of disbelief flashes across Killian's face. "Neither was I when we were on the boat, and neither was Melara when the snakes attacked us in the canyon. Did he toss us aside? No. He carried her out of that canyon, and he saved me from certain death as I was being pulled into the lake. That is the whole point of traveling together. When one of us falls, the others come to pick us back up."

Lorena ponders Killian's words as she studies the elves. Killian, sad and angry. Darian, frustrated. And Melara, sitting patiently, smirking, twirling a dagger in her hand. "And what do you have to say about this, Melara? You are never without an opinion, but now you sit quietly."

Melara lets out a long sigh. "Isn't it obvious?"

"Isn't *what* obvious?" Lorena asks.

"Why his 'betrayal' hurt you so badly."

"If you have something to say, spit it out."

"I saw you in the ice cavern with John . . ."

Lorena's face floods with a multitude of emotions. Embarrassment. Confusion. Frustration. And finally, rage. She takes a step toward Melara, looking to act on that last emotion. But before she gets the chance, she is interrupted by a sound in the distance. It comes in slow beats, every two to three seconds. Unsure of what is coming, the elves ready their weapons and prepare for a fight. They remain quiet and on high alert as the sound gets closer. Lorena racks her brain trying to figure out what type of enemy could be approaching. *Warriors? Unlikely. Centaurs? Maybe. Climour? Oh, I sure hope not.* When it's almost on top of them, Lorena makes out what it is . . .

Poof!

Kaigen suddenly appears behind her, and she raises her sword to his throat out of instinct.

"Well, this isn't the warm welcome I was expecting," says Kaigen.

Lorena drops her sword. "Haven't seen you in a while."

"I had some matters to attend to," Kaigen says as he surveys the other elves. "Did I come at a bad time?" The elves trade looks as Kaigen registers that someone is missing. "Lorena . . . where's John?"

"Yes, Lorena, where's John?" says Melara.

"He was a liability, so we left him behind."

Kaigen rubs his temple in thought as he looks toward the ground. "Hmph." A long pause follows before Lorena responds.

"Is that all you have to say—"

"You left John behind!" Kaigen yells. "This man was given to you as a gift, simply dropped into your lap. He helped you get farther on this journey than you have ever gotten. And now, you're telling me he's a liability? How stupid are you? Do you even want to kill Balloch? Do you even want to liberate this land?"

After his words stop echoing all around them, Lorena asks, "Are you done—"

"No, no, no. You don't get to speak yet," he interjects. "Clearly, this was your decision alone. What caused you to make this choice? What could have possibly happened that made you abandon him after all he's done?"

"I didn't abandon him. He let me—I mean, *us*—down."

"Ohhhh. Now I'm understanding. You always did have a soft spot for a woodsman."

The rage floods back to Lorena as she takes a swing at Kaigen with her sword. He dodges it easily, and she takes another. He teleports behind her, and she whips around with another swing, but he's already teleported higher up the hill. Screaming with anger, she hurls her sword toward him. He teleports one last time behind the twins, and the sword travels through the cloud of purple and sticks into the ground where he was just standing.

"Are *you* done?" says Kaigen. Lorena doesn't bother turning to face him. She storms up the hill without another word.

***

Unbelievable . . . Kaigen thinks as Lorena distances herself from the group. Three pairs of confused eyes are all staring at him now, and rightfully so, given the intensity of her outburst.

"What was all that about?" asks Darian.

"It's a long story," says Kaigen.

"Well, we've got a long way to go," Melara says as she starts after Lorena.

They walk at a relaxed pace, knowing they won't catch her anytime soon, and knowing they don't want to.

"Nineteen years ago, even though I had only just met the king, he assigned me to lead a group of soldiers to the southern parts of the island. Our task was simple: find and kill anyone who threatened Balloch's rule. I didn't want anything to do with that, though, so I sent the soldiers off in different directions and told them that I alone would search the forests of the woodsmen.

"I'd heard stories of their beauty, and I would not be let down that day. The forests were full of thriving plants and animals, completely untouched by the king's wrath. I walked for hours, admiring everything in my path, until I came to a small hut in the middle of the forest. Intrigued, I crept toward it. I didn't have any bad intentions, but it must've looked like I did, because the next thing I knew, an arrow had pinned me to a tree." Kaigen points to a small scar on his shoulder. "That's the only weapon that has ever pierced my skin, and can you guess who I have to thank for that?"

"Lorena?" guesses Killian.

"Lorena," Kaigen confirms. "And I just froze there, more from the shock than the pain, as Lorena walked toward me, with a woodsman at her side. As they grew nearer, I could tell they were deciding whether or not to kill me. They never would've been able to, obviously, but I decided to hang around and see how things would play out. He thought I was a thief, and she agreed. So he took his axe and attempted to remove my head."

Kaigen laughs out loud. "Boy, was he in for a surprise. Before his axe even hit the tree, I had a knife to Lorena's throat. I was a little annoyed, so I told them I worked for the king and that I was going to report the woodsmen to Balloch for colluding with a known insurrectionist, and that he would come and burn their forests to the ground."

Killian shoots him a concerned look.

"What? I'm not proud of it," says Kaigen. "Well, I'm a little proud of it . . . Funny thing is, I had no idea you all were plotting to usurp the king. I was just boasting for sport, and she bought it. She pleaded with me not to tell the king and to keep their relationship a secret. You see, the woodsmen and the king had an understanding; they stayed out of each other's way. And if he found out that a woodsman was fraternizing with an elf, especially an elf with her intentions, he would no doubt assume the worst and set out to destroy them. He's a very paranoid man."

Melara's forehead crinkles. "You're making this up. We all met you the same day—the day we caught you spying on us in our village."

"Seventeen years ago, right? Is she still sticking to that story?"

Melara's anger boils over. "She would've told us about you! And she would've told us about a relationship with a woodsman!"

"Would she, though? You had only just met her that year, and this story has a troubling end that I'm sure she would want to keep quiet."

Melara pulls back. "Troubling end?"

"Oh yes . . ." Kaigen confirms. "And I wasn't spying on you. I was coming to warn you of the king's threat of death for any known insurrectionists."

"'*Warn?*' More like threaten," Melara retorts.

"Eh . . . Take it or leave it."

"Whatever. Just finish the story."

"Very well. Apparently, she had never told him of her plans to overthrow the king, and although you all hadn't even attempted to make The Ascent yet, to him, it reeked of revolution. And this was a revolution the woodsmen wanted no part of. The two fought for a while before he told her he needed space and then asked for a week to mull things over.

"When she returned, he was nowhere to be found. Instead, she found three of the king's soldiers waiting."

"He sold her out?" says Darian.

"Indeed, he did. But they didn't know who they were dealing with, and they never stood a chance. All three were dead in a matter of minutes, and when the woodsman returned home, she killed him too."

"I cannot believe she never mentioned any of this," says Melara.

Kaigen shrugs. "Everyone has their secrets."

"But she told you?" Melara questions.

Kaigen smirks, "Not exactly. When the woodsman said to come back in a week, I took that as an invitation for me as well. I watched the whole ordeal unfold, almost intervening at one point, until I realized she didn't need my help. I've admired her ever since."

After Kaigen's story is finished, Melara is still shaking her head. "Assuming all of that is true, and she's kept it from us this entire time, there's still one thing I don't understand. If she has such an aversion to woodsmen, why was she so accepting of John when he first arrived? After all, she thought he was a woodsman."

"Yes, but she wouldn't have wanted you all to know about her past with the woodsmen. It is not her proudest moment."

"Wait!" shouts Darian. "She wasn't totally accepting, remember what she said when we first met John? 'Relax, we have no quarrel with the woodsmen, at least not *this* woodsman.'"

Melara thinks back. "How the hell did you remember that?"

"I just remember thinking it was odd," he replies.

Kaigen is certain Lorena won't be pleased he shared her story, but if he's being honest, he doesn't care. Her ignorance regarding John's importance is still tugging at his last nerve. "None of this matters if we cannot get back together with John. I don't care what Lorena says about any of this. We do need him."

"Agreed," the twins say in unison.

"Kaigen, I've never really cared for you," Melara says bluntly. "Ever since we met, you've been shifty, never sticking with us for too long. Sure, you'd pop in occasionally on our journeys, but it was always brief. Lately, though, we cannot seem to get rid of you. It's almost as if you care."

"Was that a compliment coming out of your mouth?" Kaigen mocks. "I never thought I'd see the day."

"Never mind that. I just want to know what's changed for you. Why the sudden passion for our cause?"

Kaigen's voice drops to a whisper. "Melara, Melara, Melara . . . I have always backed your cause. But look around you. Look where you are. Look at how far you've come. Doesn't it all seem a bit more real? You ask me what changed . . . I'd start by asking yourself the same question."

"John," says Killian emphatically.

"Exactly. Now, I'm not saying he's the only reason you're all standing here. But you cannot deny that he's shifted your odds. And not only that, hasn't he changed you all as well? You've come a long way from the disheartened group of elves I found sitting at the base of Mhorelia."

"He's right," says Darian.

"Indeed," Killian agrees.

Melara still isn't convinced. "Why do you whisper when you speak of our cause? If you are so against the king, then join us. In fact, why don't you go into his chambers tonight and slit his throat while he sleeps, just as he did with Cavarus? That way, we can be done with this whole mess. And since we are speaking of it, why haven't you done this already? Why didn't you take care of this twenty years ago?"

Kaigen knows the answer, but he mustn't say it. He has already told the denaros about his son, and if he told the elves as well . . . *Too risky.* A voice from the trees saves him.

***

"Kaigen, you certainly have a way with people," Lorena says as she steps out from the tree line. "Why is there always yelling when you arrive?"

"Just sharing old stories . . ."

"My apologies for not sharing it sooner. I was ashamed of my actions with the woodsman, and I swore from that day on, I would never let my feelings get in the way of our end goal again. Let me assure you all, the ice cavern was merely a moment of weakness."

"Moment of weakness?" Melara says in disbelief. "Lorena, it is not your feelings that concern us. We all deserve happiness, and if John grants you that, as well as being an asset to our cause, then that's even better. Why do you think none of us have expressed any concern about the two of you?"

Lorena scans the faces of Melara, Killian, Darian, and Kaigen. "You knew? You all knew?"

"I spoke to John about it in the cavern," says Melara.

"I saw you two on the boat," Killian says.

Darian puts his arm around his brother. "Killian does not keep secrets from me."

Kaigen shrugs his shoulders. "I knew from the moment you told Melara she could put an arrow between his eyes."

Lorena attempts to hide her embarrassment with anger. "If you all knew, then why is this the first I'm hearing of it?"

"Like I said, we don't care about that," says Melara.

"She's right," says Darian. "We care about Mhorelia."

"And each other," adds Killian.

"So, what do you say, Lorena? Can you put your pride aside?" Kaigen asks.

Lorena takes a seat on a rock nearby. She holds her bow in hand, running her fingers over the limbs. Cracks have started to form along the belly; it yearns to be rubbed in bomma fat and left to soak it all in. Her gaze moves to the twins, then to Melara. For an elf, twenty years should have little effect. But their faces look worn, their bodies bruised and scarred.

"I appreciate the kind words from you all, I do. And I will admit the positive impact John has had on our ascent. But he has not been with us through it all. Through the defeats, the suffering, the heartache, the loneliness. He has not suffered as we have, and therefore, he has not earned the right to falter the way he did. You all say he's the Chosen One. Well, the Chosen One is supposed to be the best of us. Someone who can look directly in the face of death itself and never waver."

Their faces drop. Killian speaks first. "Is there nothing that could change your mind, Lorena?"

"Killian . . . You always see the best in people. Your heart is full of second chances; it's infectious. But he would have to do something drastic to change my mind, to prove to me that he is, in fact, *the Chosen One*."

PART III

THE CHOSEN ONE

Chapter 22

The past twelve hours were grueling, but the rain is finally letting up now. It started only half an hour after John left Leon's, serving as a constant reminder of how much he misses home. Once John left the military, he no longer had to make the sacrifices he'd once been forced to make. If it was raining, he went inside. If it was too hot, he turned on the air conditioner. And if he was tired . . . he took a nap. He even could've started a family, something that was never really an option during his years with The Undesirables. Not that it would've been impossible; it's just that he was always away, often in danger, and once, he even had to seduce someone while on a mission . . . It wouldn't have been fair to anyone. But after spending the night with Leon and his family, it's all John can think about.

With nothing standing in his way this past year, he could've pursued those goals of dating, finding love, and even starting a family. So, why hadn't he? Maybe it's that nagging feeling that he doesn't deserve it. After all, if you spend enough time making sacrifices for others and putting their happiness in front of yours . . . it doesn't take long before you think you don't deserve happiness yourself.

Deciding it's best to push those thoughts aside, his attention turns to dinner. He eats the rest of what Gwyen packed for him while resting his back against a large tree trunk, its roots protruding from the ground. With the rain gone, all he can hear is the sound of droplets falling from leaf to leaf, branch to branch, until they hit the forest floor.

The forest itself has temporarily ended, just as the rain has. He sits right on the edge of what appears to be a path, stretching as far as the eye can see to his left and right, but only about a hundred feet in front of him. After that . . . more forest. *Weird placement for a path. It almost looks man-made.*

John pulls out the gift Leon gave him, a bundle of arrows. He'd gone on and on about how sharp they are, being made from a special material only found in the mountains where the Cliff Elves reside. But as John examines them, he can't see any difference between these and a regular arrow. Exhaustion beats out curiosity as he lets his eyelids close and the tree's roots cradle him to sleep.

In his dreams, he's riding a horse on his uncle's ranch. He's all alone; the wind is whipping past him as he takes the animal as fast as it'll go. They may only be traveling at about twenty miles per hour, but that feeling of connection between human and horse as you're galloping across the countryside . . . It's exhilarating. "Whoa, there," he says as they slowly come to a stop. John leans forward, resting his head on her shoulder. He can hear her heart pounding. "Good work, girl. Now let's get you home."

As he picks his head up off of her, he still hears pounding, only it's not her heart . . . It's hooves. And they're getting closer.

John's eyes slam open, and he jumps behind the tree trunk, lying as flat as he can. He peeks over the roots, trying to get a glimpse of the commotion. The rain has started back up, and three centaurs have arranged themselves in a semicircle with their backs to John. All three have spears drawn and are surveying the opposite tree line. *What are they waiting for?*

His question is soon answered. In the distance, an uproar of grunts and howls echoes through the forest. As it nears, it's accompanied by the sounds of branches snapping and trees being felled. Suddenly, a flash of fur bursts from the trees. "Is that . . .?" John says aloud. Fifteen feet of black-and-white fur stretches across the most ferocious yet majestic creature John has ever seen . . . an alterian. Its power is noticeable, even from afar. Defined muscles show through a thick layer of fur, and knifelike claws pierce into the ground beneath it. John is drawn to its striking blue eyes that glow in the darkness.

It lets out a deafening howl before jumping into action. In just one long leap, the alterian gets close enough and clamps its jaws around the neck of the nearest centaur. Blood sprays across the grass as the headless centaur falls to the ground. Another centaur hurls his spear into the side of the alterian, and it lets out an earsplitting yelp, but that only angers the beast. The now defenseless centaur doesn't stand a chance. The alterian launches its body into the centaur, mounts it, and bites down on its skull. John cringes as the sound of the *crunch* cuts through the rain.

Blood drips from the alterian's muzzle as it slowly creeps toward the final centaur—the spear still protruding from its side. The centaur pulls back his arm, spear raised, ready to throw. The alterian tenses its muscles and crouches down, eyes narrowed and lips pulled back, baring its razor-sharp teeth. A tension hangs in the air as John watches on in anticipation. As the rain falls down around them, neither making a sound, the alterian lunges. But before it can tear the centaur to shreds, another creature comes barreling out of the woods and slams the alterian into the dirt.

The way this new creature slaps the ground as it walks. How it grunts and beats its chest. Its sheer size. John knows instantly what he's looking at . . . a climour. Kaigen was right; it bears a striking resemblance to a gorilla. The only noticeable difference is the size, as it stands much taller than any gorilla John has ever seen.

Although the alterian lies still on the ground, John can make out its chest rising and falling from the tree line. The creature is barely hanging on, and after the hit it just took, he's shocked it's alive at all. The climour and centaur walk side by side toward the beast. John can't make out what they're saying, but they appear to be arguing. The centaur is yelling something at the climour, and the climour is responding with a series of unintelligible grunts. It almost looks like the centaur is pleading to spare the alterian, but the climour isn't going to let that happen . . . Without warning, it swings its massive arm into the side of the centaur, sending him flying into a nearby tree. Dead on impact.

Now it's just the two of them.

John's heart races as the climour approaches the vulnerable alterian. His brain is doing everything in its power to keep him behind the tree, hidden away from danger.

But his body won't listen.

In an instant, he's up and running, closing the gap faster than he thought possible. As the climour raises its arms for the death blow, John hurls himself into its chest. He bounces off of the creature and staggers backward—body aching, head throbbing, and his left ear is ringing badly, like he got hit with a concussion grenade. It, on the other hand, is unmoved, as if John had just thrown himself into a brick wall. Not only that . . . now it's pissed.

"You've got to be kidding me," John says aloud.

He ducks the first punch thrown by the beast and hightails it into the woods. Still delirious and completely night-blind, John frantically bolts through the trees, branches slapping him in the face as he goes. He hears the trees being crushed behind him, the climour hot on his tail.

The next moment, he's thrown into the open again. Not the path he was just on, though, this is a clearing somewhere inside the forest. Trees crash down in the distance to his right. *How am I going to get out of this one?* Then he sees them—berries, their red hue shimmering in the moonlight. Hundreds of them hang from bushes, scattered around the clearing. *I wonder—*

Everything goes quiet, bringing him out of his thoughts. But the blissful silence lasts only for a second, and now it's coming back his way. He sprints through the clearing, zigzagging and hurdling bushes as he goes, taking care not to brush them. He's barely forty feet into the clearing when the climour emerges from the forest, bloodied, angry, and racing toward him, uprooting bushes as it runs. Although John had a head start, the beast is quickly making up ground.

Run, jump, dodge, run. This goes on for what feels like an eternity. John has cleared the bushes now, but the dense forest lies in front of him. All he can do is hope that he's heading back toward the path, and that his plan has worked.

Fortunately, John bursts into the open a few moments later—lungs burning, legs screaming, blood pumping. A full sprint for that amount of time has left him drained. He looks toward the woods from which he just exited, worried that the last thing he'll see in his life is an apelike creature lunging toward him before he's pummeled to death by its giant fists.

But today will not be his last.

The climour stumbles out of the woods in a frenzied confusion. Blood drips from hundreds of cuts along its body, staining its thick gray fur. It thumps its chest in frustration and leaps toward John. But its footing isn't right, and it lands face-first in the mud. Grunting loudly and slapping the ground, it crawls desperately toward John until its body stops moving altogether.

John falls to his knees—partly from fatigue and partly from relief. His plan worked. It took a bit longer for the thorns' toxin to take effect, but it finally brought down this massive beast.

As he sits for a moment to catch his breath, he sees the alterian move, clearly in pain. All he wants to do is stay where he's at and rest, but he gets up and moves toward it instead. John runs his hand over its matted fur, feeling its chest rise and fall. The creature is still alive, but only just, and is struggling to hang on. Smeared with blood and covered in blotches of mud, this animal has seen better days. John's eyes turn to his own body now. He's soaking wet from head to toe; he's got lacerations on every bit of exposed skin, and yet . . . he doesn't seem to care.

It's funny, on a normal day, if you get even the smallest amount of dirt on your hands, or you spill a bit of drink on your shirt, or you cut your finger with a knife, you immediately tend to these things. You wash your hands, you dry your shirt, and you get a bandage. But there comes a point in any person's life where the little things keep adding up, and you think, *Why bother? It's only going to keep getting worse. Something else is bound to go wrong again soon.*

John continues to stand over the alterian, with all of these thoughts swirling around in his head, but one, in particular, keeps coming back to him. Not just in this moment, but ever since he arrived in Mhorelia. *What else could possibly go wrong?*

That's when he hears a tree fall behind him, jolting him out of his thoughts. He doesn't even hurry to turn around; he knows what he's going to see . . . a climour, ready, willing, and able to tear him to pieces. But when he turns to face the attacker, he lets out a long, discontented sigh. He was wrong; it isn't one climour . . . it's two. And they do not look happy.

"Fantastic . . ." John says aloud.

The ground shakes as they walk toward him. John balls up his fists in a half-hearted attempt to appear ready to fight.

"Well, let's get this over with."

Snap!

He barely hears it over the pelting of the rain and the grunting of the climour. But it is unmistakable as the sound hits his ear. Something falls from the sky and pierces the ground in front of him. A sword. John has no time to admire its crafts-manship as the two beasts run toward him. He grabs the hilt and runs at the climour to his left. It takes a big swing—like a careless boxer going for a knockout punch in the first round. John drops beneath the fist and lets his blade slide effortlessly through the torso of the climour. The creature lets out a barbaric cry as it falls to the ground.

The second one walks toward it and nudges the dead body, almost looking sad. But the look doesn't last long as the climour picks up the body and tosses it at John. Unprepared and with no time to react, he is knocked down and trapped under the weight of the corpse.

The creature thumps its chest and lets out a roaring grunt as John struggles to free himself. Slowly, it walks over to John. It doesn't need to hurry; even this seemingly feebleminded creature knows that John won't be able to lift the weight of the dead climour by himself. But still, John struggles, trying to wriggle and shift even the smallest amount so he has breathing room to defend himself.

The climour bends down over John, their faces only a few inches apart. Its horrendous breath stings John's nose as drool drips from its mouth. It grunts angrily at him; the sounds are impossible to understand, but John doesn't need a translator. It stands tall and raises its fists in the air as John desperately claws at the ground beneath the climour, trying to locate his sword. A glint to his left seals his fate—the sword lies just out of his reach. It's no use now. He closes his eyes and tries to find some sense of peace before the fists come down upon him.

The climour lets out a scream, and John winces, but he feels nothing . . . He slowly opens his eyes and looks around. The climour is gone, and a slew of horrific noises are coming from somewhere in front of him. John wrestles with the body, but it's blocking his view, and he can't seem to get a glimpse of what's happening. Then the screaming stops, and John is filled with a different sort of terror. *I should've stayed hidden in the woods,* John thinks as he prepares for his imminent death yet again.

But the face that appears next is one he did not expect; the alterian, its face now covered entirely in the blood of its enemies, is staring down at John. Its jaws clamp slowly on the neck of the dead climour, and it tosses the body off of John like a paperweight. He lies helpless in the mud, his body shaking, possibly from the cold rain or from the fear inside of him. It doesn't matter, though; all he can do is lie in wait, to see whether this beast sees him as a friend or a foe.

Before the alterian can do anything else, its front legs buckle, and it falls to the ground.

John freezes for a moment before rushing over to the creature. His eyes dart back and forth between the dead bodies of his enemies and the alterian that lies before him. He should leave; he knows he should. The mangled bodies that litter the ground around him are all the motivation he needs. More could come, and he is in no position to fight them off.

But once again, he finds himself trying to save the alterian. He places his ear to the beast's chest, finding its heartbeat rapid and its breathing shallow. He feels along the length of its body, trying to find some reason for its condition. Although the climour hit it rather hard, its ribs seem to be intact. The spear that still protrudes from its side isn't leaking blood, and it doesn't look like it hit any major organs. So, what's the problem?

"Kaigen!" John turns and yells. "Kaigen! I know you're out there!" But there's no response. "Figures . . . I'm on my own again," John mutters. "First he saves me, and then he disappears. Just like when the denaros poisoned me . . ."

That's it!

He sprints to the tree line and grabs his pack, riffling through it. "Come on, where is it?" he says aloud, letting out a sigh of relief as his fingers curl around the glass vial.

He hurries back with the antidote, hoping there's still time. His hand grips the spear. "Sorry, buddy, this is going to hurt." It lets out a loud yelp as he yanks the spear from its side. Slowly, John uncorks the vial and dumps its contents into the wound. *Now we wait . . .*

As John finishes off the unconscious climour, the rain subsides. His numbness has worn off now, and he's starting to feel the full effect of the cold. His body is shivering as he grabs his belongings and piles them next to the alterian. He could go off and try to start a fire or build a shelter, but the wood is all too damp, and he lacks the energy for any of it. Ultimately, he decides to lie against the warm body of the alterian for the night. The slow rise and fall of its chest lulls him into a slumber, and just before the night takes him, he feels its tail curl up and rest on top of his body.

***

You'd think the hard ground or the wet clothes would hinder John's ability to sleep well, but exhaustion is a hell of a drug. A soft growl rouses him as the sun rises on another day, silhouetting the figure standing in front of him. John isn't alarmed, though; the shape is all too familiar.

"You really don't like to listen, do you, John?" says Kaigen.

"Good morning, sunshine," John replies.

"When we first met, I told you that if you ever saw an alterian, you should turn and run. I guess I should have been more specific. You should turn and run *away*."

The alterian emits another growl. "It's okay," says John, as he pats the neck of the beast. "He's a . . . friend."

"A friend? Well, count me lucky. And all I had to do was save your life for the fourth time."

"Is it four now? I'm not sure you can count lending me a weapon, and then leaving me to fight alone . . . Let's call it three and a half."

"I had to be sure nobody saw me assisting you. I came forward only when I was sure there weren't more centaurs waiting in the shadows."

"What made you so sure the centaurs were all dead?" John asks.

"None came to kill you while you slept. That was a pretty good indicator," answers Kaigen.

John laughs. "Always the charmer, aren't you? Any chance you're going to tell me why you couldn't be seen helping me? It's not like the king could kill you, even if he wanted to."

"My reasons are my own, for now."

"Okay, then, how about you tell me who this sword belongs to?"

"I took great risks in getting that for you. It belonged to Cavarus Umor, the once great king of Mhorelia. If Balloch ever found out . . ."

John's eyes move from the sword to Kaigen, waiting for him to continue as the silence lingers—hoping maybe Kaigen will let him in and tell him whatever secret he's been hiding. But he'll have to wait a little longer.

The alterian jumps to its feet and barks at Kaigen.

"Well, look who's up and feeling better," says Kaigen. "I cannot believe you used that ointment on an alterian, especially when there was a great possibility that it would rip you apart the second it was able."

The alterian rubs its muzzle against John playfully, almost knocking him over. John smiles wide as he scratches it behind the ear. "Honestly, it wasn't a conscious decision. I just had a feeling, and the next thing I knew, I was running toward it."

"Well, she does seem to like you."

"She?"

"Oh yes, only a female has eyes like that. The males tend to have darker, less noticeable eyes."

"Are the females the friendlier ones?"

Kaigen raises his eyebrows. "John, there is no such thing as a *friendlier* alterian." He points to the two of them. "This . . . doesn't happen."

"I don't understand. What are you saying?"

"I'm saying that if you, or the elves, needed any more proof that you're the Chosen One . . . you've got it."

CHAPTER 23

"Our scouts say the elves are making better progress than ever, but the outsider is no longer with them," informs Hale, the king's top advisor and leader of the Mhorelian army. "They split up after the cliffs."

"Is that so . . ." says Balloch. "Maybe Kaigen is on our side after all."

They sit in a room at the far corner of the castle, away from the noise of a feast that started hours earlier and is nowhere near finished. They needed time to think, and they needed time to drink. Each holds a tall glass of scotch—single malt, courtesy of Kaigen's last trip to Earth—and stares into a fire that burns low in front of them. Normally, the king would use this room to bring one of his lovers to spend the night. But it's been converted into a war room, covered in maps of Mhorelia and empty liquor bottles.

Balloch takes a sip of his scotch. "And what of the outsider? Has there been any word about his whereabouts?"

"None. But now that he's alone, he's as good as dead," Hale assures him.

"I have thought that many times since he arrived, yet still, he lives," mutters Balloch. "Walking on *my* soil. Breathing *my* air." His hand is shaking as he looks into the flames. "He should be dead!" With a flourish, he throws his glass into the fire.

Hale doesn't flinch. He's used to this behavior from the king. In fact, his nonchalance toward the king's frequent outbursts is one of the main reasons he was appointed as his top advisor. Instead, Hale quietly grabs another glass and fills it to the brim.

"He will be dead soon enough," says Hale. "But we have another issue."

"What's that?" Balloch says, taking a swig of his fresh drink.

"Someone is killing our scouts."

"Who? And how do you know?"

"Two of the five groups that we sent out looking have not checked in. And they know the consequences of being late . . ."

Balloch takes another sip, mulling over Hale's words. "So, you're telling me we have another enemy out there?"

"It would appear so. And given the training and weaponry that our scouts possess . . . it must be a deadly enemy."

The king walks to an open window, peering out into the blackness below as a candle illuminates him. He takes another sip, and a mischievous grin forms on his face. *Grrrrrr.* A low growl comes from the grounds that the window overlooks. "Let them come. Let them all come. We have deadly weapons of our own . . ."

Hale nods. "I like your attitude, but I have a different idea. What if we enlist the help of the denaros? That one you asked to enchant the door between our worlds—what was his name?"

"Ellioch."

"Yes, Ellioch. Maybe he would send the outsider back to where he came from."

Balloch shakes his head. "Doubtful. They're too honorable a creature, the denaros. John broke the spell, so they'll assume he is meant to be here."

"Still, if we could persuade Ellioch, it would put an end to our problem without question."

Balloch throws back the rest of his drink in one final gulp—he drinks it so frequently, scotch might as well be water to the king at this point. "Very well, send for him. He'll most likely be found in their Northern Sanctuary, about a half a day's ride from here. But in case Ellioch is useless to us, I want a backup plan." Hale nods.

Balloch finds his way to a table in the corner and riffles through a couple of maps, stopping when he gets to a map showing the Enchanted Lands. Under the light of a candle, they both study it with intensity, trying to get a leg up on their enemy in any way they can.

While there is only one path leading to the Enchanted Lands—and to Balloch's castle, blocked by a gate he had erected long ago—there are several paths that branch off down the mountain. The elves could use any of them to reach the king, making it impossible to plan a surprise attack. Well, impossible isn't the right word, really; it's just a bad idea. But that has never stopped Balloch.

"How many men do we have left?" Balloch asks.

"To fight? We still outnumber the elves at least fifty to one," Hale responds, confused at what he's getting at.

"I don't mean men with swords. I mean true fighters," spits the king.

Hale's head drops, as he knows what the king is on about now. Besides the select group of soldiers that Hale has personally been leading for decades, the military force behind Balloch is not what it used to be. Not entirely Hale's fault—they haven't had a worthy enemy in years—but still, it isn't a great look for the head of the military to get complacent.

"We've got four dozen formidable men at least, but the rest can handle their own. I promise you that," says Hale.

Balloch remains silent, but his mind is running wild. *Why must everyone be so useless to me? A trained military should've been our primary concern! These elves should've been dealt with years ago!* A sudden realization surfaces in his mind. He has been far too lax about these elves, and especially about John. Not taking them seriously, and thus, not using the force necessary to deal with such an opponent has been a mistake. *I will not make that mistake again.*

"Send all forty-eight to intercept them. I do not want them making it to my front gate," says Balloch.

Hale looks up in shock. "My king, I don't think that is our best course of action. If they fail, who will be left to protect you?"

"I still have my guards. Ten strong and the best fighters Mhorelia has to offer"—the king's eyes narrow—"because *I* never let them stop training . . ."

Hale brushes off the insult. "Still, if we are to send anyone, let us send our lesser soldiers."

"And have them be slaughtered like the rest of them? We have already tried that, sending untrained archers and wayward centaurs to hunt a trained killer. Make no mistake, John is the Chosen One. And I will not let my arrogance be my undoing. Send them all." He slams his hand down on the map. "Send them down every path that leads to us. And do not let them slip through your fingers."

Hale shifts uncomfortably as he scans the map once more. "Balloch, I understand where you're coming from, but there must be at least twelve routes they could take."

"Well, then, four soldiers per route, I suppose," Balloch jabs back, annoyed at Hale's line of comments. "Shall I plan the attack as well?"

Before tensions can rise any higher between the two of them, someone comes banging on the door. "Balloch! Balloch!"

"Stop that banging or I will remove your hands!" he hollers back. It ceases immediately—the king does not make idle threats.

"My-my-my king . . ." the voice stammers behind the door.

"Oh, spit it out," says Balloch.

"It's just . . ." the voice starts again.

Balloch steps to the door and swings it open. "What?"

The young man standing at the door pushes aside his noticeable fright toward the king and whispers something into his ear. Balloch remains still, his gaze unmoving, staring straight ahead into the darkness of the corridor. His hands ball into fists and begin to shake.

"Hale, one last thing . . . Bring me Kaigen."

CHAPTER 24

Poof!

Killian jolts awake and lunges at Kaigen, stopping just short as he registers he isn't a threat.

Kaigen doesn't bat an eye. "You're jumpier than usual."

Killian knows he's right. The elves parted ways with John three days ago, and every day since, Killian has gotten more annoyed. Partly due to Lorena's dismissal of the painfully obvious fact that John is a *necessary* addition to their group. But mostly, it's because nobody's listening to him. Lorena wasn't wrong. Killian does always try to see the best in people, but is that a reason for them not to take him seriously? He doesn't think so, and it's starting to put him on edge.

"You ever feel like you're smarter than everyone around you, yet no one will listen?" Killian responds.

"Ha! Every single day, kid," says Kaigen. He nods at Lorena, who's asleep next to Darian and Melara. "I take it she still isn't budging on John?"

"No. And it's infuriating," Killian says as they both take a seat by the now smoldering fire.

"I like this side of you. But what happened to the young and innocent Killian that everyone else seems to admire?"

Killian shakes his head. "Oh, he's still in there, but I'm beginning to think that's the problem. Maybe my youth takes away from my leadership."

"Isn't your brother only four minutes older than you?"

"That doesn't matter. He's got a gravitas that I lack. When people hear me speak, they just see a naive little boy."

"I think you may be selling yourself a bit short. But if you truly believe that, why don't you tone down the playfulness and try to grow up a bit?"

Killian leans back onto his palms and stares into the dawning sky. "What's the point?"

"The point?" Kaigen says, confused. "The point is to be taken seriously."

"No, that's not what I mean. What's the point of life if it's so rigid? If you cannot have fun or make a joke? Almost every being you meet in Mhorelia is stiff . . . plain . . . They take life too seriously. And I get it to an extent; we're in hard times. But is that an excuse to compromise who I am . . .? No, I don't think it is. If people want to underestimate me because of my attitude toward life, then so be it."

The two remain silent for a moment. A look that could almost be described as admiration flashes across Kaigen's face as they stare into the coals, and this confuses Killian. He hasn't been this forward with his feelings in a long time, and it makes him uncomfortable. "What, no snarky remark? No quips? You're supposed to be the dreadful one, you know?" Dreadful isn't the right word, and he immediately feels bad after saying it, but Kaigen doesn't seem to mind.

"Bit hypocritical, don't you think?" he responds.

"How do you mean?" says Killian.

"You sit here, gushing about how no one will take you seriously because of the way you act. But I can't have a softer side? You see the joy in everything, and I have a sarcastic comment for everyone. We are who we are because of, or in spite of, what we've been through. But those traits alone do not define us."

Killian instantly feels remorseful. "I-I'm sorry . . . You're right . . ."

"I know. Lucky for you, you're not the smartest person around when I'm here." They both laugh. Lorena rolls over but doesn't wake, still in a deep sleep. "And don't worry, I have a feeling she'll come around soon. Just give it a little more time."

Maybe it's the small moment of bonding between the two, but Kaigen's reassurance leaves Killian feeling hopeful. "I'll take your word for it," he says. As the morning inches closer, Killian lies back down, hopeful he can sneak in another hour of sleep before the others wake. "Oh, Kaigen. I almost forgot to ask. How did you fare in looking for John?"

Kaigen waits for a moment before smiling. "Couldn't find him. But don't worry, I'm sure he's fine."

***

Killian is happy to wake gracefully several hours later, finding sleep much easier after his conversation with Kaigen. But when he rolls over, Kaigen is nervously pushing the coals around in front of him.

"Something on your mind?" asks Killian.

Kaigen doesn't look up; he just keeps moving the coals around. "It's nothing." He points to the other elves. "Did you drug these three? They haven't moved since you dozed off."

"They each drank some Ethereal Root tea; they'll be up shortly. And what about you? Did you rest at all?" Killian knows the answer. The dark circles below Kaigen's bloodshot eyes make Killian wonder just how long he's been without sleep.

"Huh? Oh, yeah. I shut my eyes shortly after you," says Kaigen as he tries to stifle a yawn. "And now I'm ready to get moving, so let's get these lazy elves up." He stands and clears his throat. "Hey!" All three elves wake in fear, rummaging around them for their weapons. Still in a daze from the Ethereal Root, it takes them a good ten seconds before they realize they're in no real danger.

Killian is trying desperately to keep from laughing, but Kaigen is making no effort at all. He's laughing so hard, he's curled over at the waist. Darian and Lorena are attempting not to care, but their faces turn beet red with embarrassment. Meanwhile, Melara's anger takes over as she grabs a nearby stick and hurls it at Kaigen, and it glances off of his right arm.

Now Killian is laughing. "You didn't even try to teleport, Kaigen?"

"Oh, come on, Killian, I deserved far worse for that," he says as the laughter slowly dies down.

Killian can't help but think that if *this* Kaigen showed himself a little more, people wouldn't be so quick to judge him. But if their discussion last night proved anything, it's that people are complicated.

"So, how was he?" asks Lorena.

"Who?" Kaigen replies, as if it's not obvious.

"John . . ." Lorena presses.

Kaigen shoots Killian a look. "John"—he drops his head mournfully—"is dead."

"What?" Lorena shouts.

Horror shoots across their faces as Kaigen waits a beat too long before adding, "I'm just playing."

Lorena doesn't hesitate in picking up the biggest rock she can find and chucking it at Kaigen's head. He teleports behind Killian. "Was that too far?"

"Why would you say that?" scolds Darian.

"Just wanted to prove a point," says Kaigen.

Killian grins and grabs his pack. "We'd better get going; we've lost enough daylight as it is." Another look of approval on Kaigen's face widens Killian's grin. Maybe it's his newfound confidence, but nobody questions his directive. They pack their things and continue The Ascent, with Killian leading the way.

As they walk up the rolling, rocky hills, he spends his time reflecting on the journey that he hopes will soon come to a satisfying end.

He and his brother grew up near the bottom of the island, so when Balloch took over, their village was a natural refuge for anyone else who was lucky enough to escape his terror. Hundreds of beings arrived in the following weeks, but one stood out among them, Melara. Killian will never forget the first time he laid eyes on her as she led a group of fifty into the village. Her clothes were stained with blood, and her eyes still blazed with ferocity from killing who knows how many on her journey south. She didn't stay long, though, quickly leaving to round up any others and bring them to safety. Two weeks later, she made her second appearance, but this time, she was accompanied by only one . . . Lorena.

Killian observed from afar as the two bonded instantly. They spent so much time together that people in the village would joke they were sisters, separated at birth. They decided rather quickly that not only did Balloch have to pay for what he had done, but that they were going to be the ones leading the charge. And it didn't take long for them to notice the twins, Killian and Darian.

Darian immediately wanted in, but Killian took some convincing. It's not as if he didn't know Balloch needed to be stopped; he just never thought he would be a part of it. Call it insecurity, call it self-doubt, call it whatever you'd like . . . Killian never felt capable of greatness.

This feeling started at a young age, shortly after his parents drowned in a freak accident. Darian took their passing better than most would, but for Killian, he'd lost his compass in life. He'd lost the two people who'd always been there for him when he needed answers, or help, or just a shoulder to cry on.

But Darian was quick to take their place, stepping in to show him the way of the healer. The two of them worked through the pain of their parents' deaths by devoting their lives to helping others, which came in very handy after Balloch's rebellion. People were soon coming in droves who needed medical attention for any number of reasons: cuts, bruises, broken bones, dehydration, hunger . . . The list goes on, and Killian helped in any way he could. The more people he helped, the better he felt.

The problem was that not everyone around him dealt with their pain in a healthy way. Most people were left bitter and depressed with their lives—rightfully so—but they took those feelings out on people like Killian. They would say things like, "Do you really think you can make a difference?" or "Why are you wasting your time with this? We need fighters, not healers." Or worst of all, they would say, "You're only doing this for yourself." Killian couldn't believe it. He was saving lives, and they were making it about themselves.

He knew deep down that they only spoke this way because they felt bad about themselves. They resented him because he had changed his life for the better. He knew this. But the problem is, if you're ridiculed and told you aren't good enough too many times . . . you start to believe it.

But there was Darian again, supporting him at every turn and helping him block out everyone else's negativity. The two of them together must've cared for over five hundred people in the first month, saving quite a few lives in the process and learning how to fix just about every ailment you could think of. But they also made time to train with a bow, at Darian's request. Like most elves, it came naturally to them, but Killian never wanted to kill—he had seen enough death in his life—all he really wanted to do was help people and make friends.

That was the ultimate decider for Killian in the end. He was still hesitant to make such a dangerous journey, let alone make it a hundred and seventeen times, but he knew this was the way he could do the most good, and he always felt at home with his new friends. They would hunt together, swim together, eat together, laugh together. You name it, they did it . . . *together.* He loved being around others who would lift him up, encourage him, and were always there to lend a kind word when he needed it.

Unfortunately for Killian, as they all walk together once again, there are no such kind words being exchanged. In fact, there is no talking at all. Sometimes, however, it's what's left unsaid that can mean so much.

The quiet indifference Melara exudes as she hangs back in the group, taking up the rear, would normally seem odd, considering she's always giving Lorena her two cents about everything. But to Killian, this looks like a subtle act of defiance. She's avoiding the discussion at all costs and proving to Killian that she agrees with him in the process.

That being said, Lorena doesn't seem too bothered by it. She's been averting everyone's gaze the whole morning. She knows she might be wrong and is too stubborn to admit it.

Kaigen isn't helping her stubbornness, constantly whistling an unnecessarily loud and obnoxious tune as they go along, hoping to antagonize her. He knows she's wrong as well, but he isn't hiding his feelings. Then again, he never really has.

Then there's Darian, standing tall and walking side by side with his brother. He's always wanted Killian to be more assertive, to stand up for himself. It doesn't take a genius to see that the pride is practically glowing from his pores.

Killian's observation skills have always been better than most, but his ability to read his fellow travelers today impresses him more than usual. Not so much Darian, no, the two of them have never needed words to communicate. When you've spent your entire life with someone, an indistinct glance can tell a whole story.

Yes, Killian is quite impressed with himself, but it's short-lived. He knows Lorena is the true leader of this group, and a leader he will undoubtedly follow to the end. If the stakes weren't so high, he'd almost feel bad for the predicament she has gotten herself into. She tossed John from the group on an impulse decision, and who hasn't made one of those before? But she won't admit she's made a mistake, and the more time Killian has to think about that, amid the silence, the angrier he gets. Finally, he can't take it any longer. "Lorena," he says.

"Shhh! Everybody quiet!" says Kaigen, cutting off the conversation before it can even start.

"What is it?" asks Darian.

"You hear that?" Kaigen responds.

The birds chirp around them, but nothing else makes a sound.

"Stop messing around," says Lorena.

"I'm not!" he shoots back angrily.

If his tone wasn't convincing enough, Killian places his hand on the ground and feels a soft rumble. "What is that?"

The confused look on Kaigen's face quickly turns to horror. "Run."

"Why?" says Killian. "What could possibly be so—"

A cloud of dust comes barreling down the mountain as Kaigen shakes his head. "Avalanche."

The dust overtakes them in a flash as they attempt to flee. Fear envelopes Killian as he runs straight downhill, with no idea where he'll end up. He can't see more than a few feet in front of his face, but he can hear the coughs and screams of the others. Then his foot catches on a root, and he tumbles a good thirty feet down the mountain. Dust is all around him now; he can feel it building in his lungs as he tries hard to breathe. Disoriented, he looks around helplessly, the screams of his companions quickly dying out. *Is this how it all ends?* he thinks, just before someone slams into him, sending the two of them even farther down the mountain.

When Killian comes to a stop, he is tangled up with Melara underneath a rocky overhang. It juts out just far enough to shield them from the dust and debris charging down the mountain. By some stroke of luck, Lorena has already found herself there, and they all lie on the ground, hacking up dust and vomit as they attempt to force air into their lungs. Melara reaches into her pack and pulls out a water pouch, dumping the contents into each of their throats between coughs. The vomiting continues until most of the dust is caked onto the ground.

When the shock wears off, Killian grunts in pain, noticing the rock shard that has become lodged in his leg. Melara, who has blood oozing from a cut above her eye and covering the left side of her face, isn't any better off.

Suddenly, Killian is on high alert, looking around frantically. "Where's Darian?"

He jumps to his feet and cries out as the pain shoots through his leg.

"Killian, you can't go out there!" says Lorena.

"You know that I must," he replies.

"Wait!" yells Melara. A shadowy figure appears in the dust that rages just outside their place of refuge.

"Darian . . .? *Darian!*" Killian reaches out to pull him to safety. But just as he does, a large object strikes his brother. It could've been a rock, or a tree, or an animal for all he knows . . . But it doesn't matter; the figure that was just in reach has now disappeared into the chaos. "Darian!"

He jumps out into the avalanche without a moment's hesitation. The objections from Lorena and Melara vanish as he enters the torrent of sounds and rubble. His ears ring from the noise as he calls out to his brother, "Darian! Darian!" He knows the odds are slim, but he just can't imagine a life without Darian. His insides are filling with dirt again, and bits of the mountain-side are pelting his body. Panic sets in as he hobbles aimlessly into the abyss, slowly suffocating.

He snaps out of his panic when his leg gives out. At first, he thinks it's the rock shard that's still protruding from his thigh; he knew he couldn't walk on it forever. But as he lies on the ground, knowing this may be the end, his eyes catch what he's just stumbled over. Through the haze, he can just barely make out what looks like hair whipping in the wind. He slaps his hand toward it and is relieved when he feels a soft body lying next to him, no more than a foot away. The feeling is brief, however, as a new thought grabs his attention. A thought so invigorating in his mind, it just may give him the strength he needs to press on. *Together till the end.*

He grabs his brother with all the energy he has left and lifts him over his shoulder, crying out in pain. Putting all of his weight on his one good leg, he slowly limps forward. There is no telling which direction he should go; all he knows is that he fell down, so he must go up. The dust stings his eyes as he pushes on; hundreds of thoughts fly through his mind at once. *I cannot go on. I won't make it.* A rock strikes him in the chest. Another bounces off of his abdomen. At this moment, he's certain that pain is all he will ever know.

But then his brother wheezes, and he's transported back to the present. He tries to clear his mind and remember all of the times his brother has saved him. There was a time, early on in their journeys, when a denaro threatened to fly Killian to the clouds and drop him to his death. Darian jumped between them and fearlessly negotiated with the denaro, admitting only after the fact how terrified he was. Then there was the time, some fifteen years earlier, when Killian ate a poisonous mushroom. Darian tirelessly searched the woods for days in order to find an elusive plant that was necessary for the antidote. These thoughts dull the pain he's going through and continue to propel him up the mountain. He is going to get his brother to safety, or die trying.

Together till the end.

Left foot, right foot, left foot, right foot. His gait begins to slow, and his steps shorten as the fatigue overcomes him. Stars appear in his eyes, and darkness comes in from all sides. The last thing he remembers before blacking out is a hand lurching toward his chest and pulling him to the ground.

***

The next memory he has is of pain . . . so much pain. Not in any one particular spot, but throughout his entire body. His legs still burn from exhaustion, and although the rock shard has been removed, and the wound wrapped tightly with a piece of clothing, it still throbs. Welts line his arms from the barrage of sand and stones, so much so that he feels as if he were still out in the storm. His head pounds from who knows what: dehydration, blunt force trauma, stress . . . It could be any number of things. And then there is the pain in his chest. Through the delirium, he can find cause for everything else, but this pain . . . this pain remains a mystery.

As Killian rolls over, attempting to sit up, a coughing fit ensues and the pain in his chest intensifies. Melara comes to his aid and lays him back down. "What happened?" he says to her.

"You fell to the ground with Darian slumped over your shoulder. Neither one of you was breathing . . . We didn't know what to do, but we thought maybe the dirt inside you was the problem. So we beat it out of you."

"You beat it out of us?" says Darian, seated in the opposite corner.

"It was the only thing we could think of. Eventually, you started coughing and retching, but it's been about two hours since then. We were worried you'd never come back around," says Lorena.

Killian chuckles. "Well, that's not technically the correct way to do it."

Lorena shrugs. "Both our healers were down, so we improvised."

"A simple 'thank you' will suffice," Melara adds.

"I suppose we do owe you that," says Killian.

"And I owe you much more, brother," says Darian.

"You would've done the same for me."

"Still . . ." Darian grabs the water pouch and lifts it to the sky. "Together till the end."

Killian does the same and reiterates the sentiment, "Together till the end," before having a coughing fit.

When the dust settles, they step out from under the ridge to see a mountain torn apart. Killian knew it would be bad, but this is much worse than he expected. The path they were taking now looks to be impassable; they will need to find another route, and an easier one would be preferable. Killian can already feel his body ache after just a few steps, and his brother has got to be worse off. A moment later, Kaigen appears in front of them, just as quickly as he left.

"You all look terrible," he says bluntly.

Melara is unamused. "You seem to have escaped the wrath of the avalanche just fine."

"And what would you have had me do? Run through the mayhem with you all? Risk my life as well, for what? Comradery?" Kaigen says back. "I knew you'd make it out. Now follow me; there is a path due west that was untouched by this disaster." Nobody objects; they just follow his footsteps in silent agony.

It's about a twenty-minute walk for people in good health, but since they are battered from their ordeal, they don't reach the path until an hour later. Kaigen was right; it remains intact and entirely usable, but as Darian lays his pack down on the ground, his body falls with it. Killian rushes to his side, helping him with his water pouch. "Well, this seems as good a spot as any to make camp," Killian suggests.

"Camp?" says Lorena. "We are not stopping. We have already lost precious time."

Killian just shakes his head, knowing that there isn't a chance in this world that they can go on like this, but he's too tired to argue. Luckily for him, Kaigen isn't tired at all.

"Have you lost your mind?" he says. "Look at them. Look at *you.*"

"I am fine, and they will be too. We will rest for half an hour, and then it's time to go."

"Lorena . . ." Darian struggles to speak, clearly exhausted from just the small distance they've walked. "I cannot keep going like this."

"Darian, we do not have time to waste. We will rest for half an hour, then continue our journey. That's an order."

"Look at us," Killian pleads. "We need time."

"This is not a debate!" Lorena yells. "We leave in half an hour, or—"

"Or what!" Killian screams. "You'll leave us behind? How long before you cast us all out on our own? How long before you're the only one still standing? We have all made sacrifices, but if we keep going on like this . . . the only thing left for us to sacrifice will be our lives. Is that what you want?"

The words ring out harsher than he meant for them to sound, but he's done apologizing. If it stings to hear them . . . it should. She should have to sit with those emotions, and feel bad for what she's suggesting, knowing or unknowing. Although, as she's stuck staring at Killian, or better yet, through him, her face doesn't show guilt . . . It shows fear.

Crack! A stick breaks behind them, and they all spin around. As it turns out, Lorena's face is showing genuine fear, for walking toward them, ever so slowly, is an alterian. Nobody moves a muscle—not that they're in any shape to fight this creature—they just stare into its eyes, hoping for even the slightest chance it might leave. But as it inches forward, Lorena calmly raises her bow and knocks an arrow. She pulls back the string quietly, but before she can release it, Kaigen's hand helps to lower the bow. All she can muster is a look of bewilderment. From her perspective, their one chance of survival is gone. But he is quick to quell her fear.

"I think you'll find this beast has no quarrel with us."

Ever so slowly, the head of a man rises from behind the alterian, with a crooked smile plastered across his face.

In her astonishment, Lorena can only get out one word: "John."

CHAPTER 25

If there was ever a time to say, "I told you so"—and John has always loved saying those words—this was it. Riding in on an alterian is all the proof John needs; he is the Chosen One, and Lorena was wrong to cast him aside. But as John slides off of the creature's back, he has no urge to boast, no urge to be the *alpha*. If he's being honest with himself, he's just happy to be around friends again. All that being said, even he is surprised at his next words: "So . . . how can I help?"

The elves eye the alterian with unease as it pulls back its lips and growls at them. "Easy now," John says to the alterian as he scratches its neck, changing its demeanor entirely. It rubs up against him and settles down on the ground, shutting its eyes after coming to the conclusion that there's no threat present.

"I knew it!" Killian blurts out.

"Knew what?" asks John, but he knows the answer.

Lorena chimes in as she circles the resting alterian: "You really are the Chosen One. Sent here to rid us of Balloch's tyrannical reign."

"No, I am here to *help*. A wise man once told me, 'It will take the efforts of many to usurp that man.'"

"And who was this man?" asks Darian curiously.

John proceeds to tell them everything that happened since they last saw each other: the forest, Leon and his family, the fight with the climour. All of it. He spares no detail as the elves listen in with wonderment, bandaging themselves up, starting a fire, and setting up camp as he speaks. Killian offers John a salve for the cuts that riddle his body, noting that he should be much worse off, considering he fought three climour by himself. John omits mentioning the massive bruising he has underneath his clothes from running head-on into one of those beasts—instead deciding to relish in Killian's pride.

When he gives them Leon's gift, they are over the moon, saying how useful it might be going forward. John still doesn't see the point of a "sharper" arrow, but if it makes them happy, then that's fine. Once he's finished with his story, the questions start coming in droves. Darian pipes up first: "How was Leon? I cannot believe he has a daughter!"

"Leon . . . he seems wise beyond his years. And I also get the feeling that he could kill me without hesitation."

"That sounds like Leon," Killian says as he stares intently at the sleeping alterian. "John . . . what made you jump between this creature and a bunch of ferocious climours? Why risk your life for something that could've just as easily killed you once it was all over?"

It was a good question. One that John had been grappling with since it happened. Throughout his whole life, he had made decisions based on logic and reason. But there was nothing logical nor reasonable about his decision to save the alterian. At best, it was reckless, and at worst, it was suicidal.

"Well, this is going to sound crazy . . . but the best answer I've got is that I felt drawn to her. It was as if my whole life had been leading up to the moment when I first laid eyes on her . . . And she was in trouble. At that point, staying hidden was not an option."

"That explanation is better than anything I could've imagined," Killian says, beaming.

Melara can't stop herself from chiming in, "You keep saying, '*her.*' Don't you mean, '*it*'?"

"No, she's a female, which makes 'it' a '*her,*'" says John.

"And how can you tell?" she retorts.

"Umm, her eyes, obviously. Males don't have eyes like that," he says, shooting Kaigen a mischievous smile.

"Hmph, well, in that case, I do not trust *her* one bit," says Melara bluntly.

"Melara, don't be foolish," Lorena scolds. "This creature is the single greatest sign we have ever gotten that our time is not wasted on this journey."

"That settles it. *Oblirian* is our newest member," John says.

"Oblirian? She has a name now?" says Melara, either annoyed or disgusted. John can't tell which.

"Of course she has a name. I came up with it on the journey back to find you all. I think it suits her well."

"Hear, hear," says Killian.

"Agreed, I like it," says Darian.

"Speaking of your journey back to us, how did you know where to go?" Lorena asks.

"Kaigen showed me the way. It was the least he could do after he left me to fend for myself against the climour," says John.

"You were there?" Lorena says to Kaigen. "And you did not assist?"

"I threw him that sword." Kaigen laughs.

Melara scoffs, "Typical. Always doing the bare minimum to help."

"What did you just say to me?" Kaigen snaps back, his jovial tone vanishing completely.

Melara is surprised, but she stands her ground. "I'm saying, you may help us at times, but you never truly risk anything to be here."

Kaigen is stuck staring at the ground, with a hateful emptiness in his eyes. Ever since John first met Kaigen, it's been quite clear to him that he keeps his cards close to his vest, never wanting to reveal too much. But whatever secret he's holding on to now, it's weighing on him.

"Kaigen?" John says. Kaigen blinks a few times and looks at John, his eyes now hollow and devoid of emotion. "Whatever you're holding on to, you've got to let it out. Your intentions have always been, for lack of better words, up for debate. It's obvious we don't have the whole story, but maybe if you'd let us in, it would help us to understand."

He shakes his head. "You couldn't understand."

Lorena disagrees. "If anyone could understand, it's this group. Every one of us has come close to losing our lives, Killian and Darian most recently of all. Look at them; they're less than a day removed from the avalanche, and they have not wavered once."

"That's all well and good," Kaigen says as he tosses a pebble into the fire. "But it's not my life I'm concerned about . . ."

"Selfless" is not a word that John would use to describe Kaigen, so who could possibly mean that much to him? Who could be so important that he would actually risk his life for them? John's mind travels back to his interaction with Leon, and then it hits him. "You have a child?"

Kaigen's stare doesn't waver from the fire. "A son . . . and he was taken from me. Stolen from me by that *vile* man who sits upon Mhorelia's throne. And if I am caught helping any of you, there is no telling what he will do to my son." His eyes shift to Melara. "You say I risk nothing to be here . . . I risk *everything* to be here."

They're left speechless, taking in this new information and mentally piecing together all of Kaigen's questionable decisions over the last few weeks.

"So, after we crossed the canyon with the snakes, when you told the centaurs where we camped, that was for your son?" asks Killian. Kaigen nods.

"And when you ambushed us on the river near Brackoa Lake?" says Darian. He nods again.

"And then there was my fight with the climour," says John.

"That, John . . . was the hardest one of all. I was certain you would perish, but I had no choice but to stay hidden in the shadows," Kaigen replies.

"I . . . I think I understand," John says.

Kaigen nods. "I appreciate that. And I would be remiss if I failed to mention that I did not leave you completely out to dry in those instances. I told Eldar to bring you to me instead of killing you. I warned you subtly about the ambush before it happened. And I gave you that sword to defend yourself from the climour. I did those three acts in defiance of the king, in an effort to keep you all alive."

"I guess this also explains why you haven't killed Balloch yourself. I'm assuming he has your son guarded at all times?" says Melara.

"That he does," says Kaigen.

"So, why risk it at all? Why not just do his bidding and let us die?" Melara asks.

He ponders this question for a moment before responding. "Just because someone is living, doesn't mean they're alive. A few days ago you asked me why I have shown a greater interest in your cause as of late . . . You asked me what changed . . . I want a life, a *real life*, for my son."

There it is again—the pit in John's stomach that refuses to go away. All this talk of Kaigen's son is dredging up his feelings of self-doubt again. Does he deserve a family? Will he ever get the chance to have children? And where would he possibly start? He glances at Lorena as she tucks one of her red curls behind her ear before dismissing the thought. *Now is not the time to think of such things.*

"There's one question I still have, Kaigen," says John. "Why hasn't the king told you to finish us off? It wouldn't be too difficult for you to kill us while we sleep."

"Oh, I offered."

"What?" Melara exclaims.

"I'm not sure you're allowed that shocked reaction, considering how many arrows you've shot in my direction over the years," says Kaigen.

Darian smiles. "Well, that's a fair point."

"And you deserved every one of them," Melara says.

"What did Balloch say when you offered to take matters into your own hands?" Killian asks.

"He said it would not be an '*honorable*' kill if he sent me . . . However, if you keep getting closer, I fear his thoughts on that may change."

A look of unease travels through the group. Part of John doesn't think Kaigen would actually go through with it, but another part of him believes he would kill every last soul in Mhorelia if it meant he could have his son back.

The silence that follows proves to be too much for John, so he relieves himself to find more firewood. A dead birch tree provides the kindling he's looking for, and he begins breaking branches from it and tossing them in a pile. *Snap!* He breaks one branch. *Snap!* He breaks another. *Snap!* This time, the sound comes from behind him, and he spins around to find Lorena.

"I'm sorry, John, I didn't mean to startle you," she says.

"You elves and your soft footsteps . . . Have you come to help me carry the firewood back?" he says jokingly.

Her eyes are trained on the ground, but she slowly lifts her gaze to meet John's. "I'm glad to see you in one piece. And I'm truly sorry about what happened before."

John reaches out and grabs Lorena's hand. "Don't worry about it. Everything seems to have worked out."

"What do you mean?"

"If you hadn't cast me out, I never would've met Leon or Oblirian. And you still might not trust me."

"Thank you, John." She grips his hand. "It's just that one can do crazy things to protect the people they care about . . ."

John looks deep into her eyes. "Are you saying you care about me?"

Lorena blushes, and happiness fills her eyes. John leans in slowly . . . but the moment is fleeting. The look of happiness turns to worry, and John pulls back. "What's wrong?"

"John, I want to lead us to glory. I want us to defeat Balloch and enter the Enchanted Lands together. And I have never questioned the possibility of that happening." She pauses and takes a deep breath. "But as we get closer and closer . . ." She looks back toward their camp, and tears fill her eyes. "What if I am leading them to their death?"

John's never seen her like this, in such despair. He pulls her in and squeezes her tight, trying to comfort her as best he can. As they pull away, he asks, "You are such a sure leader. Why do you doubt yourself now?"

Her voice gets louder as she speaks, tears filling her eyes once again: "Look at what we have encountered over the last few weeks: the snakes, the centaurs, the ambush, the brackoa, the widaps, the climours, and now the avalanche. The closer we get, the more dangerous this journey becomes. How many times can we cheat death before death wins out?" She grabs his shirt and pulls him close, her voice now filled with desperation: "Promise me you're with us till the end."

John is caught off guard. "Wh-what? Why are you being so—"

"Just promise me, John!"

"Of course I'm with you till the end. How else am I going to get back home?"

She pulls away. "Oh . . . yes."

"What now?"

"It's just . . . I've been so caught up with my end goal of killing Balloch, I forgot for a moment that your goal is to get home."

"Lorena . . ." he starts.

"No, no, it's fine. I-I should get back to camp. Here, let me grab some of that firewood for you."

As she walks back to camp, John takes a seat on the felled tree and inhales deeply. He takes in the smell of pine in the air, the greenery all around him, and the sun slowly making its way across the sky. At this moment, one could almost forget they were in a different world. He sits for a long time, reflecting on his time in Mhorelia while also thinking about his life back home. Would anyone be looking for him? How long has he even been gone?

The days have all begun to meld together, and what was it Kaigen said? Ten years here is a hundred and fifty on Earth. So, even if it has only been two weeks . . . Have they moved on? Assumed he died on his hike in Scotland? Did they hold a funeral? Who would've even shown up? These thoughts start to overwhelm him. Feeling his anxiety kicking in, he figures now is as good a time as any to meditate.

By the time he finally opens his eyes, the sun has almost crossed over the horizon, but the meditation has done its job. Feeling more relaxed, he strolls back to the camp, surprised to find only Kaigen awake by the fire.

"And where did you disappear to?" Kaigen asks.

"I needed some time to myself."

"Didn't get enough of that during your 'banishment'?" says Kaigen jokingly. John just shakes his head and dismisses the comment. "What is it, John?"

John exhales softly. "I knew when I first got here that I was on the clock, but it's just now setting in that even if we accomplish what we've set out to do . . . what life will I have back on Earth to return to?"

"What life did you have before?" Kaigen says rather bluntly.

"I had a good life," says John, somewhat offended. "I had a stable job, friends at work, and a decent apartment to go home to."

"Were you happy?"

"What?" John asks.

"I've spent years in your world, mostly observing your people. You all live very different lifestyles, but the most common I've seen is what you've just described. People going to their jobs, then going home. To their credit, some of them do look happy.

But what fascinates me is that the vast majority just look run-down and miserable."

John thinks for a moment. "You may have spent time in my world, but you do not understand it. For some people, that's just their lot in life. They've spent so long doing one thing that they have no way out."

"Nonsense. You can always change your path in life. One must simply make the decision and commit."

"It's not that simpl—" John starts.

"It is that simple. The only thing holding them back"—Kaigen points to his head—"is in here."

"Why are you telling me this?"

"Because I have watched you closely since you arrived. And you can deny it if you want, but you've enjoyed your time here."

"I've almost died multiple times."

"And in doing so . . . you've also lived."

John doesn't want to admit it, but Kaigen sort of has a point. The best moments of his life were working with The Undesirables, and he had countless near-death experiences back then. But this is not his home . . . He has to get home. *What life could I possibly have here,* he thinks, stealing a glance at Lorena.

"If you've spent years on Earth, why don't you ever bring anything back?" John asks, changing the subject.

"Would you?"

"Of course I would. If your math is correct, Earth advances fifteen times faster than Mhorelia. We've got guns, vehicles, medicine . . . all of which could help you on your quest to defeat Balloch."

"That's true; those things could help us," Kaigen acknowledges. "But given enough time, those inevitably become genocide, climate change, and an opioid epidemic. Not to mention I could never get a car through the door to Mhorelia . . . Advancement and growth are good, and your world has seen a lot of both, but they will eventually be your downfall."

Another good point, albeit very depressing, John admits to himself. Genocide, climate change, opioids . . . Those are just part of a laundry list of atrocities brought about by advancements in society that were supposed to bring good.

"But what about smaller things, like a flashlight or a box of matches?" John asks.

"I've thought about it, but if Balloch found a flashlight lying around the castle, he no doubt would wonder what else Earth has to offer. It's better for everyone if I only bring back scotch for the king, and keep the rest a secret."

"Fair point."

"And look around you, John. Lush forests, clean air, no technology. Isn't this better?"

Now that Kaigen mentions it, John hasn't looked at a screen since his phone broke during their first fight. And to be honest, he doesn't miss it one bit. In fact, not having that device attached to his hip is a weight off his chest, like a leash has been cut and he's freer because of it. Why do we need to be so connected all the time, anyway? Kaigen's right—again—this is better.

John smiles. "You know, Kaigen, you're smarter than you look."

Kaigen leans back and rests his hands behind his head. "Everyone realizes it sooner or later."

John laughs, then realizes the rest of the group has been suspiciously quiet this entire time. "What happened to the elves?"

"Looks like the events of the day finally caught up with them."

"Hmm . . ." John says as he lifts Killian's cup and takes a whiff. "And you're sure spiking their drinks with Ethereal Root had nothing to do with it?"

A mischievous look forms on Kaigen's face. "What can I say? I needed some time to myself, too."

CHAPTER 26

"Wake up," a soft voice whispers into John's ear. He lets out a long moan and stretches the full length of his body—the telltale sign of a good night's sleep.

"What time is it?" he asks Lorena.

"Time?"

He chuckles to himself. "Sorry, it's an old habit from back home." Time isn't really a concept that's used here in Mhorelia, at least not the way it's used back in the United States. There are no alarm clocks, no 7 a.m. meetings, no roosters crowing. You wake up when you wake up, and you go to sleep when you go to sleep. *Island Time, all the time.* He always liked his routine back home, but this new way of life is growing on him—although he could do without the frequent near-death experiences.

He sits up lazily to find everyone else is already awake. Lorena and Melara are making up packs for their journey, complete with enough food to make it all the way to the king. The twins are having some sort of archery contest to see who's a better shot. Two trees stand alone, with several arrows stuck into each. Judging by the number of arrows in the tree opposite Killian, he appears to be winning. Oblirian is at their side as well, nudging them playfully as they shoot. *Nice to see them getting along.*

It's been a week since the avalanche, and everyone has healed up nicely. Well, that might be an overstatement, but they're all definitely benefiting from the time spent not fighting. A few more days of rest would be preferable, but the anticipation of being this close to their goal has led to the decision to trek on. At least, that's how Lorena put it. If it were up to the twins, John is pretty sure they'd be content to stay here for another month. Without the thought of death or despair, the two of them have really come into their own—cracking jokes, playing games, and telling campfire stories from decades past. But nothing good lasts forever.

As John's morning fogginess leaves him, he notices someone is missing. "Where's Kaigen?"

Lorena points up the mountain. "This path we are on splits into many, and we have not traveled them for years. He went on ahead to scout out the best route to take."

"Hopefully one with no chance of another avalanche," Melara adds.

Poof!

"Perfect timing," says John.

"Thanks for joining us, John. I thought you might sleep all day," says Kaigen.

"Enough chitchat. What did you find?" asks Melara.

"Always straight to the point with you . . . All four paths leading east were decimated by the avalanche, so those are out. The four to the west were left unscathed, but they are a much farther journey, given the terrain. Then we've got this path straight ahead of us, which branches into another four paths later on, all of which are viable options."

"So, straight ahead it is," Lorena says decidedly.

"Well . . ." Kaigen trails off.

"What is it?"

"The safest route for us could also be the safest route for others . . ."

"What are you getting at? Did you see anything suspicious?"

"A few dead bodies in the aftermath of the avalanche. They appeared to be soldiers."

Lorena ponders this for a moment. "Those could've just been scouts out on patrol. We are nearing the king, after all."

"Maybe . . . But it could also be a search party," says Kaigen.

"A search party?" Melara says. "Even the king isn't desperate enough to send soldiers out hunting."

"Maybe in the past. But with John by your side, there is no telling what he will do," says Kaigen.

John considers the options. "So, you're saying the west will be safer, but it will be harder on all of us to travel? And the path leading north would be an easy climb, but we could be walking into a trap?"

Kaigen nods. "That about sums it up."

"I'll take that risk," says Killian, having now joined the conversation. "I don't know what I will be capable of with my leg still not fully healed."

"Agreed," says Darian. "I can still feel the dirt clinging to my lungs. The easier the climb, the better."

The look of doubt in Kaigen's eyes makes John uneasy. It may take longer to climb going west, but the thought of dealing with an ambush sounds worse, even with an alterian by their side. He decides to keep his thoughts to himself, at least for now.

It doesn't take long for them to reach the forks in the path. After a full week of rest and a good meal, they're making great time. John can see the destruction of the avalanche even without taking the paths leading east. Thirty-foot trees have been uprooted and tossed down the mountain like twigs—Kaigen was right; that way is not an option.

John finds his way to the front of the group, where Kaigen leads, with Oblirian at his side. "She seems to be taking kindly to you all now. She hasn't growled once. That must be a good sign."

"Alterian are very intuitive creatures. Once they have sensed who is a friend and who is a foe, they do not waver," says Kaigen.

"So, *no* more growling at you? Well, that's kind of a bummer."

"Ha! Sorry to disappoint you, but if she growls now, we're in trouble."

Once John is sure they're out of earshot of the elves, he asks, "So, what makes you so worried about heading north?"

Kaigen looks behind to check the elves again. "I have known the king for a long time, John . . . This feels like a mistake."

"Then say something."

"What would you have me say? Their minds are made up."

"Just . . . I don't know . . . Reason with them."

"*Reason* with them?" Kaigen chuckles. "They're a thoroughly unreasonable bunch."

"You've got to try," John pleads, becoming increasingly frustrated.

"Alright, alright. Calm down," Kaigen says as they reach the point where the path splits. Before going any farther, he addresses the elves. "Listen here, I must insist we take this path to the west."

"But we have already decided on a path," Darian remarks.

Kaigen rolls his eyes as he looks at John. "Look, I know the king. I know how his mind works. I know his tendencies . . . We are most definitely walking into a trap."

"The king is a madman; you couldn't possibly predict his actions," says Melara.

"Yes! The king *is* a madman," says Kaigen. "And a madman is exactly the kind of person who would send his best warriors out hunting us, instead of waiting for us to get to him."

The group falls silent, all of them fearfully aware he's most likely correct. Finally breaking the silence, Killian speaks up, "We may be walking into a trap, but we will be walking into it with an alterian, and the Chosen One. Not to mention that if the king is truly as mad as you say, he could just as easily have sent men down the western paths."

"That . . . is a valid point," Kaigen says, conceding. "John, lead the way."

After they walk a ways, they come to another fork in the path, where John chooses to go left. Then, after another hour of walking, they get to the final fork; John points them to the right this time.

He hears whispers from Killian about how John can sense which way to go . . . If only he knew these were just wild guesses.

The longer they walk, the slower time passes. Again, John would have no way of knowing, but the sun is sluggishly making its way toward the opposite horizon. He's completely wrapped up in his thoughts again, so much so that he doesn't notice Lorena has made her way to his side.

"John," she says, causing him to flinch. "Sorry, I didn't mean to startle you."

"That's becoming a regular occurrence."

Her face sports a lopsided grin.

"No worries, though," he says. "My mind is just elsewhere today. Speaking of . . . How are you doing?"

"Why do you ask?"

"Well . . . when we spoke yesterday . . ." John trails off.

"Ah yes. Don't think too much about that. I was just on edge from the events of the day," she says back, unconvincingly.

"Lorena," he whispers, "you don't have to pretend like nothing is wrong. Or that nothing is going on between us." As soon as the words leave his lips, he immediately regrets saying them. Who is this man who is so open with his feelings? Not John, at least it has never been before now. And the timing is all wrong. She's clearly going through something, and he is professing his love to her?

"John," she says sternly. "You need to forget about yesterday. From now on, there can be no distractions. And you and I . . . We're a distraction." She picks up her pace to leave him with that comment.

He runs his hand over Oblirian's soft fur, hoping it will comfort him. Not a chance. Such a quick conversation, but not at all harmless. The pit in his stomach grows deeper once again. Suddenly, he's mad at himself. Why did he put himself out there like that? He hasn't done that in years, and he's been able to avoid these types of feelings for just as long. Against the advice of his therapist, he decides to push these feelings aside and press on. He'll deal with them later . . . probably.

Killian and Darian snap him out of his thoughts. "What was that about?" Darian asks.

"Nothing," John says back.

"Don't worry about her," says Killian. "She's a complicated person on her best days, and this journey puts a lot of pressure on her."

"Seriously, it's all good," John reassures them.

"I know, I know. It just hurts me to see her like this. She has such a big heart, and she's been forced to hide it away. In a different lifetime, things would've been drastically different for her," says Killian.

"The same could be said for every one of you," John points out.

"A fair point," says Darian. "But after hearing stories of her as a little girl, it's been hard to witness what she's had to transform herself into."

John finds himself feeling for her once again. They haven't had such different lives, the two of them. Both had their parents taken from them at a young age. Both gave up on normal a long time ago. And both have spent most of their lives fighting. The only big difference is that Lorena didn't have much of a choice.

Darian interrupts his thoughts. "Hopefully, when this is all over, she will return to the girl she once was."

"Maybe we will all be able to return to the people we once were," Killian adds.

It's a nice thought, one that brightens John's spirit, if only for a moment. What follows quickly extinguishes that light. Oblirian emits a low and troubling growl. It rises quickly and catches the attention of the rest of the group.

"Come on, Oblirian, I thought we were becoming friends," Killian says playfully.

"Killian, that growl was not meant for you," Kaigen says abruptly.

They stand on level ground. A steep hill lies in front of them, and trees rise to their left and right. The elves are spinning in circles, desperately trying to spot their foe. A chill runs down John's spine, and panic courses through his body. Kaigen was right; they've walked into a trap.

For what feels like an eternity, the only sound they can hear is Oblirian's growl. Standing beside John, she offers a small amount of comfort amidst the fear bubbling up inside him. She quickly turns her body to face the slope in front of them, her growl intensifying.

"What is it, Oblirian?" says John. A pebble bounces down the mountain and hits his chest. A dozen more roll past him. "Kaigen, tell me this isn't another avalanche."

"No, no, we would feel a rumble. This is something else," he responds.

That's when they spot it: a mass of rocks, boulders, and logs careening toward them. They have only seconds to act.

"Look out!" yells Darian.

John, Kaigen, and Lorena jump to the right side of the path. The others flee to the left.

"Wait!" shouts Kaigen. "We must stick together!"

But it's too late. In no time, the mass is hurtling past them. Luckily, the thick trunks of the trees are stopping anything from entering the woods that they've taken refuge in, but the path is impassable for the time being. Kaigen's face shows both disappointment and anger.

"What just happened?" John asks.

Kaigen grunts. "They've done it . . . They split us up. And he sent his best warriors to do the job . . ."

"What are you talking about, Kaigen?" says Lorena.

"He sent a few men to set the trap while the rest wait in the woods for the hunt." Kaigen motions to the dense forest in front of them. "This is how he trains his best."

John and Lorena both draw their swords. "What do we do?" asks John.

"You two take care of whoever lies in wait . . . I'll deal with the men up top," he says, then vanishes.

So many feelings are swirling around in John's body, he can't seem to pinpoint any of them. After spending most of his life doing the hunting . . . being hunted doesn't sit well with him.

"We press forward, slowly," says Lorena. "Keep the path to our backs." John nods.

Every step John takes brings more angst. Any tree could be harboring their assassins. His grip tightens around his sword, and a bead of sweat trickles down his neck.

Then suddenly, John hears a noise. A scratching coming from a particularly large tree standing in front of them. John taps Lorena's arm and points to it. She nods. They make their way forward, stepping carefully to avoid making a sound. When they are within striking distance, she points to herself, then to the left of the tree. Then she points to him, then to the right. He nods. A countdown isn't necessary; they both leap around the tree and swing their swords.

Bark flies and a squirrel scurries up the tree in fear. They both let out a nervous laugh. "Watch out, Lorena, those little guys are biters," he says jokingly. She laughs again and playfully shoves him backward.

An arrow pierces the tree where he was just standing.

John turns around and raises his sword to deflect the long blade crashing down toward him. The man is quick to steady himself and swings again. Their swords clash, and he kicks John onto his back. John has barely enough time to roll away as the man drives his sword into the ground where he was just lying. They both rise and take a step back, giving John his first chance to get a good look at his attacker. He must be seven feet tall and close to three hundred pounds, all bulk. *Fantastic . . .*

To his left, he notices Lorena locked in a fight with another man, much smaller but incredibly agile. He'd love to help . . . but he's got his hands full.

"Hmph, the Chosen One . . ." the man says in a gruff voice. "We'll see about that."

He steps toward John, and they strike swords repeatedly. The man's speed with a sword is unlike anything John has ever seen. It quickly becomes clear that he cannot defeat this man without some sort of trickery. As if to emphasize that point, he dodges a swing of John's sword and punches him square in the jaw.

But this gives John an idea . . .

They square up again. This time, John spins his sword in front of him in a figure-eight pattern, the man's eyes following it intently.

"I thought this was going to be a challenge," says the man, before charging at John.

"So did I," says John, tossing his sword in the air. The man's eyes follow it once again. In one fluid motion, John unsheathes his dagger and hucks it into the man's throat. The look of shock in his eyes pleases John. But as he walks over to the man—now pawing at his wound as blood oozes through his fingers—John's sense of pride is diminished. He pulls the dagger from his neck and wipes it clean.

Before he can check on Lorena, she tackles him to the ground. An arrow whizzes past them both.

"Have you forgotten about the archer?" she says, now lying on top of him.

They both roll behind a nearby tree. "Must've slipped my mind. I was a little preoccupied with that behemoth over there," John says.

She is unamused. "Hopefully, this archer is the last one. But I must find my bow if we are to have any chance of survival."

"There." John points to her bow, lying ten feet away, painfully out in the open. She pokes her head around the trunk. Another arrow flies by.

"John, I need that bow."

"Well, go grab it, then."

"I'll have at least two arrows in me before I have time to send one in his direction," she snipes.

"Well, then, what do you suppose we do?"

She thinks for a moment. "I need you to be a distraction."

John sighs. "I was afraid you'd say that."

"I just need enough time to grab my bow, locate the enemy, and put an arrow between his eyes."

"Oh, is that all?"

She grabs his face and pulls him close. "John, I will not let anything happen to you."

All notes of sarcasm leave John's mind as she stares into his eyes . . . "Don't miss."

And with that, he's off and running. The first arrow comes so close to John's ear, the sound could've been mistaken for a bullet. *Back on the battlefield again,* he thinks as he sprints through the forest. After a thirty-second burst, he dives toward the nearest tree, an arrow thudding just behind him. As he sits there panting, another strikes the ground to his right.

"Any day now!" he yells before fleeing from cover. Seconds after leaving his safe haven, he realizes he's made a mistake. The trees have thinned tremendously, and there is nowhere else to hide. He abruptly darts to his left, hoping to throw off the shooter. No such luck. Looking into the distance, he sees a flurry of green. At first, he isn't sure what it is, but he quickly figures it out. His eyes focus on a figure, a man cloaked in green, raising his bow. *This is it.*

But then he sees another color. Red. Blood shoots out from the man's neck as Lorena's arrow hits its mark.

John falls to the dirt, his eyes closing without thinking as he tries to catch his breath. When they open, Lorena is standing over him, holding out her hand. "Get up; now is not the time to rest. We must find the others." She's right, but oh how he desperately wants to just lie there. If he ever finishes this journey and gets home, he'll never take a lazy Sunday for granted again.

As they approach the path, the rocks have ceased falling. *Kaigen must've done his job.* But then a woman screams; *Melara.* They bolt onto the path to see Oblirian rip the throat out of her attacker. Then a soldier follows Darian out of the woods, where Killian is waiting with his bow drawn. His arrow splits the man's skull.

Good, that must be the last of them, John thinks. He surveys the group; it's not a pretty sight—bruised and battered would be an accurate description—but at least they're all alive.

Lorena helps Melara to her feet and pulls her in for a hug. "Are you okay?" Melara nods.

Kaigen puts his arm around John as Oblirian comes to their side. "Nice work, John. Balloch's warriors are not an easy bunch to kill."

The twins tap their bows together.

"Nice shot, brother," says Darian.

"Together till the end," Killian replies.

Before they can react, an arrow strikes Killian's chest, sticking out both sides . . . and time stops.

Chapter 27

"No . . ." Darian breathes as his brother falls to the ground. "Nooooo!"

John's eyes instantly scan the tree line for the shooter, spotting him about a hundred feet away, but Kaigen is already on it. Even from a distance, John can see Kaigen beating the man senseless as he cries out in anger. *Good. Let him suffer.*

Then his focus turns to Killian, and the gravity of the situation sets in. *No one survives a wound like that . . .*

Melara falls to her knees, unable to form words. The rest are just as shell-shocked, watching as Darian cradles his dying brother in his arms. John takes a step toward him, but Lorena grabs his arm. Their eyes meet, and she shakes her head.

"Killian . . ." Darian can barely get out his name. "You . . . you cannot . . ." He struggles to get the words out, his voice wavering as he holds back tears.

Killian still looks disoriented as he stares at the arrow protruding from his chest. "Wh-what happened?"

"Everything is going to be okay, my brother," says Darian, blinking away tears.

"Brother," Killian chokes out, "I . . . I'm not ready to leave you."

"I know," Darian whispers. "I'm not ready either . . . We were supposed to be together till the end, remember?"

Killian's lips form a smile. "Brother, I'll always be with you . . . in here," he says as he points to Darian's heart. "I love you."

Tears stream down Darian's face. "I love you, Killian. And I will never forget you." Killian's body goes limp, and Darian curls over him, sobbing in agony.

John joins Melara on her knees, his own legs giving out. Killian is dead. The one person in this world who was the epitome of good. All he can think about is that it isn't fair as his brain is overcome with sadness and anger. Lorena kneels beside Darian, placing a hand on his back as she wipes away tears from her face. For the next few minutes, nobody says anything. John just stares blankly into the woods until something catches his eye.

A stagglehorn.

It slowly and calmly approaches the group. The elves notice it, too, its eyes curiously scanning the scene. It bends a knee toward Darian, sniffing him intently, then scampers off into the woods.

Before John can even begin to piece together that exchange, Kaigen returns. He drags the barely breathing man by his shirt collar and drops him next to the group. His face is already swollen and bloodied from the beating, and one of his arms is clearly broken. Kaigen didn't hold anything back. *Good.*

"What should we do with this one?" Kaigen says.

"We should question him," says Lorena.

Darian's sadness turns to anger. "No, he dies *now.*"

John agrees with Lorena, and he's confident the others do as well, but nobody objects.

"Fair enough. John, your sword," says Kaigen.

"No . . . He dies by my hand," says Darian. Without a second thought, he grabs John's sword and shoves it through the man's chest. He holds it there, staring into his eyes, his rage unparalleled. Then he simply lets it go and falls backward, cradling his head in his hands. John watches as the man dies in front of him. But before the man dies, he grasps Kaigen's shoulder and pulls his face toward him, whispering something into his ear. John can't make out what he said, but the look of horror on Kaigen's face says enough. Without another word, Kaigen vanishes, and the man drops dead.

John can feel the lump in his throat growing as he holds back tears. Again, nobody speaks for quite a while; they just stare into the nothingness in front of them. *The thousand-yard stare . . .* That's what it was referred to back in the military. Wiping your mind of all thoughts in an effort to feel nothing at all. It's effective, but only temporarily.

Melara breaks the silence first. "What . . . What do we do now?"

All eyes shift to Lorena, but she's still stuck in a stunned trance. Then they look at John—as if he would know what to do. He says the first thing that comes to mind. "We should have a funeral."

"Yes, that's a good plan. A funeral," Lorena repeats.

"But . . . where do we bury him?" asks John, looking around.

"No. That's not how we do things, John," says Melara. "Here in Mhorelia, we burn our loved ones and let their spirits float up into the sky."

"A funeral pyre," John says to himself. "Are we sure that's a good idea?" he says aloud.

"It could bring a lot of unwanted attention our way," Lorena cautions.

"Good," says Darian, finally removing his head from his hands. "Let them come."

Over the next hour, they silently gather everything they need for the pyre. They find most of the wood in the rubble, but John goes deep into the forest to gather some of the larger supporting logs—at least that's what he told the elves. He needs some time to himself, some time to process everything that has happened. After half a mile of walking, he plants his back against a tree, slides to the ground, and breaks down. His mind travels back through all of his memories of Killian. In the short time that they had known each other, Killian had confided in him, helped him, placed his faith in him, and constantly made him laugh. John's weeping turns to silent sobs as he recounts these memories.

Slowly, his crying ceases, and he lifts himself up. Two logs lie next to him. He grabs them both and throws one over each shoulder. If Killian's death affects him this deeply, he can only imagine how the others are feeling. *Best to keep moving and help in any way I can.*

The pyre is nearly complete when John returns. All that's left to do is put the remaining logs in place, then lift Killian to the top. John leans his two logs against the far side of the structure and forms a sort of walkway. Darian and John then carefully lift Killian's body and place him on top of the pile.

"May I have a moment with my brother, John?" Darian asks.

"Of course, Darian."

John stands on the ground by the others as Darian perches atop the pyre, whispering to his brother. A tear slides down Lorena's cheek as she watches. John puts his arm around her, and she lets her head rest on his shoulder. Her arm finds its way around him as well, and she squeezes him gently.

"Thank you," she whispers.

As the structure goes up in a blaze, they all stand stoically beside it. There will be more time to grieve later, but for now, the tears have stopped. Only emptiness surrounds them where Killian's presence used to be.

Darian lifts his pouch of water. "A thousand years would have been too short a time spent alongside you, brother."

"Here, here," says Melara.

"Here, here," Lorena and John say in unison.

The fire dies down, and John is suddenly aware of how hungry he is. He offers to cook dinner while the others talk among themselves, thinking it best to give them some space. In his alone time, he is reminded of Kaigen's absence, and a question surfaces in his mind. *What caused him to leave so abruptly?* After another moment, however, the answer seems obvious. *Must have to do with his son.* He thinks about the last look Kaigen gave him, the terror in his eyes. The king knows Kaigen has been helping them; John is certain of it.

As they sit down to eat, Darian holds up a small jar of ashes. "I'm going to bury these back home under his favorite tree. A white willow, I believe it's called. Kaigen brought it back from John's world as a sapling. He gave it to us as a gift . . . Killian loved that tree."

"Kaigen gifted you a sapling?" asks Melara.

"Yes, shortly after we met. The tree is known to have many medicinal properties, and he felt we could use it to help heal our people," says Darian.

"Why have you never spoken of this?" Lorena asks.

"He made us swear we'd never tell. Something about his image being tarnished if people thought he had some good in him," says Darian.

Everyone laughs, and for a moment, they forget their grief and sadness. But the moment is brief . . . "I'm going to get some sleep," says Darian.

"Do you need anything?" says Lorena. "Anything at all?"

"No, no. Just some rest," Darian says as he saunters away from the fire.

"He didn't even touch his food," Lorena whispers.

"I know," says Melara. "I'm worried about him."

"I'm worried about all of us," says Lorena. "In all the years we've done this, I never thought it possible that one of us would perish. Well . . . I knew it was possible, but I never accepted it as a reality."

"Not only that, but now we have Kaigen to worry about," Melara says.

John tilts his head to the side. "Why would we need to worry about him?"

"He most certainly retreated to the king because of some newfound knowledge. I'm guessing the king knows of his 'traitorous' actions."

"I gathered that much," says John.

"Well, what would stop the king from forcing Kaigen to slay us all?" she asks. "Maybe not now, but once we reach the gates, we must prepare for that scenario."

"I guess I hadn't thought of that," says John. "After everything that's happened, and after everything we've been through . . . I don't know if I *could* kill Kaigen."

"More like you don't know if you'd be able to . . ." Melara says bluntly. "You are a gifted fighter, John. But he's in a whole other league."

"I held my own when I first fell through the door," says John defensively.

"Yes, but he was only toying with you," Lorena points out. "And if his son's life is at stake . . . he'll hold nothing back."

John doesn't want to admit it, but he knows they're right. Even if all four of them fought Kaigen at once, he'd still have the upper hand. "In that case, we need to be on high alert until we reach the castle. And then we must save his son at all costs. It is the only way we can ensure he'll be on our side." Lorena and Melara nod in agreement.

After they've eaten their fill and the fire dies down to embers, they curl up to get some rest. It's a cold night, and John would love to sleep next to Lorena for warmth . . . But it doesn't seem right, and she was very clear about her feelings. He offers to take the first watch—and to be honest, he's happy to—promising to wake Melara in a couple of hours. He knows he won't get much sleep anyway; his insomnia is slowly creeping in, as it always does when someone close to him dies. When his uncle died, he didn't sleep for days. And when The Undesirables passed . . . that nearly killed him.

He spends the time thoroughly cleaning his blades, reliving the kills as he cleans. The dagger actually makes him smile, remembering the slick way he killed his attacker. But it fades quickly—his next memory is of the man pawing at his gashed neck. Those feelings, however, are not nearly as bad as the ones that surface when he cleans his sword. The anger in Darian's eyes as he stabbed his brother's killer, he'd never seen it in either of the twins. They aren't vengeful people, and John worries that this will change Darian forever.

These thoughts are driving him crazy, prompting him to take a stroll to the nearby tree line, but taking care that he stays close enough to keep watch over the elves. Staring into the trees, he stands conflicted. Part of him hopes there is someone lying in wait—a fight would take his mind off of things for a minute—but another part of him is sick of all the bloodshed.

As dawn breaks overhead, he knows he's been on watch for too long. If he doesn't wake Melara soon, she'll be furious with him. But as he kneels beside her, he glances at Darian—his body lying covered and facing away from the rest of them. John can't help but wonder if he got a wink of sleep last night—he knows he wouldn't have. In the event he was up all night, John decides it would be best to share a few words with him before the others rise. He wants at least a brief moment of privacy to share his sympathy with him.

John crouches down and places a hand on his shoulder. But it's rock hard . . . It's not his shoulder at all. He rips the cover off and finds a pile of rocks and logs arranged in the shape of an elf . . .

Darian is gone.

Chapter 28

Darian moves swiftly through the trees with only one thought on his mind: *Those men are going to pay.* It didn't take long for his sorrow to turn to anger; all he had to do was picture the arrow jutting out of Killian's chest. No matter how hard he tries, he can't get the image out of his head, adding nonstop fuel to his rage. His brother, his kind and selfless brother, is dead. And these men . . . these *savages*, live on . . . It's not right, and Darian is going to make things right.

When dawn approaches, he's put at least five miles between him and the others. They must know he's gone by now, and they'll surely be out looking for him. It wasn't easy to sneak away; he had to be sure the elves were asleep—they definitely would've heard him as he left. But John, well, his ears are not as sensitive as the elves. And what a stroke of luck that he left his post to wander among the trees. It was the perfect moment to escape, and he took full advantage. His thought process is simple: Head west and kill all the king's men, then return to the others—or die trying. The more he thinks of a life without Killian, the more he decides that the latter doesn't seem too bad.

Once he's through the woods, he stumbles upon one of the paths Kaigen mentioned. It's wide and much more treacherous than the route they chose to take, but not as bad as he expected. Multiple rock ledges yield a difficult path, but they could provide cover or shelter if necessary. The steepness of the hike finally gets to him, and he stops underneath an overhang for his first break of the excursion. Once the first bite of jerky touches his tongue, he remembers how little he ate last night. He feeds his ravenous appetite by quickly devouring four more pieces of meat and half a loaf of bread.

He felt a little bad about taking so much food with him, but the others will understand. As he takes a few swigs from his water pouch, he looks out from under his hiding place. From this spot, who knows how many thousands of feet up, the view of Mhorelia is breathtaking. He can see the far-reaching edges of the island and the different regions spread throughout. A sense of calm moves through him as he admires the land.

"Beautiful, isn't it?" he whispers aloud. He looks to his left, and that calm turns to grief . . . Killian is gone.

Then, in an instant, Darian's senses heighten as footsteps approach. He listens carefully to see how many; only one pair, it seems. *Why would one man be traveling alone?* Then he hears a stream of liquid berate the ground directly above him. *This man is relieving himself . . .* Darian knocks an arrow as the stream sprays out over the ledge under which he hides. The second the man stops, Darian takes one step out from under the ledge and releases an arrow upward through the man's jaw. Quick, clean, and satisfying—the only three words to describe this kill.

But then Darian panics. The man falls from the ledge, and he has no way to stop him from slamming into the ground and tumbling down the mountain. The noise of his armor clanging as he rolls is louder than Darian would've hoped. If others are nearby, they undoubtedly heard it. He leaves his cover and sprints for the tree line, due east. Before he disappears off of the path, he sees three other soldiers running down the mountain toward him.

They've spotted him.

Lucky for Darian, these soldiers are not as nimble as an elf. He bounds through the forest without making a sound, the clinking of his enemies' armor getting farther and farther behind him. A wide grin forms at the thought of them stomping through the forest with no hope of ever catching him. But then another thought arises in his mind, and his feet stop. *I'm leading them right to the others.*

Darian scans the tree in front of him. *Thick base, lots of branches, very tall . . . Perfect.* In seconds, he's thirty feet up the tree and sitting upright on the thickest branch he can find. There he waits, not making a sound. Then the soldiers arrive, huffing and puffing. They stop under Darian's tree to regroup.

"I hate elves!" one of them yells. "When we catch him, I am going to rip his legs clean off his body!"

"Where is Henry?" says another.

"Dead. I was about to throw a rock at him while he was having a wee, when an arrow went straight through his head."

The other soldier grunts. "Filthy elves."

Darian readies his bow, knowing if he doesn't act, he will have led them straight to the others. If there was ever a time to strike, it's now. He peeks over his branch for a better view; two have bows, and they're covered from head to toe in armor—not great odds. His heart pounds as he weighs his options. He'll have to kill them all before he's detected; otherwise, they'll have time to regroup or fight back. Even with the high ground, three versus one is risky . . . And these men are Balloch's best.

He knocks an arrow and points it at the largest soldier, aiming for a slit in his armor right below the neck. If he misses this shot, he'll be dead before nightfall.

Inhale, exhale, inhale, hold . . .

But before he releases the arrow, a whitewing lands gracefully beside him. He loosens his grip on the string as the bird stares into his eyes. For a moment, he forgets about the men beneath him. *You were all supposed to fly south,* he thinks. The bird blinks at him, cocks its head sideways, and then flies away. Darian's eyes well up, *Killian?*

"Let's continue this way. He can't run forever," says the soldier, bringing Darian back to the present.

He swallows hard and blinks the tears away, aiming back to the slit in his enemy's armor. His bow hand is shaking wildly, and his mind is in complete disarray. The soldiers press on, due east . . . It's now or never.

Inhale, exhale, inhale, hold . . .

At the last moment, Darian lifts his bow and fires back toward where they came. The arrow silently flies past several trees before landing in one just before the western path.

All three soldiers perk up. "What was that?" yells the leader.

"It was back toward Henry," says another. "That dirty elf doubled back."

"Let's go!" he grunts. They sprint toward the noise, and Darian lets out a deep sigh of relief. What was he thinking? Taking on four of the king's men in broad daylight is downright reckless. What he needs to do is wait until nightfall. Yes, that's what he'll do. He'll track them until the sun sets and then kill them while they sleep.

Trailing the men proves easier than Darian originally thought. They may be warriors, but they're also clumsy and exceedingly loud. Constantly smacking one another and yelling profanities, their voices carry at least a quarter mile. And when they aren't talking, their heavy footsteps carry almost the same distance.

They give up on pursuing Darian rather quickly and make for their camp, stopping only once to shoot an unsuspecting animal from afar. The accuracy of the soldier with his bow—and at such a long range—reassures Darian he made the right call not to engage earlier.

Day turns to night as he stalks them to their camp, taking care not to be seen or heard. He waits quietly from a distance as they skin their dinner and roast it over a fire. The smell of the food wafts into Darian's nose, and his stomach rumbles. Deciding that he might be here a while, he sits behind some bushes and removes a loaf of bread from his bag. Some nearby berries make a nice spread, and he smiles as he takes his first bite.

"The sweetness of the berry complements the savoriness of the bread in such a way," he can hear Killian say in his mind. The thought of his brother brings a wave of sorrow, and his feelings of loneliness continue to grow as he sits in the darkness.

"No," he mutters to himself. "I must not get distracted."

He peers over the bush for another look. The men have poured some sort of drink and appear to be getting drunk . . . very drunk. *No matter,* he thinks. *The more they drink, the easier this will be.* All he has to do is wait for them to drink themselves to sleep. But the more they drink, the louder they get, and soon, Darian can hear them as if he were sitting right beside them.

"Why was there only one of them after us today?" says the leader.

"Hmph, maybe they split up to hunt us all down?" says another.

"Ridiculous!" yells the third. "This close to the king, they would stick together."

"He's right," the leader says. "And I got a good look at the elf before he disappeared into the woods; it was one of the brothers. Those two would *never* go out alone."

"So, you're saying the rest may be dead?" the second soldier replies.

"Maybe not all of them . . . but definitely the twin," he says back.

After a brief pause in the conversation, the third soldier raises his glass. "I'll drink to that!" Laughter rings out through the woods.

Darian's blood starts to boil, and rage consumes his thoughts. *These men do not deserve to die in their sleep. I will put an arrow through two of their necks, then witness the fear in their leader's eyes as I slit his throat. Yes, I will be the last thing that he sees before it all goes black.* He rises defiantly and knocks an arrow. A stone's throw away, but in the darkness and their drunkenness, not one of them notices. He pulls the drawstring back to his cheek, his eyes narrow. The only dilemma on his mind is who he should kill first.

"Don't," a voice whispers behind him.

He spins around and points the tip of his arrow an inch from John's face.

"You should not have come here," says Darian.

John raises his hands. "Did you really think we would not search for you?"

"This is my task, and mine alone."

"But it doesn't have to be," John pleads.

Darian shakes his head. "You cannot stop me."

"I'm not here to stop you. I am here to help you."

Darian thinks for a moment. "They die by my hand, understood?"

"Understood. Give me two minutes to sneak in close, then take the first shot. I will move on your mark."

Darian crouches back down as John slinks away into the night. He aims back at the largest one, suddenly annoyed that any of them will have a quick death, but so be it. Once he spots John in position, he slows his breathing and whispers into the darkness, "I take pride in knowing this breath will be your last . . . Die slow."

He releases the arrow.

Blood sprays from the man's neck, and John jumps into action, piercing the leader's back with his sword. The last standing soldier gets a swift kick to his chest, sending him into a nearby tree. His body sticks into the broken stump of a tree branch, leaving him hanging a foot off the ground.

Darian slowly strolls toward the carnage. "Nice work, John. I'll take it from here." The man stuck to the tree grabs at the branch protruding from his rib cage, his hands trembling. He coughs up blood as Darian pulls an arrow from his quiver, which quickly finds its way into his left shoulder. A second arrow sticks into his right shoulder. Then Darian pulls out a third.

"Darian," John says.

"Just hold that man down and make sure he doesn't die," Darian spits at John before sending the third arrow into the soldier's head.

He drops his bow and unsheathes a dagger, turning to the leader—John's sword still lodged inside of him. Darian bends down to meet the soldier's gaze. "Do you know who I am?"

The man's breathing is labored and drawn out; his eyes avert Darian's gaze. "I know who you are . . . You're one of . . . those misguided elves . . . set on taking back . . . Mhorelia . . ." He meets Darian's stare. "But let me . . . tell you something . . . You will *never* take back the—"

Darian slits his throat, staring into his eyes until the light goes out.

With all the men now dead, Darian wastes no time and begins to retrieve his arrows. "John, thank you for your help."

"I'm just glad I found you when I did. We need to leave now, though. The deal was that if we found you, we were to meet back before nightfall."

"You go back, John. I'm not finished," Darian replies, now gripping a handful of arrows.

"What?" John says back, confused. "Darian, you can't keep doing this. The path you're on does not lead to anything good. It just leads to more emptiness. Trust me."

"I don't care."

"Darian, we are all hurting, but don't let your brother die in vain. He wouldn't want this."

"You barely knew my brother! How could you know what he would want?"

John doesn't retreat; he doesn't give in. He just keeps his eyes trained on Darian. "You're right. I didn't know your brother as well as you did, obviously. And I wouldn't dare compare my feelings to yours. But one thing I do know, Killian would never want any harm to come to you."

The hostility Darian has been feeling is still very much at the surface of his being as he stands opposite John—who's clearly bracing for a fight. But as Darian looks at the dead bodies surrounding him, and the blood pooling at his feet, he feels only sadness. Tears well up in his eyes, and the arrows fall from his hand.

"Why did it have to be Killian?"

CHAPTER 29

"Where is he?" Kaigen shouts, his voice echoing through the halls of Balloch's castle. "Where is my son?" He teleports from room to room, desperately searching for Isaiah. His heart drops when he finds Isaiah's room a mess, with furniture knocked over and covers ripped from the bed. "Son? Isaiah?" he whispers.

Then a scream rings out from the training grounds. A child's scream.

Kaigen looks out the window in horror to find Isaiah tied to an archery target. Balloch stands across from him, bow in hand, while Hale and a crowd of soldiers watch from the side. Kaigen teleports in front of Isaiah just as the king is raising his bow. "Stop!"

"I was wondering when you might show up," the king says.

"Please, Balloch. Don't do this."

"I told you what would happen if I ever found out you were helping the elves."

"Balloch . . . I-I-I wasn't—"

"Did you think I wouldn't notice that scoundrel Umor's sword is missing? You gave it to *him*." Balloch pulls back the drawstring. "Now move."

Kaigen knew it was a risk stealing Umor's sword, and now he has a decision to make. Hold his ground, or fight them all. He looks back at his son, shaking in fear, then turns to Balloch. "I'm not going anywhere."

"Very well, then," says Balloch, letting the arrow fly.

Kaigen grunts as it sticks through his left shoulder.

"Daddy!" screams Isaiah.

"It's okay, son. Daddy's going to be okay," Kaigen responds.

"Well, this makes things interesting!" booms Balloch. "How many arrows can I put into your body before you teleport far, far away from here?"

Kaigen raises his arms and gestures toward himself. "Let them come, *my king*."

Balloch knocks another arrow and points it at Kaigen's head.

"I love you, my son," Kaigen whispers to Isaiah.

Nobody moves as Balloch and Kaigen lock eyes. All that can be heard are the whispers of Balloch's men and a soft breeze, blowing a few stray pieces of straw over the space that spans the two of them.

The crunch of gravel underneath Hale's boots breaks the silent tension as he marches up to the king and whispers into his ear. Kaigen watches as Balloch's smile turns into a scowl. They exchange a few more whispers, and Balloch lowers his bow. "You are of no use to me dead," he yells to Kaigen.

The frustration instantly consumes him. "I am of no use to you at all!" he yells back at the king, ripping the arrow from his shoulder and tossing it on the ground in front of him. "I am done letting you use me."

"Is that so?"

"It is."

"Well, let me give you an ultimatum." Balloch hands Hale his bow and slowly walks the distance between him and Kaigen. "You'll stay here and assist me when needed, or . . . I'll kill your son."

Kaigen leans in so their faces are mere inches apart. "If you kill my son, then I'll have nothing to lose."

Balloch tilts his head. "Then it appears we are at an impasse."

Kaigen's fist balls up, and he wants nothing more than to send a right hook across the king's jaw. But he lets out a deep exhale and unclenches his fist instead—better to bide his time.

Balloch's eyes move to the wound on Kaigen's shoulder. "Nasty cut. We'd better get that fixed up. I cannot have you bleeding out now."

"I'll be fine," Kaigen says, not willing to admit the pain stemming from the puncture.

"Nonsense. You really are a stubborn one." The king turns to the crowd. "Isla, see to it that this creature's wound is taken care of."

"Save it. I don't want any of your people laying a finger on . . ." Kaigen starts, but he trails off as a woman steps forward. Unlike the men around her—all wearing uniforms signifying that they fight for the king—she wears a long green dress. An elven dress.

"You look surprised, Kaigen," mocks Balloch.

Kaigen keeps his eyes on her, but says nothing.

Balloch continues, "We found her wandering around these parts about a year ago. She was all alone, claiming to be lost. My first thought was to kill her, for obvious reasons. But after discovering she was a healer, I gave her the choice of pledging her allegiance to me, or death. She proved to be wise enough to choose the former.

"It was difficult at times, but we took every step possible to hide her from you. I always suspected you were helping the elves, and I couldn't have you telling them we have one of their kind among us. Nor could I have you relaying information between Isla and the rest of them, assuming she was a spy. But I see no harm in the two of you getting acquainted now. After all, you won't be leaving us anytime soon. And she has since proved her loyalty in many different ways . . ."

Isla avoids Balloch's gaze. "Kaigen, is it? Come with me. I'll fix you up."

As she escorts Kaigen to a room he's visited once before—the only other time he was badly injured—he's fighting off the irritation of how easily the king wounded him. If the circumstances were different, the king and all of his subjects would be lying lifeless on the ground. But there is no sense in dwelling on that fact; Kaigen is more interested in this elf he now follows.

He sits on the bed and eyes her up and down. "Isla, is it?" She nods, laying out medical supplies as he continues his inquiry. "What did he mean when he spoke of your loyalty?"

"I do what I have to do . . . Same as you," she says.

"Same as me?"

"The king used to whisper around me, but he has since become rather comfortable in my presence. He speaks plainly of you, and all that you have done for him."

Kaigen clenches his jaw. "I did what I had to do." She nods in agreement. "So, you've been serving the king for a year now?"

"I do not serve that man. I serve the people of Mhorelia."

Kaigen chuckles. "I'm sure he sees it that way, too."

"I don't care how he sees it. That is the truth."

"My apologies, I didn't mean to offend you. People like us . . . we're survivors," Kaigen says, attempting to sound a bit more empathetic.

"You didn't seem to care about your survival earlier," Isla says as she starts to stitch his wound.

Kaigen doesn't even flinch as the needle pierces his skin. "You misunderstand me. I don't do any of this for my life; it's all for my son. Everything I do, I do for him."

"How admirable," she replies. "But what would life be for your son if he didn't have his father?"

"It wasn't an easy decision, but one I came to a long time ago. My life for his, *always*. And if it comes to that, I would hope one day he could understand why I did it."

She continues to stitch up the hole in his shoulder, dabbing the blood every so often as it drips down his arm. "That boy of yours, he's a good child."

"You've spoken with him?"

"I've patched him up a few times. Nothing major, just some cuts and scrapes from playing around the castle. For what it's worth, he seems to have a good outlook on life, given the circumstances."

"Thank you; that's good to hear."

She ties the last bit of twine off as she finishes the stitching. Then she wraps his shoulder with a thick cloth, pulling it just tight enough to apply a bit of pressure. "How does that feel?"

"Good as new." She moves to the door, but Kaigen grabs her arm. "I'd love to hear more about your time here, if you wouldn't mind staying a little while longer?"

She smiles. "I'd like that. But first I want to hear about your travels with the elves."

They sit side by side for the next hour, discussing everything that happened over the past year. He tells her about their quest and about all the adventures he's been on. She's very inquisitive about the elves, asking about how they met and what they're like. Although their mission to usurp Balloch is well known throughout Mhorelia, little is known about them specifically. He goes into great detail, speaking of their history and their backstories—her eyes lighting up when he speaks of Melara. But he doesn't ask her about it; instead, he moves on to discuss the fights they've had, the creatures they've encountered, and the laughs they've shared, and he tells her all about John.

She had heard murmurs throughout the castle about the Chosen One, but nothing concrete—the king had taken great care to keep any details a secret. The only thing Kaigen doesn't mention is Killian. Not only does he not want to dredge up those feelings in front of a stranger—albeit a pleasant and beautiful one—he isn't sure he can trust her yet, and he cannot let the king find out about Killian's death.

When it's her turn to talk, she tells him about her time living in the castle. It seems Balloch had gone to great lengths to ensure she and Kaigen never crossed paths. He had a cabin built for her in the forest, quite far from the castle. Guards kept watch on her at all times, and she was only to come see the king when he was certain Kaigen would not be around.

"I'm guessing you do not know much about the comings and goings around here, given the watch that Balloch has placed on you?" asks Kaigen.

"I should be offended," Isla responds with a smirk. "The soldiers around here are clueless, and I am an elf, after all. I did most of my snooping around at night, after the soldiers had finished their food and drink. And when the king had me visit the castle, I was always observing." She leans in close and whispers, "Balloch is up to something."

"I don't mean to offend you again, but Balloch is always up to something."

"That may be, but let me ask you this. How often does Balloch have a denaro visit him?"

Kaigen's eyes widen. "Ellioch? He hasn't called on him in years. You're sure of this?"

"Indeed. I saw the creature fly toward the castle at dusk about ten days ago. Since then, nothing."

She must be mistaken. Would Balloch really kill Ellioch? he thinks. "And you're positive the denaro never left?"

"Absolutely. Like I said, I've been keeping a very close watch since then. What do you think is going on?"

"I'm not sure. But if the king had Ellioch killed, I must find a way to alert the rest of the denaros. This may even sway them to join our cause, and we could use all the help we can get."

Isla flashes a look of concern. "You think the elves will fail if they go it alone? Even with the help of the Chosen One?"

"All I'm saying is that they are greatly outnumbered, and the odds are stacked against them. Any help they can get is not only appreciated, but necessary."

"Count me in," says Isla. "I've been lying in wait long enough."

"You know, I like you, Isla. Which is odd because I usually find elves to be hardheaded and tough to be around for long periods of time."

She chuckles. "I'll take that as a compliment. You're not so bad either . . . Despite what the men around here might say about you."

He lets out a laugh. "Pleasant *and* funny—that's a combination you rarely get in anyone. I'm finding it harder and harder to believe that you're actually an elf. That you're from the same family as those stubborn elves that I have been forced to travel with."

"Well, I can assure you that I am an elf. But I am not part of their family. At least not Lorena's or the twins'. I am a Cliff Elf, like Melara."

"A Cliff Elf?" Kaigen says, surprised.

"Yes. That's why I have stayed so far north for all these years."

"Hmm . . . I knew you and your kind were hunting past the cliffs, but I didn't know any of you were located this far north. Why were you traveling this close to the Enchanted Lands all alone?"

She leans in once more, whispering as quietly as she can into his ear: "I was not alone."

<h1 style="text-align:center">CHAPTER 30</h1>

Hope. That's what it is, the feeling that's rising in Kaigen. If the Cliff Elves are alive, then they will fight alongside John and the elves. And if the denaros choose to side with them as well . . . the scales start to tip in their favor.

"Do you know where the other Cliff Elves are?" Kaigen asks in a hushed voice.

"Not exactly," says Isla. "We meet up every time the moon is at its thinnest, exchanging information under the cover of darkness, just outside the castle walls."

Kaigen's head tilts. "If you can escape your guards and meet with the elves outside of the castle, why do you bother coming back here at all?"

"The king's men found me when I was out on a scouting mission. But before they could get to me, I hid my bow and anything that might signify I was a Cliff Elf. I made up a story of how I was a healer who had gotten lost looking for herbs, choosing to give myself up in order to stop them from searching for the rest of us.

"If I disappear now, he will send search parties after me. At least this way, my family can go on hunting without having to watch their backs."

Kaigen is beaming with admiration. "You really are one of a kind. I would've ditched this place long ago." She elbows him in the side and looks away, failing to hide her blushing cheeks. "The next new moon is almost upon us. Do you think you could get the word out that John and the others are on their way?"

"I would be honored," she says.

"In the meantime, I need to find a way to prove that Balloch killed Ellioch. And once I have the proof, I'll need to get that information to the rest of the denaros."

The unmistakable sound of armor clapping together approaches. The door flies open, and Balloch stands before them. "Well, look at you, all bandaged up, Kaigen." He turns to Isla. "A fine job as always. You may go now; your services are needed on the grounds." She nods and leaves the room swiftly. "Kaigen, something has come to my attention that I had not thought of before. I need a way to guarantee that you won't teleport off to see your friends when I'm not looking."

"You have my word, Balloch."

"Ha! Your word is garbage around here. No, no, no. I've got a better idea. Lucky for me, your little parlor trick is rather messy. So, if I see even a wee bit of purple residue lying around this castle . . . I'll kill your son. And another thing, you had better stay close to me for the time being. Because if I ever need you, I am going to holler out your name for all to hear, and if I do not hear you coming . . . I'll kill your son. Is that clear?"

"Clear."

"Good! Now let's try this out," Balloch says as he walks out and shuts the door. "Kaigen!"

Kaigen takes a deep breath and opens the door. "Yes, my king?"

"Very good, you are starting to get the hang of this," says Balloch with a wry smile. "Now I need to go prepare for your friends. For now, you may do whatever you'd like, but stay close." He winks before exiting down the hallway.

Kaigen slowly shuts the door behind him. Blood begins oozing from his wound again—at that moment, he realizes his body is still being consumed by the tension he feels in the king's presence. He tries to relax, but every time he thinks about Balloch, he sees only red. A small table sits in front of him, where

Isla's supplies were sitting a moment ago. He slams his fists down onto it, sending wood splintering in every direction. Satisfied with the results, he takes a deep breath and heads toward his living quarters. First he must rest, and then he'll formulate a plan.

Memories of Killian flood back to him as he tries to fall asleep, causing only more anguish. When he does finally doze off, his sleep is restless, filled with fears for the people he cares about: John and the elves will have to finish their journey alone, unknowingly walking into ambush after ambush; Kaigen will have to fight against them in the end, not knowing if he could really kill any of them; and then there's his son, trapped in this colossal mess.

He wakes covered in sweat, not convinced he got any sleep at all. The bags under his eyes are becoming more defined every day; he doesn't need his reflection to tell him that. Another hour of sleep would be beneficial—the stress and fatigue of his life are wearing him down bit by bit . . . But no matter, life goes on.

Deciding it's best that he make appearances throughout the castle, he spends some time wandering the grounds. The looks he gets from the inhabitants vary greatly. Some show shock; others show confusion, and some have no reaction at all. But most just have a general look of disdain. The king has clearly exaggerated when sharing the details of any traitorous acts Kaigen has done. Nobody says anything, though, and that delights Kaigen. He may be hated by most, but he's still feared by all.

Hunger sets in, and he finds his way to the dining hall. It's full of people, all sitting down to enjoy one of the daily meals provided by the Enchanted Lands. Kaigen scans the food—meats, grains, fruits, vegetables, and even desserts—all set up buffet style. The way they all gorge themselves while most of Mhorelia starves makes him sick. He plates his food and walks to the nearest table, with six soldiers seated around it, leaving no room for a seventh. But this is Kaigen's favorite table—placed near a window overlooking a dense Mhorelian forest—and this is where he'll be sitting.

A burly man sitting closest to Kaigen swallows his food and grumbles, "Move along, traitor."

Kaigen drops his plate on the table. "I think I'll be taking this seat, Captain."

"And I think you'd be wise to find another," the man says. "Or would you like us to *make you*?" The other five soldiers shift in their seats uncomfortably, slowly locating their weapon's hilts.

"I wouldn't make promises you aren't willing to keep," Kaigen taunts.

The man scoffs and looks back at his food. "You wouldn't fight us. Not while the king holds your son captive."

Kaigen leans in close. "Are you willing to take that risk?"

A palpable tension lingers as the men contemplate a fight. The captain takes another bite and chews it slowly, mulling over his options.

Oh, how Kaigen wants this . . .

The captain abruptly stands and kicks his stool behind him, getting face-to-face with Kaigen. But after a short standoff, he spits at Kaigen's feet. "You're not worth my time," he says, then grabs his tray and leaves. Kaigen stares at the other men, who still look tense and terrified.

"And what are you all waiting for?" he says.

They quickly grab their trays and scuffle away. Two of them drop their utensils, but nobody looks back—following the captain like a bunch of lemmings. Kaigen takes a seat and grins. "Cowards," he whispers to himself.

While he's happy his presence still causes unrest among these people, that won't help him with his plan. He needs to find a way to locate Ellioch without being seen. And then find a way to prove to the denaros that Balloch had Ellioch killed. This would be an easy task if he could teleport, but it's too risky; he'll have to find another way. Normally, the view from this seat at his favorite table would be enough to calm Kaigen—it has so many times before—but today, his anxieties are winning out. With guards stationed everywhere—all of whom will be on high alert—the task seems insurmountable.

Lost in his thoughts, a hand on his shoulder startles him. "How'd you sleep?" says Isla.

"I'll manage," he says, breathing a sigh of relief.

His stomach fills with butterflies as she sits down next to him, a feeling he hasn't felt in a long time. *It's because she's been so kind to Isaiah,* he tells himself, but he knows it's more than that. "You shouldn't be seen with me. I don't want to give the king any reason to punish you."

"Relax, Kaigen. I do not fear Balloch. Besides, I'm just here to check on your bandage." She winks and examines his shoulder. "Now tell me, how much progress have you made?"

Kaigen looks away, embarrassed. "None at all. Unless you count making a few more enemies as progress?"

Isla laughs. "I don't mean to shatter your illusion, but those men never really cared for you."

He smirks. "An astute observation," he says, his smile quickly fading. "To be truthful, I just don't see how I am going to walk these halls without detection. The king has men standing at all corners, and as you said yourself, these men *do not* care for me."

Isla tightens the bandage around Kaigen's wound. "I may have found a way around that."

He perks up. "How do you mean?"

"The king has a feast planned for tomorrow evening. A way to boost morale before the Chosen One gets here."

"Why does he feel he needs to boost morale? Everyone seems to be thriving here."

Isla lowers her voice. "Ever since the Chosen One showed up, the king has been rather preoccupied with him. He's been pushing his soldiers to the brink of exhaustion—ten hours a day, every day—preparing. There have been murmurs floating around the castle that he's lost his mind, that his paranoia borders on madness. He told the soldiers that the feast is a reward, but that is not the case . . . He fears a mutiny."

Kaigen stifles his laughter. He knows more than anyone just how mad the king truly is. John showing up may have worsened his madness, but it was always there. "If there's a time when the halls will be unguarded, that's when I must act. How much time do you suppose I'll have?"

"I would guess most of the night, but people may come and go as they like, so stay vigilant."

A thought pops into Kaigen's head as he takes a bite of food. "What if he requests my services at the feast?"

She chuckles. "He wants to *boost* morale. I can promise you that you won't be invited."

Kaigen nearly chokes on his food as the joke catches him off guard. They both laugh for a moment, but Kaigen stops suddenly. Balloch has entered the dining hall, followed closely by the captain that Kaigen harassed earlier . . . and neither of them looks happy.

"I'd better go," says Isla.

"Wait. Before you go, how did you come by this information about the king? I wouldn't have guessed that he would share his personal thoughts with you," Kaigen says.

Her eyes drop. "I've had to do terrible things since I arrived here. Things to make the king happy. And when the king is happy, he talks . . ."

She leaves hastily. Kaigen's eyes are trained on Balloch now, a ferocity building inside of him. The two men approach him with an attitude that sets him off immediately. "You cried to the king like some petulant child?"

The captain steps back, and Balloch steps between them. "Easy now, let's put that knife down," says Balloch.

Kaigen looks down, finally realizing he's still gripping the knife in his hand. He tosses it aside. "Sure thing. I won't need it," he says as he takes another step toward the captain.

"Whoa, whoa, whoa. Let's not lose our heads," Balloch says as he pushes Kaigen back. "Now, the captain tells me that you were being rather hostile earlier and that you took his table. Is this true?"

Kaigen's lips slowly curl upward. "It is."

"Now, I cannot have you running around and pestering my men. Whether it looks like it or not, you're a prisoner here. And you will treat your guards with respect."

"Prisoner . . . Is that so?" says Kaigen.

"It is," says the king. "Now I need you to apologize to this man, or face the repercussions of your actions."

Kaigen's face turns hot with hatred. "You want me to apologize?"

"I do, and I will not ask you again," Balloch warns.

"Fine," Kaigen says through gritted teeth. He grabs his tray of food and makes his way to the captain's side, mustering up his most patronizing tone. "I am *so* deeply sorry for threatening to kill you earlier. I hope you will find it in your heart to forgive me . . . *Rat*."

Kaigen doesn't wait for a response. He just trudges off to his chambers and scarfs down the remainder of his food. Figuring it's best to let things cool off, he lies in his bed and lets his mind wander. However, as the time passes, his thoughts keep coming back to the same thing . . . Isla. Her beauty, her tenacity, her laugh. Everything about her reminds him so much of his beloved Marion. The thought of her brings back feelings he has tried to push down for a long time. He closes his eyes, relenting to those feelings as exhaustion sets in, a single tear falling down his cheek.

Chapter 31

Nightfall came hours ago, and the others are sure to be getting worried. John can only hope they stuck to the plan—once you are back at the campsite, you do not go out again. Nothing worse than everyone wandering around in the darkness.

He almost made that mistake years ago on a mission in South Africa. Jenny and Lucy were out doing recon, set to return to camp no more than two hours later. The night went on, however, and they did not return. John couldn't get the idea out of his head that they might be lying dead in a ditch somewhere. It was two in the morning when he decided to go out looking. Carl and Ben pleaded with him to stay, stalling him for another ten minutes. Thankfully they did, too, because just as he was about to leave, the twins returned unscathed. Apparently, they had gotten stuck in the enemy's camp and had to wait until everyone went off to bed in order to escape unnoticed. It was a valuable reminder of the importance of patience, one he tries to keep with him at all times.

Keeping with that theme, John waits patiently for Darian to open up. In the past forty-eight hours, he lost his twin brother, and he brutally killed five men—he *needs* to open up. Holding on to that much pain alone . . . it's bound to take a toll on him.

But after a while, it's clear he won't be opening up on his own, which puts John in another dilemma—he's never been great at consoling others. It's not that he isn't compassionate; he has just always struggled to find the right words. He tries many times with Darian, opening his mouth to speak, but nothing comes out. It takes Darian speaking to end the empty silence.

"John, you don't have to say anything. I know what I did, and it will not happen again."

He hadn't realized his attempts to speak were so noticeable, or misinterpreted. "It's not that, Darian . . ."

"Oh," says Darian, stopping to place a hand on John's shoulder. "Please do not feel as though you have to comfort me."

"I don't feel as though it's my job, or anything like that. I just—"

"It has nothing to do with it being your job to comfort me," Darian interrupts, "and everything to do with the fact that you are suffering too. You all are. Just because he was my brother, does not mean that you have to be strong for me. We will get through this *together*."

At that moment, John realizes he hadn't taken as much time to get to know Darian. Killian was cheerful and fun—an easy combination to bond with. But Darian was always the more stoic one, strong and honest too. And this maturity . . . this empathy . . . it almost brings John to tears. "I miss him, Darian."

Darian wraps John in his arms. "I know, John. I miss him too." John holds the embrace longer than he expected before wiping his eyes and continuing on.

Darian and John can see a fire in the distance as they approach the camp. Much to John's relief, he hears voices as they grow nearer. Concerned voices, but voices nonetheless. He calls out with the signal they had agreed upon: the hoot of an owl. *"Ooo. Ooo."*

Melara sends the signal back, signifying that everything is alright to proceed. John tries not to laugh, but even though Melara is the best at producing a convincing owl sound, it still sounds brutally off-key. Darian looks to John in amusement. "What dying animal is that supposed to be?" John laughs even harder as they emerge from the forest.

Melara and Lorena stand unamused, staring at the two of them as they approach. Oblirian sleeps by the fire, seemingly apathetic toward the whole situation. John can see the worry plastered on Darian's face—he knows he messed up. Hoping to get ahead of it, he dives right in. "You have to understand, I was grie—"

Lorena thrusts her arms around Darian and squeezes him tight. "I'm so glad you're alright!"

John pulls Melara aside. "You were right; he went looking for trouble."

Melara shakes her head. "And did he find it?"

John nods. "But I don't believe he'll go looking again."

"Good," she whispers emphatically, then heads to Darian. He opens his arms for another hug, but she just shoves him in the chest. "Don't you ever run away again, understood?"

"Understood," he says.

"She's right; we need to stay together," says Lorena. "Now more than ever."

"Understood," Darian says again. "I just—"

"Why you left is not important," Melara cuts in, "as long as you don't do it again." She throws John and Darian each a rag. "Now clean the blood off yourselves and join us around the fire."

John hadn't noticed the blood, but as the fire now fully illuminates them, it's impossible to miss. They find a nearby stream and wash themselves as clean as they can. The thin crescent moon casts a faint light upon the red water running off of John, and he can't help but think how much more bloodshed is yet to come.

Once they are sufficiently washed, they head back to camp and have a seat next to Oblirian. She lays her head on John's lap, and he runs his hand over her fur, giving him a little bit of comfort after a long and taxing day. No part of him wants to discuss what's coming—some shut-eye would be better—but he knows they must. "So, what's next for us?"

Lorena starts by flattening a patch of dirt in front of her. "We are here"—she draws an "X" in the dirt, followed by a straight line—"and if we travel up this path that leads straight ahead, we will get to the king's gate in a day's time." She then draws a line to signify the gate, and behind it, a bunch of circles. "He will likely keep most of his army behind the gate, with maybe a few guards to sound the alarm if we are seen. It is of the utmost importance that we remain undetected."

"Is that gate the only entrance?" asks John.

"Unfortunately, it appears to be," Lorena responds. "The forest around the castle is so dense, with vines so thick, that it is known to be impassable. And where there is no forest, Balloch built a wall so smooth and so sturdy, it is neither scalable nor breakable."

"Kaigen mentioned that to me when I first got here," says John. "Could we go around the wall?"

Darian shakes his head. "Did Kaigen also mention that the ground drops off at the edge of the wall?"

John thinks back. "I believe he did say something about a 'thousand-foot drop.'"

"One cannot be sure of the exact height, but if you fell from there, you would most certainly perish," says Lorena.

"So, we cannot go through the wall, we cannot go around the wall, and we cannot go over the wall . . . Could we go under the wall?" asks Darian.

Lorena shakes her head again. "The wall is so thick, and the ground so hard, it would take at least a full cycle of the moon for us to dig beneath it."

Melara shrugs. "So, our only option is to take out the guards at the gate? And then what? Knock?"

"Knock? That's your best solution?" John says. "Are you saying that you never had a plan for what you would do once you reached the gate?"

Lorena's shoulders slump and she looks toward the ground. "I suppose we never had the liberty to look that far ahead."

The frustration among the elves is mounting. John didn't mean to stir the pot any more than it already was, but to leave home without a full plan . . . Foolish. He attempts to rein in their emotions by moving the conversation along. "Say we find a way inside, then what?"

Lorena lets out a sigh. "*If* we can make it through the gate undetected, we will be vastly outnumbered, and Balloch will certainly be ready for us."

John chuckles. "So basically, they have the unstoppable force *and* the immovable object?" Confused faces stare back at him. "Sorry, just a paradox we sometimes reference back home. It's not important."

"Is there anything we have that could give us an edge in this battle?" Darian asks in a defeated tone.

"Nope," says Melara.

"Well, that's not entirely true," says John.

"How so?" Lorena asks.

"As it stands, we have the element of surprise. And that will always give us a leg up," John says.

"How do you suppose we have the element of surprise?" Melara asks. "Didn't you hear Lorena? Balloch knows we are coming."

"True. However, he doesn't know *when* we are coming. If I were him, I'd assume we would attack at night, and use the cover of darkness to our advantage."

They all nod in agreement.

"Well," John continues, "why don't we attack at dawn?"

"John," Darian says, mulling it over. "That . . . that could actually work."

"Not only will they not expect it, but they will have stayed up all night in anticipation of our arrival," adds Melara.

"Yes! They will be exhausted and caught off guard. That could definitely give us a much-needed edge," says Lorena.

Their faces are beaming as they sit with a new glimmer of hope. But Lorena's smile quickly fades into a frown. "Even if we catch them off guard, we will still have to fight through waves of Balloch's men. It might not be enough."

"She's right," says Melara. "Even if we surprise them, even if we find a way into Balloch's castle, even if Kaigen somehow remains on our side . . . we are still outnumbered."

"It makes me wonder if we should even attempt it," says Darian.

Nobody outright agrees with Darian's comment, but nobody dismisses it either. All this pessimism is giving John a headache. They have faced the worst odds imaginable at every step of this journey, and now that the end is finally within reach, they are speaking of throwing in the towel? It's not lost on him that this is the point where Killian would normally spread his feelings of optimism throughout the group. But Killian is gone, and someone needs to step up.

John stares into the fire as he speaks, the flames dancing in the reflection of his eyes. "We are not giving up. We have come too far, and you all have given far too much for this cause. I stumbled into your lives by chance, and all I wanted to do was get back home. But that is no longer my objective. You all have shown me a beautiful new world, a world that has been taken from you, and a world that *must* be taken back. It's times like these when you have to ask yourself what matters most, and to me . . . that is you. So tomorrow morning, I'm going to march toward that wretched man who calls himself a king and take back the land that was stolen from you . . . Now who's with me?"

"Yes!" Darian blurts out. "I will follow you anywhere."

"As will I," says Melara.

"Here, here," says Lorena.

"That settles it," John says. "I say we all get some rest before we begin the final march. I know I could use it."

"Agreed," says Lorena.

"And maybe a plan will come to us in our dreams," says Darian.

John suppresses a laugh after realizing he's not kidding, and they all turn in for the night. It doesn't take long for John to fall into REM sleep, his subconscious mind taking him to places he hasn't been in years. He relives several missions he went on with The Undesirables—some pleasant, and some unpleasant. The most vivid of them is his trip to the Amazon rainforest in South America. They had been walking for days in the dense undergrowth, the humidity never dropping below ninety percent, and John couldn't take it any longer. He and Carl found a thick patch of trees and started climbing, maneuvering from branch to vine as they went. It must've taken close to forty-five minutes to make the climb, ascending over one hundred feet in the air. But when they reached the canopies of those trees, they experienced a bliss unlike any other.

Truthfully, the humidity probably wasn't much different at the top of the trees than at the bottom, but it sure did feel like it. Both of them sported ear-to-ear grins as they looked out over the roof of the forest, their claustrophobic feelings receding. It felt as if they were breathing air for the first time in their lives. In fact, from where they were sitting, it was almost as if—

John bolts awake and crawls to Lorena, shaking her shoulder gently. She whips around and barely restrains a punch aimed at his temple. "Sorry! It's just me," he whispers.

"What is it, John? What's wrong?" she says, her brow furrowed in concern.

"Nothing. Nothing is wrong. It's just . . . I think I know how we can get past the king's gate."

CHAPTER 32

Kaigen's dreams the night before were filled with memories of his beloved Marion, intertwined with thoughts of Isla. The similarities the two of them share are uncanny, and their reminiscence gave him the first good night's sleep he's had in weeks.

Now he flips his dagger by the blade, catching it by the handle as he sits on his bed. Over and over, he flips the weapon, wondering why the king never made him relinquish it. Probably another power play—Balloch knows he would never dare use it while his son is still the king's captive. As he waits, his sadness for Marion wanes; now, instead of feeling grief, having her presence in his mind drives him forward. That, and the last words she ever said to him: *"Keep him safe."*

A knock on the door brings him back to the present. His mood rises at the thought of Isla on the other side of the door. But it sinks quickly as a guard enters with breakfast.

"The king thought you might be hungry," says the guard. "You didn't show up to the dining hall this morning."

"Decided to sleep a little later. Wanted to conserve my energy . . . in case I need it."

"Hmph," the guard grunts. "Well, get out while you can, because the king doesn't want you around later tonight."

Kaigen makes his best attempt to feign confusion. "And why is that?"

"None of your concern."

So Isla was right.

The breakfast he received from the guard is a lavish one, filled with fruits, meats, breads, and a large cup of juice—yet another feeble attempt from the king to show he cares, or at least put a speck of doubt in Kaigen's brain. Either way, it won't work. Kaigen's mind was made up about the king long ago, and it isn't changing because of some delicious food spread. If anything, this is yet another reminder of the king's monstrosities, eating like this every day while others claw for scraps . . . It's despicable. There's no reason he shouldn't eat it, though—he's already feeling stronger from the meal he had yesterday. Bite by bite, he savors it; the fuel he will need for the fight that is coming.

***

The castle is still bustling by late afternoon, and Kaigen is getting restless. Being cooped up in his room has given him time to formulate a plan, but now he just wants to act. The plan is simple: sneak out when everyone is at the feast, then find evidence that Ellioch has been murdered. Completing this task isn't as simple, but he's got an idea of where to start. Isla has assured him that Ellioch's body has not left the castle, and if that is true, there are only three locations where the king could hide a body of that size without someone accidentally stumbling upon it: the Dueling Aisle in the southeast corner of the castle, where soldiers can battle with wooden swords to see who is the better fighter; the Western Tower, a tower that is said to be haunted and is seldom occupied; or the High Hall of Contemplation, a wide open area at the top of the castle where King Umor would go anytime he sought peace.

Since the Dueling Aisle is the closest to his quarters, and will have the least amount of prying eyes, he will start there. But first, he needs to find Isla and see if she got the word out to the other Cliff Elves. The only question is how to speak with her without the king becoming suspicious—he refuses to let anyone else he cares about get hurt.

He tries to walk normally as he strolls through the castle. It's one of those things you never have to think about until you're walking with an ulterior motive. He gets a few side glances from passersby, but nobody questions him. Assuming he's free to roam the common areas, he tries the dining hall first, but there's no sign of Isla. Then he checks the training grounds, with no luck. But as he passes the throne room, he hears her voice—such a striking voice. Relief comes to him, but just as he's about to enter, he hears another voice, Balloch's. He stops short of the entry, knowing he has no reason to be there, and no real reason to seek out Isla.

His heart is pounding, and he can feel his shoulder wound pulsing in pain with every beat. He had forgotten how much of a burden it was to be injured, but as he stares at the bandage, another thought comes to mind—the painfully obvious solution to his problem. Without giving himself time to talk himself out of it, he reaches across his shoulder and rips the bandage off, stitches and all.

Blood pours down his arm—much more blood than he had anticipated—and he lets out a silent groan in agony. But again, he mustn't enter right away. It would be too much of a coincidence if the bandage was just barely torn off. He quickly retraces his steps for the last hundred feet, dripping blood along the stone floor as he walks. Then he drops the bandage in a dimly lit corner of the castle and sprints back to the doorway, yelling Isla's name as he runs.

He bursts through the door, and she immediately runs to his side. "What happened?"

"Caught it on a stone a ways back . . . Can't see a thing in these hallways," he lies.

She eyes the gash on his shoulder. "I can stop the bleeding, but I'll need my other supplies to sew you up. I only have my small bag with me."

"Helping the king with a splinter, I suppose," mocks Kaigen.

"Watch that snarky tone," Balloch spits back.

Isla wraps his shoulder with another white cloth. "Why didn't you teleport to me?"

"I had no idea where you were. And besides . . ." Kaigen looks toward the king.

Balloch laughs. "Ah yes, I may have banned teleporting for the time being."

She shoots Balloch an annoyed look.

"Fine. Go, go! I cannot have him bleeding out in my throne room," says Balloch. Isla and Kaigen hastily take their leave. "Wait!" he yells at them. "Once you are done, send him to his quarters. I do not want to see his face for the rest of the evening." She nods, and they swiftly exit before he can yell out any other demands.

Not a word is spoken until they get to her supply room, as neither of them is sure who could be waiting around each corner. Once inside, she slams the door and ushers Kaigen onto a cushioned bed, with white linens laid out upon it.

"Why would you tear these stitches out?" she asks as she cleans the wound before reapplying the stitches.

He shrugs his shoulders. "Tear them out? Didn't you hear? I caught them on a stone."

She shakes her head. "He may have bought that, but I'm not as naive as he is. Now drink this; you must be in a great deal of pain." She holds out a vial of liquid.

"No. I need my head clear for the rest of the night," he says, pushing the vial away.

"Suit yourself. But how do you plan on finding anything when you are to be confined to your quarters?"

"Never mind that; I will find a way," he assures her. "It's more important that you got word to your friends on the outside. So, did you?"

"Keep your voice down," she says as her eyes dart to the locked door. "I was able to get a message to them last night. They are going to find a high point in the surrounding trees to survey the castle for the next few days. If John and the others arrive, they will be ready."

"Good, then all I have to do now is find Ellioch," Kaigen says as she finishes the last stitch in his shoulder.

She wraps a larger cloth around the wound, tying it snug. Before he can stand, she places a hand on his cheek and leans in close. "Kaigen, whatever happens . . ." She pauses as they stare into each other's eyes.

Then there's a hard knock on the door. "Open up! It's time to pack it in for the night," yells a guard.

"Just finishing up!" Isla yells back at him. Then, turning to Kaigen, she whispers, "Just be careful."

She rushes out past the guard, who then escorts Kaigen to his room. Usually he would have a few quips for the guard as they walk, but he follows in silence instead, his only focus on the task at hand.

Once inside his quarters, the door slams behind him, and, much to his dismay, he doesn't hear the guard leave. *Well, this changes things . . .* "Balloch has you on guard duty tonight, I see," he says through the door. No response. "Well, just don't come into my room, and we won't have any problems."

"Hmph," the guard grunts.

Unfortunately, the only other option—besides killing the guard—is to go out the window and scale his way down. Not great, but not impossible. The walls on the front of the castle may be a smooth surface, but not as much care was taken on the back walls where Kaigen's room is located.

About an hour later, the last rays of sunlight set behind the castle walls. *Time to get to work.* Kaigen looks out his bedroom window and sighs . . . About a thirty-foot drop—it wouldn't kill him, but he would definitely break something. The thought does cross his mind to leap from the window and then teleport, but that still leaves a small chance of leaving behind some purple residue. A chance he isn't willing to take.

Once he's shrouded in darkness, he quietly places a chair under his door handle and starts his descent down the wall.

Without the light of the moon, he has to move almost entirely by feel. Some of the rocks were laid better than others, so traversing the wall proves to be harder than he thought. Five minutes in, and his forearms are burning. Fear creeps in as he looks down and sees what little progress he's made. But then, he catches a break; his foot brushes up against a bulky, poorly placed rock, jutting a full six inches out of the castle wall.

Finally, he can rest for a moment. Making sure his full weight is on the rock, he removes one hand at a time, straightening and flexing his forearms to give them some much-needed relief.

But the rock suddenly breaks free.

He slams his arms against the wall, managing to grip one rock with his right hand, barely able to hang on. His legs flail at the stones beneath him, desperately trying to find footholds. After a few seconds, he manages to secure himself. They're small holds, but they'll have to do.

"What was that?" a voice calls from around the corner of the castle wall.

Kaigen freezes. If they discover him now, it's all over. Two men emerge, looking curiously into the darkness as Kaigen flattens himself against the wall.

"I swear I heard something," the voice says, now directly beneath him.

Kaigen's arm is burning, and he can feel his grip loosening from the rock he now perilously clings to. Maybe he could drop down and kill them quickly enough... No, it's too risky; someone could hear. But then, just when he believes he can't hold on any longer, he forces himself to remember who this is all for. For his new friends, for Mhorelia, and most of all, for Isaiah.

He glances down just as one of the men trips on the sheared rock. "Ow, what is this?" the man blurts out.

Kaigen has to think fast. As the two men bend down to examine the rock, he quietly breaks a small piece of stone from the wall with his free hand, then hurls it backward. It clinks against something in the darkness, and the men jump up, drawing their swords and walking toward the noise.

"Nothing to be afraid of," one of them says nervously.

"Whoever you are, show yourself!" yells the other.

A small animal scurries between their legs, and they both hack at it wildly, catching its back half before it can escape. "Ha! Didn't realize you were afraid of a little rodent," mocks the man.

"Shut up!" says the other. "Let's just get back to the feast. I'm starving."

As they round the corner, Kaigen allows himself a heavy exhale of relief before finishing his downward climb. Once he's on the ground, he walks around the opposite corner of the castle, taking care to keep close to the wall. The Dueling Aisle has a long row of windows at ground level, the closest of which Kaigen jumps through to investigate. Nobody seems to be around, so he makes quick work of the room to find nothing.

Next up, the Western Tower—a tall tower with a small entryway at its base, but a large trapdoor at the top. If Balloch were keeping the body here, he would've had to meet Ellioch at the top of the tower and kill him there. It's unlikely, but absolutely possible.

After running a short distance across a small courtyard, he finds the door unlocked. Two small vermin attempt to dash between his legs. He stomps on one of them, killing it, its blood coating the floor. "Disgusting," he says quietly, wiping his foot off on the doorframe.

A circular staircase lines the inside of the tower, with windows every twenty steps. Looking up through the center of the staircase, he can see the trapdoor is wide open, giving him a clear view of the new moon. That, along with the thin rays of light shining through the windows, is the only means of illumination. He'd love nothing more than to just teleport to the top, but the stairs will have to do.

Step by step, he climbs the dilapidated tower. A thin layer of dust coats the inside, webs cover the walls, and every creak of the staircase sounds like a whisper from a forgotten era. A chill runs down Kaigen's spine, and he grabs hold of his dagger. It's not as if he believes the tower to be haunted, but he can't deny the ominous feeling that hangs in the air.

When he's about halfway up the staircase, the trapdoor unexpectedly slams shut, and what little light it allowed in disappears. The only light left is the crisscrossing beams coming from the windows. Kaigen quickly conceals himself in the shadows of the tower; that door didn't close on its own. *What could it be?* The answer soon comes to him; well, actually, it sticks to him. He barely touched one of the webs that line the walls, but he can't seem to move his arm . . .

Spiders.

Terror flows through Kaigen's body like water through a riverbed. He *hates* spiders. Luckily, his fear of them as a child forced him to learn everything there is to know about them. Like how they can't see well in the dark, and how they rely on smell and touch to find their prey.

He has to act fast; just by touching the web, he's already alerted the spider to his position. A pebble lying two stairs above him will do the trick. He grabs it and flicks it down toward the rodent carcass at the bottom of the stairs, sending a vibration pinging through the web. Hopefully that, and the smell of the dead body, will be enough. All he can do now is wait.

The sounds of it descending through the tower will haunt Kaigen forever. The sound of it slowly unspooling its web, the way it rubs its legs together, the slow chattering of its teeth . . . It takes everything in Kaigen's power not to teleport far, far away from here.

He steals a glance as it crosses the shadow he has retreated to. Every detail about the thing makes his skin crawl: its beady eyes, its thick fur, its pointed legs. He doesn't even allow himself an exhale as it moves past him in the darkness. He just reaches out with a quickness he didn't know he possessed, and cuts the lone silk strand, without making a sound. The noise that follows is one that finally pleases him—the spider falling to its timely death. But just to be sure, Kaigen cuts his other arm free, detaches a hefty stone from a nearby window, and hurls it to the bottom of the tower. A muffled crunch soon follows—another pleasing sound.

He sprints the remaining stairs, knife in hand in case his last victim has friends nearby. When he reaches the top, he throws the trapdoor open and happily exits the tower, but Ellioch is nowhere to be seen. Staring across the courtyard, he's now at eye level with the High Hall of Contemplation. *Of course, it had to be there,* he thinks; the hardest place to access unnoticed. The High Hall of Contemplation has a flat roof, supported by eight tall pillars instead of walls, and is open to the elements, with one large staircase leading down into the castle. It's the only place that really makes sense, as Ellioch could just fly right in.

He stands no chance of climbing the steps from within the castle; he'd have to pass about a dozen places where guards could be stationed, let alone the king's feast. No, the only way in is by teleporting, but he mustn't leave any trace. He isn't concerned with the tower—no one is visiting its viewing platform any time soon—but for the High Hall of Contemplation, he'll have to try the roof, then climb his way down.

Kaigen leaves quite a bit of residue where he teleports to, but nobody will notice from below. Now there's the matter of climbing down. He leans over the edge, and his stomach sinks. "How am I possibly going to get—" *Oh no . . .* He's interrupted by a thought, a terrible, disgusting thought. He teleports back to the tower before he can talk himself out of it, returning moments later with his hands now wrapped in the spider's webs.

Mentally blocking out the feeling of the webs clinging to his hands, he finds the corner of the roof and hangs his body over the edge. His hands stick without issue to the stone pillar, making his descent to the bottom a swift one. Safely there, he does his best to remove the webs, first cutting at them with his dagger, then scraping them on the floor. Some pieces remain, but he'll find a way to wash them off soon enough. Now it's time to find Ellioch.

The openness of this place has always made Kaigen rather uncomfortable—there's nowhere to hide. He dashes across the open floor and locates the staircase. Peering down into the darkness, he can't see much, but the coast looks to be clear. There are no lamps lit, nor torches hung. Windows line the wall, but they're no help to Kaigen's sight. As he creeps into the room, his eyes slowly adjust. The benches that line the wall begin to take shape, the door to his left becomes visible, and lying directly in the center of the room . . . Ellioch.

Kaigen kneels before the creature and places his hand on its chest, wishing it would rise. But it won't. There's no telling the time of death; a denaro's magic stays with it long after it's gone, so it can take years to see even the faintest bit of decay.

A somber mood overtakes Kaigen. He didn't know Ellioch all that well, but he knew the creature to be kind at heart. And although he thinks the denaros can be stubborn at times, they truly are a majestic species.

His mind remains in a trance for some time. He knew the likelihood of finding Ellioch murdered, but a part of him still thought he was just being paranoid. That the king would never do such a thing. But the proof is right in front of him. Proof that the king is just as sick and ruthless as he had previously thought. It's also proof that the king is getting desperate.

Kaigen has to find a way to get word to the other denaros, but how? He looks around, not exactly sure what he's looking for, but hoping to find something useful. As he backs away from the body, he knocks over a bucket that's concealed in the darkness.

"Did you hear that?" comes a voice from beyond the door.

Kaigen's brain snaps back into focus. *Of course there would be guards . . .* His mind reels. Should he leave? Where would he go? The guards would no doubt find the evidence he was here. So, what then? Hide? A key slides into the door, and the lock turns. Right as the door swings open, Kaigen quickly lifts Ellioch's wing and pulls it over himself.

Sounds are muffled under the wing, but he can hear at least two men searching the room.

"Is someone there?"

"I can't see a thing."

"What's that over there?"

"It's that creature, you moron."

"No, not that! I meant behind the bird!"

One of the men trips over the denaro and cries out. "I cut my leg on the talons!" He kicks it. "Stupid bird!"

Kaigen is trying as hard as he can not to make a sound. Lying vulnerably on his back, he longs for the time when he could just rise and kill them both. But if they find him out, that may be his only option.

"This is no use. We need the torches."

He hears their footsteps as they run out of the room. When he can no longer hear them, Kaigen jumps out from under the wing. There's a light at the end of the hallway; he doesn't have much time. Bending a knee, he takes a handful of feathers and cuts them off with his dagger, whispering an apology into Ellioch's ear. Then he closes his eyes, snaps his fingers, and the feathers are gone.

Now he must escape. Maybe he can climb back up the pillar? At the end of the hallway, the men are rounding the corner. There's no time. He runs toward a nearby window and dives out of it. As he plummets toward the ground, he can only hope the purple powder he leaves behind will be spread thin enough and go unnoticed.

Poof!

He falls onto his bed with a thud. Purple covers the floor.

"What was that?" yells the guard outside his door.

"Nothing! Just tripped," Kaigen yells back as he frantically swipes the powder under his bed.

"Open up!" the guard replies as he attempts to open the door. The chair Kaigen wedged under the handle holds him out . . . for now.

He grabs a blanket and keeps sweeping. "One second!" But as Kaigen looks around the room, he knows that no amount of time would be enough to hide this mess.

"I said, *open up!*" the guard yells again, slamming into the door and bursting into the room.

The two lock eyes, and before the man can speak, Kaigen's dagger is stuck between his eyes. He drops dead instantly, his red blood mixing with the purple powder on the floor. Kaigen stares at the scene before him and sighs . . .

"I told you not to come into my room."

CHAPTER 33

Dawn is approaching, and John stands at the base of the densest forest he has ever seen. An array of weaving vines connects the trees, barring him and the others from going any farther. He places his hand on the nearest trunk, and his eyes follow it to the top.

"Are you sure about this?" says Lorena.

"I don't see another option," he replies.

Melara looks to the skyline, which grows more orange by the minute. "We must go now if we are to make it to the wall before dawn."

Oblirian brushes up against John. He places his head on hers and brushes her soft fur. "You must stay here and wait for our signal." Oblirian growls back at John. "I know, I know. We won't be long, though. Do you see that path?" John points to the path leading onward. "A short distance down that path is Balloch's gate. We'll find a way to open it so that you can join the fight with us." Oblirian backs away and lies down in the grass.

"She will wait for us," says John.

"It's amazing how fast you two have bonded," says Lorena.

"There's just something about her."

Melara clears her throat. "Eh-hem . . . Whenever you two are done *chitchatting*, we've got a forty-foot climb ahead of us."

And so, with each of them grabbing a vine, they start their ascent. Even after taking only what they deem necessary—weapons, water, a bit of food, and a small amount of oil if they need light in the forest—their climb is slow-going. John had expressed his concern over bringing the oil—the last thing they need is a forest fire when they're trapped inside of it—but he was overruled. Some of the vines are nearly as thick as the trees they encircle, forcing them to jump from one to another and travel deeper into the forest. Half an hour in, and they've gone much farther forward than they have vertically—thick clumps of vines and branches blocking their way up. A feeling of claustrophobia grows in John's mind, and as he surveys the others, the same feeling shows on their faces as well.

Another half hour and they reach a cluster of limbs and vines that serves as a floor for them to rest. Sweat drips down John's face as he finishes what's left of his water pouch. Heavy breathing is all he can hear as they sit to catch their breath. Then a small stream of light shines through the canopies of the trees and hits Lorena's face. Her eyes sparkle as it passes over them, and John is filled with a sense of relief. "We must be nearing the top."

Melara stands. "And we are also running out of time."

Darian does the same. "She's right. If we do not arrive soon, Balloch will have time to change out his guards, and they will be much more rested than we are."

John sighs. *Once this is all over, I'll never take downtime for granted again.*

Lorena extends her hand and helps John to his feet. "Let's go kill a king."

The last bit of forest proves easier than the first—the vines and branches serving as stairs that they can walk over, rather than cling to. It's not long before they reach the end, thirty feet off the ground with only a wall of thinly woven vines separating them from Balloch.

John peeks his head out past the vines to get a lay of the land. The forest extends to his left until it meets the wall that the others spoke of. To his right, he can see the gate, followed by more forest, and then more wall. Directly in front of him stand the outer walls of Balloch's castle. They're remarkably imposing and utterly impenetrable, except for a massive set of wooden doors at the front. An oddly placed tree has grown between the gate and the castle walls, but John doesn't think too much of it. What he is searching for are guards, and he doesn't see any.

Melara notices this as well. "We must have just made it—"

The front doors of the castle slowly swing open, and two rows of soldiers file through them, led by Hale.

Melara sits back against a tree, defeated. "There goes our chance at a surprise attack."

"Not necessarily . . ." Darian says as he watches the king's men.

They walk in perfect unison until they reach the large, misplaced tree that looms over everyone. There they get into formation, four rows of twenty-five at least. Even though they don't all look like soldiers, John still doesn't like those odds, and there are sure to be more inside the castle. "Are you seeing something I'm not?" he says to Darian.

"Kind of a weird spot for a tree, isn't it?" Darian points out.

John takes a closer look at the tree, standing just a bit taller than all the rest that surround them. "Well, yeah. But I don't see what that has to do with anyth—"

Then he recognizes it. It's a Tree of Light.

Darian grabs his bow and takes a knee. "Look, I know it's a long shot, but what if we use that tree as our diversion?"

Lorena grabs her bow as well. "A Tree of Light's bark is tougher than most. The only arrows that will penetrate it are the ones given to us by Leon."

Melara removes them from her quiver. "We have ten shots. Let's make them count."

John is completely confused. While he recognizes the tree, he doesn't quite see how that helps them.

"You still have that lighter, John?" asks Lorena.

John's eyes widen. "Oh, you all are crazy . . . You're going to blow up the tree?"

"Got a better idea?" says Melara.

"Aim for the light spot, halfway up the tree," says Darian.

Then suddenly, Hale starts screaming at his soldiers. "Today, we stand as one! To stop a group of tyrants from taking what is rightfully ours!"

The group of soldiers follows his words with a loud chant: "Ooo! Ooo! Ooo!"

"Time your shots with the chants," Lorena says.

Hale continues, "They walk with an outsider, one who does not belong in our world!"

"Ooo! Ooo! Ooo!" they chant as the arrows fly, hitting the tree in quick succession.

"So I stand before you to ask, who will fight alongside me as these traitors threaten our way of life?" Hale shouts.

"Ooo! Ooo! Ooo!" Three more arrows strike the tree.

"Who will lay down their lives to protect Mhorelia and its rightful king?"

"Ooo! Ooo! Ooo!" *Thud, thud, thud.*

There's only one arrow left, and the tree is still not leaking oil.

Lorena drops her head. "I really thought that would work."

"We've got one last shot. I'll take it," says Melara. She rips a small piece of cloth from her cloak and wraps the arrow's head with it, dousing it in oil. "Remember when you said I shouldn't bring this, John?"

John raises an eyebrow. "Is now really the best time to gloat?"

"Given our current circumstances, I may not get another chance," she says back with a smirk.

John removes the lighter from his pocket and holds it up to the arrow. "I can't believe this trusty little guy has lasted this long. And to think I bought this on a whim." He pushes down on the spark wheel . . . and nothing happens. Melara starts to open her mouth. "Don't say it," says John. "Just give me a minute." He flicks the wheel frantically. Sparks. Sparks. Sparks.

Flame.

Finally, it lights, and John lets out a sigh of relief as the arrow's tip is engulfed in fire. "I told you it would work."

Everyone gives in to a brief laugh, but it dwindles as the reality of the situation sinks in. If this arrow does not ignite the tree, they are out of options. Hale will surely notice a flaming arrow, and then it's four against hundreds. Melara pulls back her drawstring gradually until the feathers brush up against her cheek. The chants of the men are drowned out by the deafening silence surrounding John. All he hears is Melara's breath. *Inhale. Exhale. Inhale. Exhale.* Then an arrow hits the tree.

But it isn't hers.

She lets up on the drawstring as they all try to locate the shooter.

"Where did that come from?" says John.

"I cannot see anything," says Lorena.

Another arrow hits the tree unnoticed, masked by the chants of Hale's army.

"Those arrows . . ." says Melara. "They are the arrows of the Cliff Elves."

"That cannot be . . ." says Darian. "Their homes were destroyed."

"And yet, they live on," says Melara. Another arrow hits the tree. "They are survivors. *We* are survivors." Another arrow hits the tree, and a beautiful black liquid oozes from it. Melara lifts her bow once more, takes aim, and lets the arrow fly, all with a smile on her lips.

John had a pretty good idea of what would happen next—he's been around his fair share of explosions—but what transpires is something he never could've imagined. The blast sends a shockwave that knocks them backward, slamming John into a nearby tree. He opens his eyes slowly and tries to take stock of the situation. His head is pounding, and there's a sharp pain in his shoulder, courtesy of a piece of bark now lodged inside of him. He rips out the shrapnel and tosses it aside. Slowly getting to his feet, he looks out toward the castle to see the fire and chaos unfolding in front of him. Men are crying out helplessly, but their screams are muffled by the intense ringing in his ears. Finally, a familiar voice cuts through the chaos . . . Darian's.

"Help!"

John spots him barely hanging onto a vine that's about to break. He lunges, grabbing hold of Darian's arm just as the vine snaps. With the help of Melara and Lorena, they pull him up and stare blankly into each other's eyes. John's wound appears to be the only major injury, but everyone is dazed.

John makes the first move, pulling his sword from its sheath. "Let's finish this."

"It looks like your girl is one step ahead of us," says Lorena.

John looks upon the carnage once more. The gate has been blown clean off its hinges, and Oblirian is finishing off the stragglers that weren't killed in the explosion.

After making the quick climb down, they're fighting alongside her, not that you could call it much of a fight. Only about ten men survived the blast, and they were badly wounded. A few arrows from the elves take out most of the remaining soldiers, leaving them standing alone on the battlefield, except for one.

Hale is crawling away in agony, the blast somehow cutting one of his arms clean off. Oblirian grabs him by the leg and tosses him toward John. But it's Melara who kicks him onto his back and kneels beside him. He can barely speak, but he manages one last sentence: "You will never defeat the mighty Balloch."

Melara meets his gaze. "Oh, but we will . . . It's a shame you won't be around to see it." And with that, she pulls an arrow from her quiver and lodges it in his heart, never breaking eye contact.

The doors to the castle are still intact, so all that's left to do is wait for Balloch's next move. Then a glint from atop the castle wall catches John's eye. He's never seen Balloch before, but the gaudy crown this man wears is evidence enough. His voice reigns down: "It's great to finally meet you, John. And you've brought friends . . . I know you have come a long way, but your feeble attempt to usurp me ends here!"

"Is that so! Well, why don't you come down here and we can finish this, just you and me!" John yells back.

Balloch lets out a bellowing laugh. "Now, why would I do that? I have an army at my disposal, as well as your *jumpy* friend." Kaigen steps forward into view, with two guards at his side. "How about this, John. I will give you this one chance to walk away. To go home. Behind this castle lies the door you seek, the one that can send you back to your world. Isn't that what you want?"

John chuckles. "Can you believe this guy." But the others aren't laughing.

With a tear in her eye, Lorena grabs John's hand. "John, you should go."

"What?" John says back.

Lorena continues, "You didn't ask to be here, and we were anything but kind to you when you arrived. Yet you stuck with us, you fought with us, and you got us farther than we've ever been. You don't owe us any more than that. If there is a chance for you to get home safe, you should take it."

The others say nothing, but the feeling is mutual.

He looks at Darian. "She's right, John. And I know Killian would want the same for you."

Then he looks at Melara, hoping for a different response. "Get out of here, John. You think we cannot do this without you?"

"It's true, you weren't the greatest when I arrived. I believe it was you, Melara, who tried to kill me. But we have gone through so much, and we have grown *together*. I have been with you through it all, and you still don't seem to get it . . . This is my home, and you are my family now." He turns back to the king. "Balloch! Do your worst!"

Balloch shakes his head, saying, "Very well," and the gates open. Ten men march forward, armored from head to toe, with not an inch of skin showing—at least on their fronts.

The elves pepper them with arrows, but they glance off the armor, not even slowing them down. John grabs a tuft of fur on Oblirian's neck and swings himself onto her back. "Lorena, see if you can get a clean shot at their backsides."

"And what will you do?"

"I'll turn them around." Oblirian and John charge the soldiers, and the elves ready their bows. The soldiers hold their ground, weapons up. But just before Oblirian plows over the soldiers, she leaps over them, and they all spin around. When Oblirian lands and turns back to face the soldiers, three are on the ground with arrows in the backs of their knees. *Good . . . There's always a weak spot.*

The soldiers immediately form a circle, with their backs to each other and the three wounded in the middle. "Oblirian," John says aloud, "we've got to break that circle." And with that, they charge at the soldiers. *Three, two, one . . .* "Stop!" Oblirian stops short, and John springs off of her back, planting a dropkick right in a soldier's chest. The man tumbles backward and knocks five of them down, throwing them into complete disarray.

But these men are trained killers, and John knows every swing of his blade must count, cutting clean through the leg of one of them before regaining his footing. He turns just in time to see Oblirian crush the skull of one man and then throw a second a clear thirty feet into the castle wall. The sound of the man's bones crunching in his armor cuts through the violence that's transpiring around him. But there's no time to think. John swings his sword like a madman, blocking blows, striking armor, all the while arrows are flying all around him. It's unclear whether they're all friendly arrows, but it doesn't really matter; he wouldn't be able to dodge them either way.

When John and the soldiers finally back away to catch their breath, the scene is gruesome. Bloodstained bodies riddle the ground—four dead, two dying, and four left standing. They split up; two stay with John and Oblirian, and two head toward the elves. John is bruised and bloodied, but when he sees the ferocity in Oblirian's eyes, he's filled with comfort. "Let's do this." They rush the two men, who, slowed by their armor, don't stand a chance. A few quick swings and bites, and the men fall to the ground, never to fight again.

But then a scream rings out and one of the soldiers kicks Darian to the ground, then sets his eyes on Melara. She shoots arrow after arrow at him, but he presses on, unfazed. Lorena is pulling her dagger out of the other man's throat and is too far away to act. Oblirian runs toward them, but she'll never make it in time. Melara grabs for another arrow as the soldier closes in . . . but her quiver is empty. He raises his sword to strike.

"Noooo!" John screams.

As Melara stands to face her attacker—determined to die with dignity—an arrow pierces through the soldier's armor. He drops to his knees, and his sword falls to the ground. She whips out her dagger and slits his throat for good measure, then turns to the tree line and blows a kiss.

They quickly gather their arrows as Oblirian finishes off the stragglers. "How's everyone doing?" asks John.

"Couldn't be happier," Darian says, in between coughs.

"And how do you feel about your decision to stay behind?" says Lorena.

"Couldn't be happier," John replies. "Melara, was that your girl who took that shot?"

She beams. "That was my Serafina. She's the only one who could make it look that easy."

John laughs and turns his attention to Balloch. "Well, we're still standing! Is that all you've got?"

Balloch lets out an unnerving laugh, and the gates open once again. But this time, it isn't ten soldiers walking toward them; it's a horde of centaurs . . . And they do not look happy. The elves form a line next to John. "It appears we are outnumbered once again, and I'm not sure we'll be able to fight our way out of this one," says John.

"You may be right, John," Lorena says grimly.

"Anyone have another trick up their sleeve?" asks Darian.

"Nope," says Melara. "I say we go down fighting, and we take as many of them as we can down with us."

John looks down the line and takes in the features of his team members one last time—something he never got to do before The Undesirables perished. "I love you all, and it will be an honor to die alongside you."

Then the ground starts to shake.

"What is that?" asks John. "Another avalanche?"

Darian places his hand on the ground, then turns his attention to the fallen gate. Destroyed in the blast, it now exists as a smoldering mess, with smoke rising high in the sky above it. "Oh, John . . . you will not get the luxury of dying today."

"For Mhorelia!" a voice thunders from behind the smoky wall.

"He came," John says under his breath.

Sundane bounds over the fallen gate with Leon riding on his back, followed by a stampede of stagglehorn. John and the elves join the charge, and an epic clash ensues as they meet on the battlefield. The stagglehorn are piercing the hides of the centaurs, but they aren't going down without a fight. The battle is a free-for-all as some throw spears or shoot arrows while others swing their deadly blades. Creatures are falling left and right from both sides, and the castle grounds have become a dust bowl. John has lost all sense of direction, swinging his sword at anything that threatens him. He can hear the shouts of his friends and the snarls of Oblirian, but he can't see them through the commotion.

Finally, there is a break in the fighting, and John allows himself a moment of rest. The dust has now completely obscured his vision, and he can hear the sounds of violence somewhere off in the distance. But something draws near. He ducks to avoid a passing centaur's attack and relieves the beast of its legs. It crashes behind him, and he raises his sword. Another follows, and he narrowly dodges its attack as it speeds by. He raises his sword once more, trying desperately to push a thought from his mind . . . But still it lingers.

What if the next creature I see . . . is Kaigen?

***

Atop the castle wall, Kaigen watches the mayhem unfold below, with Balloch at his side. Two guards are positioned behind him, with spears trained on his back. He wants so desperately to join the battle, to fight alongside his friends. But thirty feet to his right stands his son—shaking, afraid, with a guard's knife to his throat. If Kaigen moves at all, his son will die—that was Balloch's promise.

But the tide appears to be turning as he watches the king's men fall. The Cliff Elves played their part, finding a high vantage point and providing fire from above. John and the elves held their own against Balloch's best warriors, slaying them in a matter of minutes—and the way Oblirian tossed them around as if they were toys, it brought a smile to Kaigen's face. Then there was the stagglehorn stampede, and Kaigen had to admit, he never saw that coming—neither did Balloch. The shock that filled the king's eyes widened Kaigen's smile even more. Yes, it appears John is winning, and now Balloch has to go and ruin Kaigen's good mood.

"Kaigen, it's time."

"Time for what?" Kaigen says, attempting to stall.

"Do not play dumb with me, boy. It is time for you to finish this."

Kaigen's eyes dart back and forth between his son, Balloch, and John. He doesn't want to fight John, but for his son . . . *No, I need to buy some time.*

"And here I thought you were an honorable king," he says.

"Oh, get off that pedestal on which you stand," barks the king.

"I'm just saying, what kind of message does it send to your troops if you can't even defeat one single man?" Kaigen says in his most patronizing tone. "A *true* king would fight with his men instead of standing up here and watching them die."

Balloch leans in close to Kaigen. "And if it comes to that, I will kill the imposter myself. But until then, get to work, and no more stalling!"

Kaigen wrestles with the idea in his mind, unsure of what to do. But Balloch interrupts his thoughts: "Fine, have it your way. Guard! Kill the boy!"

"Wait!" Kaigen yells, pushing the guards aside.

Then a thundering sound pierces his ears: "Oooooooooooo!" And Alura comes flying toward the castle.

They came! is all Kaigen has time to think before Alura unleashes a blast of wind into the castle wall, creating a crack down the center that separates him from Isaiah. The shockwave that follows puts everyone off balance, including Isaiah's guard.

Kaigen quickly teleports to his son, removes the guard's knife from his hand, and kicks him off the castle wall. He drops to a knee and hugs his son tighter than he ever thought possible. "Are you hurt?"

"I'm okay, Dad," says Isaiah, not wanting to let go. "What do we do now?"

That's a great question, he thinks, realizing he hadn't put much thought into it. He looks around frantically. The king is already gone—no doubt holding away somewhere until the fighting is over. The battle still rages on below, but Kaigen refuses to leave his son, not until he knows he'll be safe. Then Kaigen spots a second denaro flying by, which gives him an idea. He looks directly into his son's eyes. "Isaiah, do you trust me?" His son nods. "Be sure to grab onto the denaro and don't let go. I'll see you soon."

And with that, Kaigen throws him over the edge of the wall. "Catch!" The passing denaro scoops him up before he can fall anywhere near the ground. Mixed emotions arise in Kaigen's mind; his son is finally safe, and yet there he goes.

But I will see him soon enough.

He peeks over the edge of the castle wall. "Don't worry, John. I'm coming."

***

When the denaros fly overhead, all fighting ceases. John looks on in wonder as Alura creates a gust so powerful, it cracks the castle wall and clears the battlefield of all dust. And with the dust gone, the true carnage is revealed. Bodies of men, centaurs, and stagglehorn are slumped over each other. Some missing limbs, others torn in half. One of the more brutal sights is staring back at John. A stagglehorn with three spears in its side lies dead, its horns stuck deep in the side of a dying centaur. It coughs up blood as John approaches, "Please . . . Plea—"

John cuts off its head—a merciful death.

The two sides have backed off to regroup. Leon leads the stagglehorn over to John and the others, and Balloch's forces head toward the castle entrance. This brief intermission allows John time to survey his team: Oblirian is covered in blood, but looks to be okay; the elves appear to be fine, aside from a deep cut on Melara's left arm, but her reunion with Serafina has seemed to suppress all notions of pain; and then there's Leon, still riding Sundane and looking like the warrior everyone said he would be.

"You really cut it close there, Leon," says John.

"Yes, well, one of my friends told me what happened to Killian. And that was the last straw," says Leon.

"Friends?" John asks.

"The stagglehorn," Darian says as he locks arms with Leon. "It's good to see you again, Cousin. I only wish Killian were still here to join in our reunion."

"As do I," says Leon. "May he rest in eternal peace."

The castle doors open and shut, allowing another wave of soldiers to enter the battle—albeit a much smaller wave, maybe twenty-five at best—led by Balloch. Leon turns his attention to the others. "This must be the last of his men. Let us make our final stand."

Chapter 34

John has been on countless missions in the past that required killing. And almost every time that John was asked to take a life, it was from long range, or under the cover of darkness. One bullet, one stab, one flick of a detonator. He often never even saw the people he was supposed to eliminate, but he will never forget them. Just as he will never forget the killing he has done here today—if he manages to get out alive—for nothing can compare to the events that just transpired, or the ones that are about to.

Two lines have formed, one led by John, the other by Balloch. Alura circles the standoff overhead, having not done much since her first attack on the castle. Sensing John's annoyance with that fact, Leon speaks up. "Denaros are creatures of great power and mystique, but they do tire. That first gust she threw would have weakened her quite a bit. And until she can regain her strength, she is just a bird in the wind."

"Well, we can't wait forever. Let's do this," says John.

But before they can act, a cloud of purple explodes in the sky. "Kaigen?" John says aloud. Several blasts follow, each one lower than the last, creating a tower of purple as he slams into the ground below. When the powder clears, Kaigen is down on one knee, with his fist in the dirt and his eyes down. But this is not the same Kaigen.

"He shape-shifted . . ." Lorena gasps.

***

Kaigen rises to his feet. No horns, no tail, just a dark-skinned, muscular man with the same devious eyes. John extends his arm, and they lock hands. "So, this is what you normally look like?" says John. Kaigen nods. "Much more approachable," John continues.

"Nice of you to join the fight," says Lorena.

"I couldn't let you have all the fun. But enough pleasantries, I've got a king to kill," says Kaigen.

"Kaigen!" Balloch shouts. "Do you remember what I told you would happen if you ever shifted back into your natural form?"

"Yeah, yeah, you'd kill me and my whole family," Kaigen says mockingly. "Well, here we are."

Balloch removes a horn from his belt and lets out a maniacal laugh. "Exactly." When he blows the horn, a *rumble* emanates from inside the castle.

"That can't be good," says Kaigen.

At that moment, a climour crashes through the castle doors, splintering them into hundreds of pieces. A broken chain dangles from a collar around its neck.

"Oh, good. He has a pet climour," says John. "Hey, Kaigen . . ."

"Yeah, yeah, I'll handle it."

And both sides charge.

Kaigen wastes no time teleporting toward the beast, hoping to keep their scuffle away from the rest of the fighting. The climour is caught off guard and catches all of Kaigen's hard right hook to the jaw. It howls out in pain and spits blood to the side, along with a few teeth. *Ohhh, that felt good,* he admits to himself—even though his hand could very well be broken after that punch. *Now let's see if it can keep up.* What follows is a series of quick teleportations, coupled with a barrage of punches, kicks, and stabs with his blade. The beast is screaming out in protest, wildly flailing its arms in an attempt to stop Kaigen's endless attacks. And unfortunately, he eventually succeeds.

Kaigen is spinning in midair after a quick maneuver places him behind the climour, and before he can react, the creature's arm whips back and gives him a solid blow to the chest. The blow instantly knocks the wind out of him, and he careens backward into the castle wall, blacking out on impact.

He regains consciousness a moment later, gasping for air, and he's surprised he hasn't been pulverized yet. When he locates the climour, it's frantically ripping objects from its side, leaving Kaigen even more confused. *Are those knives?* Then suddenly, Alura swoops in and flicks her wing toward the climour. Her feathers turn to blades as they leave her wing and stick into the thick skin of the beast.

"You got my message?" he says to Alura, still very much in a daze from the climour's punch.

"Hmmm, I did indeed. And it's a good thing I showed up when I did," she says in return.

"I was handling it."

"Hmmm . . . And how do you plan on *finishing* it?"

A bit of rubble becomes dislodged from the top of the castle wall and falls behind Kaigen, giving him an idea. "Go help the others. I've got this." She nods and takes off, leaving Kaigen alone with a very angry climour. "Looks like it's just you and me now." He picks up a nearby stone and throws it at the beast—still going berserk over the knives in its back. It immediately stops its frenzy, cocking its head toward Kaigen. *Well, that got its attention.* Then it slaps its hands on the ground and rushes Kaigen. He backs away slowly, toward the castle, taunting the beast: "Come on! Come on!" And right before they collide, Kaigen vanishes.

Poof!

The climour smashes into the castle wall headfirst. If that collision isn't enough to kill it, the large stone parapets falling from above will surely do the trick. They bury the beast in an instant, never to be feared again.

***

John's body count is piling up. There's no way he could determine the exact number, but if he had to guess, it's probably around triple digits. But those kills don't matter, and John has his sights set on the only one that does, Balloch. The man has a small army surrounding him, with archers and swordsmen taking out any stagglehorn who comes near. A small group stands beside him with what appears to be only one job: to shield him from any arrows that fly his way. In order to kill him, John will need to get in close, and that will require a diversion.

He yells to Lorena, "We need to surround him! Take the rest of the elves and circle behind." Then, to Leon, he says, "Take your stagglehorn and go the other way; we will hit him on all fronts!" They do as they're told, quickly flanking the king's inner circle from all sides. *Now it's my turn.*

"Oblirian!" he yells. A moment later, he's on top of her and they're circling the battlefield. "We need to find a way to break through his men," he says aloud. Still circling, the Cliff Elves send a storm of arrows toward Balloch's men, and all of their shields go up. "That's it, Oblirian. Not *through* his men, but *over* them."

He pulls up short as he reaches the Cliff Elf giving the commands. "Serafina, I suppose?"

"What do you need from us?" she replies.

Straight to the point, he thinks, *just like Melara.* "I need you to send another shipment of arrows on my command. Can you do that?"

"With pleasure," she answers confidently.

Poof!

"And what of me, John?" says Kaigen, appearing at his side.

"If you haven't had enough fun yet, I'd love for you to clear a path for me. Then give me as much time as you can," John replies.

Kaigen nods his approval. "Let's end this."

John cracks his neck on either side with two satisfying *pops*. "One. Two. Three." Oblirian takes off toward the shrinking circle of Balloch and his men. Kaigen teleports in front of the two of them, knocking down anyone who stands in their way. Oblirian covers the distance in a matter of seconds, and when she's about fifteen yards away, John calls out, "Serafina! Now!" The arrows fly, the shields go up, and Oblirian springs over them. John leaps off of her back and lands next to Balloch while Oblirian crashes into the backs of his men, sending the protection circle into complete disarray.

The fighting bursts into chaos around John, but he's locked in on Balloch. The two men draw their swords in unison.

"We finally meet, face-to-face," says Balloch. "A peasant and a king, a failure and a leader, a man that will soon be forgotten and a hero that will forever live on—"

John cuts in: "The Chosen One . . . and a dead man."

Balloch scoffs, "We'll see about that."

Their swords clash. John may have been the top student in his swordsmanship class, but Balloch is no slouch. Blow after blow, the blades bounce off of each other, and John can't seem to gain the upper hand. Balloch knocks him off balance with a spin move, and John takes an elbow to the jaw. He steadies himself as Balloch laughs in his face. "Are you going to make this a challenge, *Almighty Chosen One?*"

One of John's strengths has always been his ability to admit when he's been bested. In his experience, others typically saw it as a weakness; he saw it as lacking an ego, and an ego will get you killed. So, as he spits blood out of the side of his mouth, a thought comes to mind. A risky thought for sure, but maybe his last chance at defeating Balloch.

"You think that wearing a crown makes you a king? *Nonsense.* You couldn't lead a flock of sheep, let alone Mhorelia."

Balloch grimaces in disgust. "I have humored you for long enough. It's time for you to die."

As Balloch advances, John tosses his sword into the air and removes his dagger from its sheath. But as he hurls the dagger at

Balloch, he knows he's miscalculated, for Balloch's eyes stay put, trained on John. In one quick motion, Balloch slices the dagger out of the air, knocking it a few feet away and very much out of John's reach. "Trickery will not work against me, John," he yells, not breaking stride. "For I am the rightful ruler of Mhorelia!" He raises his sword for the killing blow, and John can only look on in terror, hoping for a stray arrow to catch him. A stray arrow never comes . . .

But a stagglehorn does.

It flies through the battle and splits John and Balloch apart, knocking them to the ground and sending Balloch's sword flying. If John had watched the sword, he would've been pleased to see it pierce the hide of a nearby centaur. But he's focused on something else—his dagger—which now lies only a foot away from where he's landed.

He jumps to his feet, dagger in hand, and races toward Balloch to administer the killing blow. But the king rolls over just in time to see him coming and plants both feet into John's chest, launching him backward. When John rises a second time, it's Balloch's turn to lunge at him, his own dagger aimed at John's throat. He slips the knife, but takes the full force of Balloch's body as they slam to the ground. John then throws his arms up to block a blow from Balloch as he tries to bring the knife down, stopping it only inches from his face. Shifting his legs, he's able to throw Balloch to the side, and they roll together, legs entangled, jockeying for position, until John finds himself on top of Balloch. Their arms are braced against each other; John's knife points down, Balloch's up. Both men are letting out primal grunts as they push with every fiber of their being, hoping the other will give in first.

John can feel the king start to relent, desperation plastered on his face as the knife inches downward, slowly making its way through Balloch's enormous beard. "It's over for you, Balloch."

"That may be so," Balloch says, "but I can still take you with me."

The fight in Balloch's arms ceases, and both knives find their homes. John's plunges deep into Balloch's heart while Balloch's enters just above John's left pec, cutting his tattoo in half and exiting just below his shoulder blade. John rolls off of Balloch, gasping for air as he stares at the knife protruding from his chest. A warm pool of blood forms around them both, and a sense of calm washes over John.

He's seen enough injuries like this to know that if he's going to live, it will take a miracle. It's poetic really; John is going to sacrifice his own life for his team, something he's always wished he could have done for The Undesirables. His mind goes to images of his old team as the world slows around him. The last thing he hears is Kaigen's voice coming from somewhere nearby: "John? John!"

Then it all goes black.

CHAPTER 35

Some say the afterlife is spent walking among the clouds, surrounded by loved ones. Others say that there exists a lush sanctuary in which all of your greatest desires are met, day in and day out. And then there are the people who say that after death, lies nothing. Only darkness, stretching on for all of eternity.

For John, it's the last one.

The only thing that's puzzling him is the pain that persists in his body, the worst of which stems from his stab wound. *Didn't realize there'd be pain in the afterlife . . . Figures.* He lifts his eyelids slowly, hoping that pain and darkness aren't the only two things on the other side. What he witnesses next looks like a scene from a fairy tale: a woman cloaked in white, with bright lights flickering off of her silky hair. "Oh, good. At least there are angels here," he says aloud. She smiles at him and giggles, prompting a smile of his own.

A voice to his left takes his attention off the angel. "Watch itttt."

"Kaigen? Oh no, you died too," says John.

"You're not dead, John," Kaigen replies. "Isla, did this boy hit his head in all the commotion?"

John's bewilderment only grows as his vision comes into focus. He's lying on a bed; next to him stands Kaigen, a small child—presumably his son—and a woman he's never met. Isla, apparently. But this doesn't make any sense. He's dead; he has to be. Kaigen continues on while John is pulled back to reality. "John, I'd like you to meet Isla, the woman who saved your life."

He gradually lifts his body up in the bed, still incredibly sore from everything that's happened. "That's, that's impossible."

Isla just smirks. "Maybe for a human. Although your wound is one of the worst I've ever seen. It's shocking you're alive; you must be quite the fighter."

"Stop boosting his ego," says Kaigen. "It did take him a full three days to recover."

"Three days!" John blurts out, along with a slew of questions. "What has happened since the battle? How are the others? Did everyone make it?"

"Easy, John," Isla says softly. "Kaigen, why don't you take him outside for some fresh air. I'm sure you two have a lot to catch up on."

"Keep an eye on Isaiah, would you, please?" Kaigen says.

"I would never give up a chance to spend some time with my favorite little guy!" she says as she picks Isaiah up and twirls him around.

John nudges Kaigen with his elbow as they exit the room. "So, what's the deal with her? Are you two . . .?"

"Never mind that; we are off to visit Lorena."

"I thought we were heading for fresh air?"

"Look, John, I'm about to go on a monologue here that will cover a lot of your questions, so please . . . no more interruptions."

"Still just as charming as when we first met," says John, recognizing the quote from his first day in Mhorelia.

John has never seen the inside of a castle before. But as they walk the halls, it's just as he would've expected: cold stones all around him; dimly lit hallways throughout; and the faint, yet inescapable musty odor of mildew—none of which is appealing to John. Luckily, Kaigen's retelling of the events of the last three days provides a welcome distraction.

"The former king's army proved to be stubbornly loyal to the man, even when all hope was lost. Leon called out for their surrender shortly after you stuck your knife into Balloch's heart, but there were no takers.

"You'll be happy to know that all of your friends made it out alive, although not completely unscathed. Melara took two deep slashes to her arm and will be unable to use it for quite a while. Darian took a spear to the shoulder, but he seems to be recovering fast. And then there is Lorena, who took two arrows to the thigh to protect Oblirian. A selfless act that'll have her walking with a limp for the time being.

"As for the dead, we lost a good many stagglehorn during the battle, and, unfortunately, a couple of Cliff Elves as well. Leon and Melara took those deaths hard, but their spirits have been trending upward since Lorena's coronation."

"Coronation?" John cuts in.

"In Mhorelia, once a leader is gone, we must appoint a new one. It has been that way for generations, and although she objected, Lorena was the obvious choice."

John can't argue with that. She's a natural born leader, and John can't wait to call her a queen—knowing how much she'll hate it.

"Her first act as queen," Kaigen continues, "was to get word to the rest of Mhorelia that Balloch's tyrannical rule has ended. And with it, the starvation and the needless violence as well. She enlisted the denaros to remove the blockades from the Enchanted Paths so that food could be delivered throughout Mhorelia once again."

"You all have been busy in my absence," says John.

"Not everyone sleeps as much as you," Kaigen says, accompanied by a playful smack on the back.

"And how has everyone taken to Lorena's rule?"

"Well, it's only been a few days, but there are already rumors surfacing from the woodsmen that a woman is unfit to rule." Kaigen shakes his head in disgust. "But if they get the chance to meet her, they will see what we have already seen: She is the *only* person fit to rule Mhorelia."

"Ain't that the truth," John says. "So, where is she now? And where is everybody else? I'm not stuck alone with you, am I?"

"You'd be so lucky. Darian and Leon have gone with the first shipment of supplies headed south. We are unsure if there are others who still give their allegiance to Balloch, so they thought it best to accompany it as an added level of protection. Also, Darian expressed interest in burying some of Killian's ashes back home."

"Under the white willow," says John.

"Exactly. As for Lorena, she has appointed the Cliff Elves as her top advisors, and Melara as her first in command. They are meeting now in the dining hall for further discussions on defending the Enchanted Lands."

"Defending? Defending from what?"

"We may be at peace now, but it has been my experience that peace does not last forever. There is always someone out there who thinks they deserve to have it all, and it is our duty to stop them."

He's right. John knows that. It's a flaw that's present in most humans he's had the displeasure of knowing. It doesn't matter whether it's wealth, power, status, or privilege . . . There are people who always feel like they deserve more, like they're better than the rest.

That depressing thought leaves him as they enter the dining hall. All eyes turn to the two of them when the door creaks open, followed by a flash of white. One moment John is standing, and the next he's flat on his back. The pain of getting knocked over is immediately replaced by happiness as Oblirian repeatedly licks his face. "Miss me, girl?"

"Alright, Oblirian, give the man some space," says Melara, now standing over him with an outstretched hand. She helps him to his feet and slaps him on the shoulder. "It's good to see you pulled through—although that does mean I lost our wager."

Kaigen grins, and John raises an eyebrow in confusion. "Kaigen, you big softie. You bet that I would live?" Kaigen shrugs his shoulders. "And Melara! You bet against me?"

"Can you honestly say that you thought you would survive?" Melara says.

John sighs. "Fair point."

Although she's kept her distance since he entered, John is fairly certain he saw Lorena smile when she first laid eyes on him. As she walks toward him—trying desperately to hide her limp—he can't help but smile, too. "You should try using a cane," he says playfully.

"For what?" she snaps back. "Would you have me appear weak?"

Her tone catches John off guard. "No, no. It's just . . . I heard what you did for Oblirian. Thank you."

Lorena reaches out and caresses Oblirian's mane. "She had already saved me twice by that point in the battle. I was merely returning the favor."

John shoots Kaigen a sidelong glance. He only shrugs. Lorena ushers the Cliff Elves out. "That's enough for today. Melara, I'd like a full inventory of our new armory, along with an updated list of supplies at our disposal."

Melara nods her head. "Understood."

Lorena then turns her attention to Kaigen and John. "Kaigen, I'd like you to see if you can locate Darian and get an update from him and Leon. And bring them some of the maps of Mhorelia lying around my new study. After our journey, I think they may be in need of some updating."

"Anything for you, *Your Majesty*," Kaigen says with an exaggerated bow. "John, I'm truly glad you're not dead."

And then, *Poof!* He's gone.

John is left staring into Lorena's sparkling eyes, nervous about what will happen next. Had he misread things? Would her being crowned queen change her feelings toward him? She can deny those feelings all she wants, but John is certain they are there. The moment the last elves leave the room, and the door slams shut behind them, he gets his answer.

She leaps into his grasp, thrusting her arms around him and squeezing him tight.

From this moment forward, until John is lying on his death-bed, old and gray, he'll remember every aspect of her warm embrace: the perfect pressure of her arms encircling him, like a thick blanket on a cold night; the way his heartbeat quickened as they held each other close; the chill he got when her red hair gently brushed up against his stubbled cheek. He'll remember it all, every last detail, until the day he dies.

Still holding him close, she whispers into his ear, "I thought I'd lost you."

They slowly pull apart, now resting their foreheads against one another, his hands around her hips, her hand gently pressed against his cheek.

"John . . . please don't go back home to your world."

"Like I said before, this is my home now, and I can't imagine a world without you."

A rush of warmth flows through John's body as their lips softly come together. Her hand lightly pulls at his hair as their passionate kiss continues. John has never felt this way about anyone, and he doesn't want this moment to end. When they do finally separate, they're all smiles as they giggle nervously together.

"You have no idea how long I've wanted to do that," he says.

"No, I think I do," she replies, followed by another laugh.

He grabs her hand. "Why don't you show me the rest of the castle? I'd love a tour of our new home."

The two of them spend the next several hours together, roaming the castle grounds in a blissful trance. For once, they can spend a moment together without the fear of an enemy around every corner. For once, they can laugh and smile as they bask in each other's company. For once, they can be happy.

Lorena shows him where they plan to build several new homes—ones that travelers can stay in when they come to visit the Enchanted Lands. Next, he's shown the place where they will build a wall of remembrance, which will have the names of the brave souls who fought and died for Mhorelia carved into the side. She tells him of her plans to unify Mhorelia by personally visiting all of its people, at every far-reaching corner of the island . . . And she plans to leave tomorrow. With the castle tour completed, they now stand outside her bedroom door, John wishing more than anything that this day would never end.

"How long do you plan on being gone?" John asks.

"I'm sorry, John," she says somberly. "I wish I could stay with you here for longer, but I must do my duties as the queen."

"I know you do." He pauses, thinking. "I suppose I should let you get some rest. You've got a long day of travel ahead of you tomorrow."

As he starts to leave her, she grabs his arm and flashes him a look of playful seduction. "And just where do you think you're going?"

EPILOGUE

John lies in Lorena's bed, her head resting on his chest. Their breathing flows in sync as a pleasant calmness pours over him. She fell asleep hours ago, and although he tried to follow suit, John has been lying awake thinking ever since. His mind travels back, thinking of all the ways his life could have gone differently. What if he'd never found hope in therapy after his discharge? What if he'd never taken that facilities engineering job in Alabama? What if he'd rejected his boss's proposal of traveling to Scotland? What if he'd chosen to hike a different trail, avoiding falling through Mhorelia's door altogether? Maybe these questions are better left unanswered, because if he's being honest, he wouldn't trade this current path he's on for anything.

Looking back on his life, John actually can't remember a time when he was at such peace—maybe when he was a child. That's not to say his time on Earth hadn't produced any good memories, but peace . . . that always seemed to elude him. And judging by what he knows of Lorena's life, the same is probably true for her as well.

Hoping to give her some much-needed rest—and because he knows he won't be getting much sleep tonight—he slowly gets up and carefully rests Lorena's head back down on the bed to avoid waking her.

John wanders out of the castle and is happy to see a familiar face staring up into the faintly moonlit sky. He sits down on a log next to Kaigen and matches his upward gaze. "You couldn't sleep either?"

"On a beautiful night like tonight, I had no desire to sleep. There's something about the solitude of the night that brings me peace."

John nods. "I get that."

The two sit in silence for a great while, simply enjoying each other's company. It is Kaigen who eventually speaks up. "I'm assuming Lorena told you about her plans?"

"She did. And I'm to believe Isla is going with her?"

"That's right. And I've asked them to bring Isaiah along with them."

"Really? I figured after all of this, you'd want to spend as much time with him as possible."

"I do," admits Kaigen, "but he's been locked up here for too long, and he needs to see the rest of the world that's out there."

"Admirable. And you can visit him any time you'd like, I suppose, if you can find them."

"Indeed, I can. But for the time being, it looks like it's going to be just you and me," Kaigen says with a smirk. "Maybe we could get into some trouble while they're away?"

"Oh yeah? You sound like you have something in mind."

Kaigen pulls a piece of paper from his pocket and hands it to John.

John unfolds it. "What's this?"

"Looks to me like a map leading toward the southern part of the island. I found it when I was searching through Lorena's study. Read the top."

Across the top, written in large lettering, is a warning:

THE GREATEST THREAT TO MHORELIA

"Greatest threat? What do you think it means?"

"I'm not sure exactly. Not much is known about those lands; I myself have only ever travelled to the edge of the Enchanted Lands that borders the southern slope."

"Why are you showing me this?"

"Well, seeing as we just saved Mhorelia from what I thought was its greatest threat, it doesn't really sit well with me that there could be another out there. So I was planning on taking a little trip down to the southern side of the island—a quick trip—just to see if there's anything we should worry about. It shouldn't take more than a week or two, and we will be back before Lorena and Isla return."

"*We?*" John cuts in.

"Well, seeing as you've got nothing to do and nowhere to be, I was hoping you'd join me."

An ear-to-ear smile forms on John's face as he looks into Kaigen's eyes.

"What do you say, John? Are you up for another adventure?"

ACKNOWLEDGEMENTS

I came up with the idea for this novel on a solo walk in the middle of April. After that day, I was determined to make Mhorelia come to life. It took a long while and was by no means an easy task to complete. So a truly heartfelt thank you is owed to everyone who helped make this a reality for me. To Anna Carlson, who listened to all of my crazy ideas and watched me spend night after night huddled in front of my computer. To my brother, Joshua Walker, the first person to read a rough draft and give me some much-needed feedback. To Jen S., my copy editor, who showed me how to correctly use a semicolon. And most of all, to everyone out there who reads this book and falls in love with the world I have created. Thank you.